"In the tradition of Ted Dekker and Frank Peretti, *Cross Shadow* is a strong, taut thriller that retains a Christian sense of optimism and hope while acknowledging the existence of great evil in the world. Huff raises the stakes on every page all the way through the white-knuckle finale—like watching an action movie through the written word."

KYLE MANN, editor in chief of *The Babylon Bee* and author of *How to Be a Perfect Christian*

"Andrew Huff's writing is as fast-paced and tight as his enticing story lines. Masterfully balancing a well-developed plot with a cast of characters you feel like you've known forever, Huff creates one page-turner after another in his Shepherd Suspense trilogy. He may be a new author, but his talented word-spinning is anything but novice and will linger long in the reader's subconscious."

BETSY ST. AMANT HADDOX, author of *All's Fair in Love and Cupcakes*

Praise for *A Cross to Kill*
A Shepherd Suspense Novel #1

"An action-packed nail-biter from beginning to end, filled with enough twists and turns to put *24* and Jack Bauer to shame! I couldn't put it down. Many thanks to Andrew for hours of entertainment and frantic page turning."

LYNETTE EASON, best-selling, award-winning author of the Blue Justice series

"A fast-paced novel that drew me into the adventure from the opening pages. The characters wrestle with faith, forgiveness, and redemption in a gripping plotline packed with suspense, action, and danger."

GLENN KREIDER, author of *God with Us*

"What a ride! *A Cross to Kill* explodes with action (right from the beginning!) and has an even better story to tell. Andrew brings each scene alive with amazing detail."

ROB THOMAS, founder and CEO of Igniter Media

"Let's hope we all now get to follow John Cross from book to book and movie to movie. What a thrill to imagine carrying Christ into every kind of job and seeing the impact it has in this page-turning story. Get to know Cross. Get to know Huff. I think we're going to be spending a lot of time with them both."

RANDY HAHN, senior pastor of The Heights Baptist Church, Virginia

CROSS SHADOW

SHEPHERD SUSPENSE NOVELS

A Cross to Kill
Cross Shadow
Right Cross

CROSS SHADOW

ANDREW HUFF

KREGEL
PUBLICATIONS

Library of Congress Cataloging-in-Publication Data
Names: Huff, Andrew, author.
Title: Cross shadow : a novel / Andrew Huff.
Description: Grand Rapids, MI : Kregel Publications, [2020] |
Series: Shepherd suspense
Identifiers: LCCN 2020000500 (print) | LCCN 2020000501 (ebook)
Subjects: GSAFD: Mystery fiction. | Christian fiction.
LC record available at https://lccn.loc.gov/2020000500
LC ebook record available at https://lccn.loc.gov/2020000501

ISBN 978-0-8254-4645-0, print
ISBN 978-0-8254-7652-5, epub

Printed in the United States of America
20 21 22 23 24 25 26 27 28 29 / 5 4 3 2 1

CHAPTER ONE

A BRISK WIND prompted Christine Lewis to draw her coat tighter as she exited the headquarters of the North American Broadcasting Channel and joined the herd of New York City natives and tourists mingling in the open-air plaza out front. Pushing past a group of senior citizens organizing a photo op in front of the network gift shop, she picked up her pace and trotted through the Forty-Ninth Street crosswalk just as time expired on the pedestrian signal.

The plaza access street between Forty-Ninth and Forty-Eighth offered a quaint block length of traffic-free asphalt perfect for a pleasant lunchtime stroll, but her meeting with her cameraman, Mike, had run over and she didn't want to miss the next B Sixth Avenue Express car arriving in six minutes. His excitement over covering a Russian tanker detained by the coast guard did nothing to distract her from her impending clandestine meeting.

Even as she marched toward the intersection, she couldn't help but imagine any number of scenarios of how her resignation would impact the network. With Mike as an exception, most of her coworkers wouldn't care. Her boss, Steven Jacobs, would be furious, but when wasn't he when things didn't go his way?

Janeen would want to come with her, but Christine didn't expect United News Network to accept terms that included full-time jobs for best friends. Still, maybe the door would open. Someday. A pit formed in her stomach as she pictured Janeen's reaction to the news of Christine's departure. She pushed the emotional farewell from her mind and searched for a happier face to picture.

John.

But he wasn't alone. She couldn't think about her budding romance with John without also thinking about Lori Johnson, her "second mother." Lori hadn't insisted Christine call her Mom. Yet. Christine laughed to herself as she imagined the impending demand.

The corners of her lips sank as she recalled the last time she'd been able to travel to Virginia to see them. How long had it been? A week? No, longer.

Three.

How had she let it go so long? Christine pulled her hand from her jacket pocket, the phone secure in her grip. As she rounded the corner onto Forty-Eighth, she swiped the screen and quickly found John's contact in video chat. It didn't take long for the call to be accepted, and after a quick pause to load, the handsome, gentle face of John Cross appeared.

"Hey," he said with a smile.

"Hi." She copied his expression and allowed herself to enjoy the richness of his hazel eyes and the symmetry of his features. "Your hair's gotten a little longer than you usually wear it."

"Yeah. I haven't been able to get to the barber." He ran his fingers through the waves of hair falling behind his ear. "Are you headed there now?"

"Yeah, on Forty-Eighth, about to the station."

"I'm glad you called. I've been praying all morning."

Christine smiled more broadly. These were the moments she treasured the past few months, however brief their sparse interactions tended to be. They'd argued many times over who bore the responsibility for the lack of communication. It was mostly hers, though she acknowledged the 24/7 nature of ministry that also pulled John's attention away from their relationship. His thoughts always seemed to be elsewhere, even when they were together.

"Where are you?" Hearing about his day always helped make the distance seem shorter.

"St. Francis Hospital. Nick called this morning. Bri's in delivery right now."

"Oh my goodness!" Christine held a hand to her mouth. "That's early. I hope everything is OK."

"So far it looks like the little guy is just eager to come. Nick's with her. I've just been in the waiting room . . . with both sets of new grandparents."

"That sounds . . . fun?"

John winked and lowered his voice. "Let's just say I'll have some great stories for my sermons. How do you feel?"

"Good, I guess? I don't know how I should feel about the most important interview of my life."

"You're going to do great. Why wouldn't the biggest name in cable news want Christine Lewis on their team? They should've offered you anchor eight months ago."

Rounding up, that made the hundredth time for the same compliment. And she doubted him every time he said it. Just because he thought she deserved the opportunity didn't mean anyone else did. They pursued her, sure, but in this business one wrong conversation could spell doom.

The piercing blare of a truck horn caught her attention, and Christine looked up to see the driver expressing his disagreement with the poor decision-making of a small sedan. She also noticed a larger-than-usual mob of pedestrians heading down the steps to the express subway station at Sixth Avenue and Forty-Eighth.

"John, I've got to go. Looks like the platform's going to be busy, and I don't want to miss my train."

"Call me after, if you can. Love you."

She hated the hesitation she felt before she replied, "Love you too." The video call ended, and she buried her phone back in her jacket pocket as she stepped into the line of people taking the stairs down.

They'd both used the "L" word too soon in her opinion, though it came easy in the early weeks of their dating relationship. Life-threatening situations tended to enhance the lure of romantic attachment. After the novelty wore off, it was apparent they'd rushed into a handful of the trappings of dating they both normally eschewed.

It left them in an awkward place where they knew what the other would do in a life-threatening situation but not what kind of movie they each preferred. Not that she wanted a normal dating relationship. A date with an ex–CIA officer tended to be anything but boring and predictable. Instead of movies or shopping, they drank coffee in between self-defense and surveillance lessons. But still.

She pushed her thoughts on the subject out of her mind and used one of John's techniques to direct her senses on the chaotic scene in front of her.

During her morning commutes prior to dating John, Christine never paid mind to her surroundings. But now, she saw a detailed map of the station in her mind. Down the stairs, veer left, straight to the turnstiles, a quick left, then right, down another flight of stairs to the platform.

With the layout pictured in her brain, she used her eyes and ears to surveil the crowd for possible obstacles. She weaved through the masses with the grace of a ballet dancer, avoiding a large family digging through pockets for fare passes, a small gathering of pedestrians admiring a busker drumming on empty rain barrels, and a lady with blue hair balancing an assortment of handbags in one hand and a cat carrier in the other.

Exactly why she rarely carried a bag anymore. Too much to deal with when trying to move fast.

She made it to the platform just as the B train rolled to a stop. She chose the car farthest from the front and moved in sync with the rest of the crowd as they boarded.

As she settled into a hard orange plastic seat near the car's center, the train pulled away from the platform. Christine checked her watch.

Right on time.

For the train as well as the crushing anxiety. The past eight months might as well have been eight years in the ever-changing landscape of national news. The attempted detonation of a chemical bomb in

Washington, DC, was old news the second a juicier political scandal was exposed. Which overhyped crisis of the moment was it? Christine couldn't recall.

Probably an "imminent threat to our democracy." She imagined esteemed NABC anchor Daniel Meyers saying those exact words to open his nightly news program, though in her opinion it was more tabloid than news. Funny how experiencing a real imminent threat made political posturing feel partisan and petty.

Her dissatisfaction with her job at NABC refused to wane. She'd suppressed her feelings for months, but she'd gained clarity in a discussion with her Bible study leader, Park Han, a few Sunday nights ago. The feisty woman's voice whispered in a shadowy corner of Christine's mind: "God's will can be seen in the pushes and pulls. You're feeling the push. Now all you need is the pull."

He pulled, all right.

In addition to the replay of her conversation with Park, she heard John's well-meaning compliments, Janeen's fictitious sorrow, and a dozen possible outcomes of her meeting with producers at the United News Network. She pressed her hand into her chest to slow the incessant beating.

Stop!

Christine drew slow, deep breaths and concentrated on the car's passengers. If she didn't occupy her ride with mental exercises, she'd only think of the many ways she was certain to bomb the interview. She scanned the crowded car to pick out interesting subjects.

Across from her sat a young adult female, Asian features, dressed in chic leggings and boots, her head buried in her phone.

An African American male, slightly younger, with long hair and baggy clothes, braced himself upright against a stanchion connecting the floor to the ceiling. Even though his eyes were closed, he grinned from ear to ear as he subtly air-drummed to whatever was piped into his bulky but fashionable headphones.

She scanned the remaining passengers, noting small details, until her eyes settled on a young adult male at the front end of the car. A drop of sweat left a shiny trail of moisture down the side of his face. He licked his lips more than once and kept his eyes on the floor. Christine sat straighter and studied him. His complexion was dark, but more from a tan than ethnicity; his frayed hair retreated from his forehead; and he wore a large faded-blue jacket. His left knee trembled, and he kept trying to bury his hands farther than they could go into the jacket's pockets.

The jacket. His thin neck looked silly protruding from it. He was more of a medium build, in contrast to the extra-large size of the jacket. His abdomen, though, filled it out.

He fit a profile—she just didn't remember which one. And yet it nagged at her. She knew she'd heard those characteristics in connection to something before. She recalled everything John taught her. Nothing. She dug further, before John, before the kidnapping. But not much before. During her time as a foreign correspondent. Time she spent with . . .

The explosive ordnance disposal unit stationed in Kirkuk, Iraq.

Christine forced back an audible gasp. She took more deep breaths to ease the increased fluttering in her chest. Her planned route to the UNN building faded into the dark recesses of her mind as she considered her startling new reality: a suicide bomber rode the 11:54 B Sixth Avenue Express heading deep into New York City.

CHAPTER TWO

MAYBE HE WASN'T a suicide bomber. She was just being paranoid. The stress of the interview plus residual trauma from her kidnapping and subsequent involvement in the attempted terror attack in DC. Her imagination just needed the right stimuli.

Christine closed her eyes and breathed through the rising anxiety. Controlled breathing, another of John's techniques he'd introduced to her to help when the panic attacks set in. She imagined him beside her. What would he think?

Her eyes snapped open. He'd want to get a closer look. Time was short with three scheduled stops between her starting point and final destination. As if it read her mind, the train slowed as it pulled up to the Bryant Park platform.

What if he got off? She would have to follow. No choice. Christine pretended to examine the transit map tacked to the wall of the car so she could monitor the man's movements without raising alarm.

A handful of the passengers readied their exit. The man shifted in his chair but remained seated. More sweat trickled down his temple. He pulled his hand out of his pocket to look at something, but before Christine could identify what it was, an elderly lady shuffled by, obscuring her view.

The train came to a full stop, and the doors slid open. The exiting group of commuters swapped places with another group of similar size boarding the train. Christine's person of interest avoided eye contact with the new passengers, though that would be as true of any other New Yorker as it would be of a suicide bomber suspect.

The distinct chime of the loudspeaker announced the imminent closing of the doors. They slid shut, the noise of the busy platform now muffled. Christine managed two more deep breaths before the train climbed slowly, agonizingly, to cruising speed.

Christine noted the time on her watch. Only a couple of minutes between Bryant Park and Herald Square, the next scheduled stop. Not nearly enough time to make a move, but each stop meant a potential escape for her suspected bomber.

It had to be now.

She stood to her feet, the rough sketch of a plan drawing itself together in her mind. If she could see what the man was holding in his pocket. Or maybe get him to stand up. She walked toward the front of the car, careful to avoid the swinging hands of the young man still air-drumming.

Did he flinch? His eyes remained locked on the floor, but he might've noticed her in his peripheral vision. She was committed to the plan now.

Whatever it was.

As she inched closer, the man straightened and finally took his eyes off the floor. He stared straight ahead, through the vagrant asleep against the glass window, and seemed fixated on the black tunnel walls speeding by. His knee stopped trembling. His thin neck still glistened.

Christine reached out her hand as if ready to open the door to the gangway. The car jostled on the tracks, and she let her body go limp.

She fell toward the man, but he quickly stood and angled away from her. With no choice, Christine crashed against the bench and tumbled onto the floor at his feet. She heard footfalls running to her side, but she lay still with her nose pressed into the cold metal.

"Ma'am, are you OK?"

Large hands wrapped around her forearms and lifted, then rotated her upper body with ease. As she turned, she saw the sweaty man's boots stepping away from her. At the last second, she caught a glimpse of what she feared: a bundle of wires tucked just underneath the man's coat.

"Ma'am, can you hear me?"

Her suspected bomber crossed the car and sat down next to the unconscious drifter. Christine ignored the good Samaritan helping her up and, feigning a groggy mental state, kept the jacket within her field of view.

"Ma'am?"

The sweaty man averted his eyes from the scene for a moment and checked on the contents of his jacket pocket, awarding Christine a fleeting view of the final piece of evidence she needed. He only pulled the shiny object out of his pocket enough to check its status, then it disappeared.

The detonator.

Suicide bomber confirmed.

"Miss, are you OK?"

Christine rolled her head back and finally opened her eyes wide enough to identify her concerned rescuer. The heavyset, clean-shaven man in the puffy green jacket waved his large hand over her face.

"Can you see me?" he belted over the rumble of the train on the tracks.

Christine mumbled and fluttered her eyelids for maximum effect. "I'm all right. I just"—she swallowed a nonexistent lump in her throat—"I just got lightheaded."

"Can you stand? Try to get off the floor and into a chair maybe?"

"I'm sorry. I'll get off the floor." She made a show of trying to rise on her own, until she finally let the man help her to her feet. Still pretending to be disoriented, she insisted they move away from the front of the car to her original seat.

The man helped her sit and continued to cradle her arm as he sat down next to her. "That was some spill," he said, his New York accent every bit as heavy as he was. "Are you OK? What happened?"

"I guess I didn't get enough sleep last night and had too much coffee this morning. I wasn't feeling great in this car, so I thought the next car might move less, I guess." She didn't want to lie, but she didn't want to panic the other passengers either.

"How do you feel now? Still lightheaded?"

The man was polite *and* thorough.

"I'm fine, really. It's passing. And I'm getting off soon."

The jostle of the train subsided, and ambient light filled the car as it exchanged the darkness of the tunnel for the open platform of Herald Square Station. The voice on the loudspeaker confirmed the stop and instructed passengers to stand clear of the doors.

"Is this your stop?"

Christine strained her neck to see if the man in the blue jacket had joined the handful of riders starting for the exit. He remained seated in his new spot, knee trembling again, his focus now on the platform.

Christine kept him in her peripheral vision as she scanned the crowd gathering to fill the train.

"Ma'am, is this your stop?"

She stole a quick glance at her phone as she replied, "I'm sorry?"

No signal.

Her companion moved his head into her view and enunciated his words. "Is this where you need to get off? I can help you out if you need to."

The doors slid open, and the masses pushed through each other.

"Oh, no, this isn't my stop. You don't have to help. I'm fine. Really."

The man grunted and furrowed his brow. "See, that's where you're wrong. I might not technically be on the clock, but helping you is exactly what I'm paid to do, ma'am."

Christine turned her full attention to the man. "Excuse me?"

The activity in the car settled as the chimes rang again and the doors slid shut.

Grinning, the man opened his puffy green jacket, and the overhead fluorescent tube glinted off the golden badge affixed neatly beside the black holster resting on his belt. "Detective Peter Rabinoff, NYPD, at your service. I'd like to make sure you don't fall again on your way out, if you don't mind."

The train rocked as it started again into the tunnel, and Christine nearly fell onto the floor once more.

Rabinoff closed his jacket and zipped it halfway up. He squinted as his grin faded. "Hey, don't I know you from somewhere?"

Christine grabbed his forearm firmly and stared into his eyes. "Listen to me. Whatever you do, don't react to anything I'm about to say. I wasn't lightheaded before. I pretended to be to get a look at the man in the blue jacket."

Rabinoff's poker face wasn't perfect, but sufficient.

"I noticed him when I boarded the train. Something didn't seem right. I saw wires hanging underneath his jacket, and he's got some sort of device in one of his pockets. I think he's wearing explosives."

Keeping his eyes trained on hers, Rabinoff leaned back into his chair and studied her face. After a few seconds, he turned his head.

Christine expelled air through her mouth and tightened her grip on his forearm. He stopped turning as she gave him a subtle shake of her head.

He waved her off and shifted in his seat to face toward the opposite side of the car. Suddenly, he laughed out loud. Christine dropped her gaze as he turned his head fully and looked down the length of the car.

Any second now and the blast would claim them.

Rabinoff turned to her as his laughter subsided and he took a deep breath. "OK, Miss Whoever You Are, ignoring the obvious fact that you've been watching too many spy movies, the man seems distressed. I can get why you thought something might be wrong. Either he just stepped out of the shower before he hopped on or he's soon to run out of any sweat he might have left."

Christine nodded. "See, I . . ."

"Are you certain you saw what you saw?"

She caught the reflection of the back of the bomber's head in the glass of the window behind Rabinoff. She held her gaze for a moment, then made firm eye contact with the detective. "Yes."

Rabinoff took a deep breath. "All right."

"What are we going to do?"

"*We* aren't going to do anything."

"But the train's about to stop again. What if he gets off?"

"I didn't say *I* wasn't going to do anything." Rabinoff adjusted his jacket, took a deep breath, then stood. He walked toward the front of the car and then, to Christine's surprise, disappeared through the door to the gangway.

What just happened? In her mind's eye, she'd witnessed Rabinoff confronting the man in the blue jacket and requesting compliance with an examination of what he wore around his waist. Her prayer for the man's submission to authority faded from her heart as she studied the door to the gangway with gritted teeth.

He'd left her. He'd left them all. And for all she knew, the bomber would detonate before Rabinoff returned.

If he ever intended to.

Christine returned to her breathing exercises to quell the anxiety building in her chest. Rabinoff wasn't just plan A—he was the only plan.

A distorted voice echoed from the loudspeaker overhead, announcing the train's imminent arrival at Herald Square. Christine prayed fervently as they slowed to a stop next to the platform.

A smaller crowd greeted the train, an answer to her prayer, and several of her fellow riders positioned themselves near the exit. Just before the doors could open, Christine saw a transit employee directing a family down the platform toward a different car.

She prayed harder.

The doors opened, and half the passengers in the car made their way onto the platform and toward the station exits. Incredibly, no one on the platform chose her car, for which she offered a quick prayer of thanks.

Chimes accompanied the doors as they slid to a close. Her only recourse was to wait for the man to leave the car and head above ground. Then she could call the police, presuming he still had some distance to travel before his intended target.

How long until the next stop? Christine checked her watch, but suddenly realized they weren't moving. She scanned the platform outside but didn't see a single person. No one else seemed to notice.

Except him.

The man in the blue jacket was shaking and sweating even more as his eyes danced frantically from the windows to his fellow passengers. Christine avoided making eye contact with him and pretended to pick at a fingernail.

The train didn't budge. The air in the car felt warmer. The air-drummer opened his eyes and dropped his hands. He frowned at the loudspeaker and said, "Any day now."

The door to the gangway opened, startling everyone in the car. Rabinoff stepped through, his green puffy jacket unzipped. The door closed behind him, and he held his hands open.

"Ladies and gentlemen," he announced. "There's no cause for alarm, but I'd like to ask that everyone remain seated." In slow motion, he lowered his left hand toward the man in the blue jacket and shifted his right toward his right hip. "Sir," he said calmly, "I'm Detective Rabinoff with the New York Police Department. There's no need to be scared. I'm not here to hurt you. I'd just like to ask you a few questions."

The man in the blue jacket, his eyes bulging and his mouth open, hyperventilated as he jumped from his seat and backed away from Rabinoff.

Without rising, Christine edged forward in her seat. Air-drummer pressed himself against the exit doors. The others stared blankly at the scene. The homeless man snorted.

Rabinoff's right hand slipped over the butt of his gun. "Sir, every-thing is fine. Please just show me what you have under your jacket. There's no need for either of us to do anything rash."

The man's jacket collar was soaked in sweat. He trembled as he came to a stop in the middle of the car. Facing Rabinoff, he pulled his hand from his jacket pocket, revealing a metal cylinder with a red switch at its peak. Wires snaked out from the bottom of his fist and disappeared into his sleeve. With his free hand, he unzipped the jacket and let the two sides part.

He wore a black vest underneath. A row of white blocks encircled his abdomen, interconnected wires poking out from beneath each one.

The smartphone girl gasped.

Air-drummer swore and backed away from the middle of the car, but a sudden jerk of the bomber's head stopped him in his tracks.

"Everybody stay calm," Rabinoff ordered. "Don't move." The gun remained holstered, his hand resting just above it. "Listen, pal, I don't know why you chose to do this, but just consider where you are and what you're planning on doing. Whatever else you think this is about, I can tell you right now this isn't going to accomplish anything."

What was he doing? That didn't seem the right way to talk down a suicide bomber. Christine held her breath as Rabinoff took a single short step to close the distance between him and the bomber.

"All you're going to do is kill a bunch of innocent people. Then they'll talk about you on the news for a few weeks, then poof. Gone. You'll never be remembered. You'll get a poorly written online encyclopedia article about your meaningless life."

Definitely not an approved negotiation tactic.

Rabinoff took another step. The bomber's thumb twitched against the trigger. He darted his eyes between the detective and the others. His breathing slowed.

"You might have noticed I haven't pulled out my weapon. That's because there's no reason to. Bomb beats gun. I'm a quick draw, but I'm not that quick. So it's on you. I'm willing to work with you on whatever will help end this with all of us leaving this car intact." Rabinoff nodded as if to prompt the bomber to respond.

A deafening silence filled the car. Christine heard the man's sweat drops slapping against the metal floor.

She searched her memory for anything John had taught her that might help Rabinoff subdue the man without activating the vest. Disarming live bombs had never come up in conversation. He mostly instructed her in self-defense.

Like what to do if someone forcefully grabbed her.

Suddenly, it came to her. Once she saw it, she pushed everything else away and directed her mind, just as he'd taught her, until only it remained. The moment. Her one opportunity.

Christine trained her eyes on the trigger in the man's fist. She estimated the distance between them. John had drilled her until he'd approved of her speed and strength, but the gap she would need to make up caused her to doubt her ability to intervene.

Pray.

She had been.

Harder.

Out of the corner of her eye, she spied Rabinoff's foot lifting off the floor. The bomber straightened. Christine teetered on the lip of her chair.

As Rabinoff lifted his foot to take another step, the bomber stepped backward, parallel to her.

She readied herself, her eyes locked on the red switch. Rabinoff was saying something, but her brain refused the signals sent from her eardrums. A bead of sweat formed on her temple.

The thumb relaxed.

Christine leapt from her chair, grabbed the man's thumb with her left hand and his wrist with her right. Just as John had instructed, she pulled backward on the thumb as hard as she could. The bone broke like a twig.

The man screamed. Rabinoff cursed.

With his thumb still pinned, Christine shoved down on his wrist with her other hand. The man fell to his knees. He opened his hand, and the detonator dropped free, dangling from his jacket sleeve by the wires running underneath.

Rabinoff appeared next to her, his weapon drawn and pointed in the bomber's face. "Stay down!" he barked at the man, then let loose a flurry of expletives in Christine's direction. "What are you, crazy? What if that hadn't worked?"

"Get it off him!"

"We might set it off. Bomb squad is on its way."

The bomber spat an insulting word through his gritted teeth.

Rabinoff pressed the barrel of his gun even closer into the man's face. "Don't move a muscle, or I swear I'll blow you away." He drew a few breaths, then kept his eyes trained on the bomber as he said to Christine, "Nice moves."

The door to the car suddenly slid open, startling the air-drummer and causing him to nearly fall out of the train. A uniformed police officer entered, his weapon drawn. "On your right," he announced as he took brisk steps into the car and next to Rabinoff.

The detective never broke his gaze as he replied, "I've got an armed incendiary device being worn by the suspect. Relieve the lady, please."

The officer rushed to Christine's side and, after holstering his weapon, wrapped his muscular arm around the bomber's and motioned for her to release her grip. She obeyed, stood up, and backed away from the men.

As she drew a deep breath, she watched the passengers flee out the wide-open doorway onto the platform. Air-drummer, smartphone girl, even the homeless man. All five sprinted toward the station exit.

Five. Plus Christine and the bomber. Seven.

That wasn't right. It was eight. Eight passengers when Rabinoff returned. How did she miss one?

Christine scanned the car and the platform outside and concluded she'd imagined the eighth person, when she turned around and saw the back door of the car standing wide open. A dark shadow jogged down into the black abyss of the tunnel.

Handler.

That was what the explosive ordnance disposal men called a suicide bomber's companion, the person responsible for making sure the bomber went through with the plan. Christine remembered two men and a woman sitting near the back. The woman was the last to flee the car. That meant it was one of the men.

"Detective," she called out, still watching the shadow run. "I think he had a friend. And the friend is getting away."

"I'm kind of busy right now."

Christine drew a deep breath and clenched her fists. She turned to take one last look at Rabinoff. He shifted his eyes from the sight on his pistol to Christine and back.

"Don't even think about it."

Christine turned away from him and rushed through the door. She took a leap from the train and hit the ground running.

CHAPTER THREE

A HANDFUL OF square yellow and blue lights spaced yards apart gave off the bare minimum of light needed for Christine's eyes to adjust to the darkness of the tunnel. The blob jogging before her appeared only a shade less black than the void beyond it.

The man moved fast, and Christine struggled to keep up. The wrong step and she'd break an ankle against the uneven metal track.

The bomber's handler wouldn't be armed with explosives, but that didn't necessarily mean he was unarmed. His job was to accompany the suicide bomber to the target and ensure a successful detonation.

If he'd been on the train, why didn't the handler intervene and stop Rabinoff? Christine couldn't think of any reason other than the train car had not been the intended target. But that possibility just begged additional questions.

Since when did suicide bombers care about *not* blowing people up?

Christine strained to examine the obscure path. Rails no wider than her foot ran parallel above uneven concrete. A third rail hugged the left side of the track nearest the wall, and she knew enough about the subway system to know that was the one with the electrical current. She stuck to a wider path just under the rail to her right, praying that no construction errors left holes for her to step in.

When she looked up, her heart jumped as she strained to catch a glimpse of the handler escaping down the tunnel. Did he know that she was behind him? Sound traveled well in the tunnels, but her footfalls competed with the rumble of a passing train in a parallel tube.

A sudden muffled crash echoed off the slick curved walls, followed by a low-toned grunt. She pushed herself faster down the lane and finally spotted the blob pushing himself up off the ground twenty or so yards ahead of her.

The ambient noise stilled, and the clap of Christine's boots against the concrete announced her presence. The handler took off in a full run. Ignoring the warning signals in her brain, Christine locked her eyes on his shape and pushed herself to pick up the pace.

The trek from Herald Square to Forty-Second Street–Bryant Park followed one of the shorter train routes on the Sixth Avenue Express. The light from the platform spilled into the tunnel as the gap again widened between Christine and her quarry.

The outline of the man grew more distinct, as did the rumble in the ground underneath her. A different rumble from a passing train. This one shook the rails on either side of her.

The 11:54 out of Rockefeller Center.

Christine didn't need a better motivation to catch up to the handler. Her calves ached as she pumped her legs. Up ahead, the Bryant Park platform shone bright, like a beacon warning her of impending danger.

The man reached the platform and lunged onto it as the twin headlights of the approaching subway train rounded a corner ahead and bored down the track at full speed.

Christine's foot slipped, forcing her to slow or risk tripping onto the track. Once she found her balance again, she ran as fast as she could.

Several people screamed, barely audible over the screeching brakes as the operator fought to bring the train to a quicker stop than usual. But subway trains weren't easy to halt.

The train was nearly on top of her. Its bright headlights blinded her just as she took the final two steps to the platform edge. Closing her eyes, she pushed down on the tiled floor of the platform with her palms and used the leverage to launch her body up and forward.

She rolled across the tile just as the train screeched to a halt right where she'd stood on the track. Her hands stopped her momentum, with her stomach against the floor.

Another scream distracted her from the anxiety of near death. She jolted upright on her hands and knees and looked up to see the man shoving an older woman aside as he fought his way through the crowd toward the exit staircase.

As she jumped to her feet in pursuit, she took note of the man's short-cropped hair, olive skin, and weathered tan barn coat. He bounded up the stairs with his back to her, making it impossible to see his face.

She elbowed her way through the crowd and up the stairs behind him. She'd lose him for good if she lost track of him in the mass of commuters. All the work she'd put in on the treadmill at the gym better pay off.

He sprinted up the two flights of stairs, through the bank of turnstiles, and up the staircase toward the exit, but the bustle of the station kept him from gaining speed. Just as he ascended the stairs leading up and out, a toddler playing with a stroller stepped in Christine's path.

She collided with the stroller and sent it and the diaper bag it was holding sprawling across the floor. The toddler's mother reached for him and shouted "Silas!" as she pulled him to her.

Without hesitating, Christine stepped over the stroller and kept running toward the stairs. The light grew brighter but a shade bluer as she charged up the staircase and exited the station. In seconds she emerged from underneath the city and onto Forty-Second Street, Bryant Park behind a row of trees to her right.

Christine scanned the crowded sidewalk for any sign of the handler. She turned to search the opposite side of the street, when she saw the short-cropped hair and tan coat of the man as he walked the perimeter of the park.

She walked fast and wove her way down the busy sidewalk. The cold air and cloudy sky didn't keep the locals and tourists away from the park. Though busy, the foot traffic on the sidewalk did little to calm Christine's fear of discovery. She tucked her chin down, puffed the collar of her jacket as much as she could, and angled her face to the ground without losing sight of her quarry.

She dug her hands into her pockets to grab her phone. A quick call to the police, with detailed information on the man's whereabouts, and he'd be in custody before he reached the end of the block.

Her heart fell. Her pockets were empty. She pictured her phone resting comfortably on top of the hard bucket seat of the train, right where she'd left it after deciding to break the bomber's thumb.

No phone. No backup. She needed to come up with a plan, or he'd get away.

They walked in tandem for only a minute before the man glanced over his shoulder. He spotted her and took off in a full sprint down the sidewalk. Christine groaned as she too burst into a run, dodging annoyed pedestrians out for a leisurely midday stroll.

The blossoming trees in the park gave way to the four-story, yellow-brick facade of the New York Public Library Main Branch. Just ahead, the handler shoved an unsuspecting male with a heavy backpack out of his way as he rounded the brick wall lining the perimeter of the building's grounds and took the stairs to the Forty-Second Street entrance.

Christine lost sight of him for a split second, then spotted him at the top of the stairs as she passed the end of the brick wall. He stood still and stared at her down the barrel of a gun. She jumped behind the wall just as he fired.

Three gunshots rang out. The bullets struck a platter resting on top of the wall just above Christine's head. She ducked under her arms as bits of concrete pelted her from above. People screamed as they scattered in all directions.

More screams emanated from the library as, Christine presumed, the man fled inside. She peeked from around the wall and, with the man nowhere in sight, proceeded to take off up the stairs, when a strong hand grabbed her from behind and pulled her back.

"Hey!" she shouted, balling her fist and raising it in the air.

"What are you going to do, hit me?" Rabinoff was all business. He held his gun high and refused to let Christine break from his grasp.

"Detective!" She dropped her fist and stared at him. "How?" she blurted.

Rabinoff held tighter to Christine. "I told you not to think about it."

"He just went inside. And he has a gun."

"We're going to take it from here."

"We?"

From every direction, police officers clad in classic NYPD navy blue descended on their position and rushed the library steps. Radios cackled with chatter concerning an active shooter.

Rabinoff tugged on Christine's arm. "We'll handle this. You head down Forty-Second to the squad cars cordoning off the block, and wait for me there. *Now.*" He added extra emphasis to his final word and urged Christine away from the scene.

She obliged, confident the city's finest were now in control of the situation. With her head low, she started down the sidewalk. More police raced by as pedestrians continued to evacuate.

Right as she reached the corner of the building where it met a terrace overlooking the park, she heard gunshots against a pane of glass on the rear of the library. A young girl screamed.

Christine raced up the stairs to check for injured bystanders. People fled from the simple iron tables and chairs on her right and down into the park. To her left, the more elegant umbrella-covered tables and chairs of the Bryant Park Café sat empty.

Halfway down the side of the building, a figure burst through a second-story window and crashed into one of the umbrellas, showering the café in shards of glass.

Christine recognized the tan coat.

The man righted himself and hobbled away from the café. Rabinoff appeared in the window frame, pointing his gun and shouting obscenities.

Christine ran to intercept the man. As she closed the gap with him, she grabbed one of the iron chairs and spun 360 degrees. She released her hold, and the chair launched from her hands.

The chair struck the man and sent him sprawling across the floor of the terrace. Christine froze, unsure of what to do following her unexpected success at stopping the man in his tracks.

The pause was all he needed. The handler jumped to his feet and aimed his gun at her.

In the second prior to the gunshot, Christine felt something unique. Before she'd met John, facing certain death frightened her. But now, with the prospect once again presented before her, Christine was at peace.

Death did not scare her. It was powerless.

The piercing explosions of the gun sliced the air in rapid succession as every last round was expelled from the clip.

The handler's body convulsed with each hit until he tumbled over and hit the ground facedown, dead.

Christine's eyes widened even farther, and her mouth fell open. She turned and found Rabinoff standing among the broken debris of an umbrella, table, and chairs. He kept the weapon aimed in the direction of the handler as he stepped to her side.

"It's OK. You're OK." He used the full length of his arm to pull her away from the body as NYPD officers rushed across the terrace to confirm the shooter had been neutralized. Christine and Rabinoff walked down the steps and onto the now vacant sidewalk.

Christine finally breathed. Once they were at an acceptable distance, Rabinoff lowered his gun, dropped his arm, and turned to face her.

"I knew I knew you from somewhere," he said. "You're that reporter. The one who was rescued from kidnappers overseas last year, right? Christine—"

She stuck out her hand as she finished his words. "Lewis. Nice to meet you, Detective Peter Rabinoff."

Rabinoff shook her hand and his head. "You must have a knack for being in the wrong place at the wrong time."

"Comes with the journalistic territory, I guess."

"Oh." Rabinoff reached into the pocket of his jacket. "I almost forgot. You left this on the train." He pulled out her phone and extended it toward her.

Christine took it. "That would've come in handy about five minutes ago."

A pair of officers approached them as Rabinoff said, "Well, I hate to break it to you, but you're going to have to come in for a statement. I hope you didn't have any plans."

The interview. Christine swiped her phone open and checked her notifications.

Two missed calls from UNN.

And fifteen missed calls from John.

CHAPTER FOUR

JOHN CROSS STARED at the black screen, a cascade of thoughts spilling from his mind. His training, though rusty, was too ingrained. He imagined every possible scenario, evaluated every possible outcome. The details were scant. The rampant speculation on the news plus the near absence of communication from Christine left holes he felt too eager to fill with absurd plots even Hollywood would turn down.

What did he know? There'd been a suicide bomber arrested on the subway. A shootout occurred at the New York Public Library. And Christine was in the middle of it all. No more, no less.

He opened the phone for the third time in the span of as many minutes, his messages app already queued. Nothing new, but he again read what she'd sent.

I'm OK. I have to make a statement to the NYPD, then I'll call. Don't worry. I'm safe. I'll call as soon as I can.

The police wouldn't have stopped her from making a phone call, but he imagined he was a notch or two down the list. She'd call her mother, then her father, just to ensure they wouldn't worry should her name come up on the news.

By then they'd be ready for her. He knew they'd be thorough, and he hated them for it. All he could do was wait.

And pray.

He stopped pacing the carpet in front of the altar and plopped onto the front right pew of the Rural Grove Baptist Church sanctuary. The television news broadcast that had interrupted a game show rerun in the waiting room at Memorial Regional Medical Center replayed in his mind.

"Breaking news out of New York City," the polished anchorman had said, coming out of a network alert graphic. "Details are just beginning to come in about an attempted suicide bombing on board a subway car. New York City police were able to intervene and prevent what could've been a violent, tragic event. Here's what we know at this hour . . ."

At that point, Cross had half listened to the report, half waited for the call to connect with Christine's phone. In between the ringing and dialing, he'd absorbed the scant information from the broadcast: a single suicide bomber, NYPD intervened, the bomb disarmed, one suspect in custody, reports of another suspect being pursued on foot.

The incoming update of shots fired at the library had prompted Cross's exit from the hospital. Nick and Bri's families had understood and wished him prayerful farewells.

He now pictured each of them in his mind and prayed for hope and blessing. Then he thought of Nick and Bri and spent twice as long asking for health for mother and baby.

His prayers transitioned to Christine, her family, even himself. His former life with the Central Intelligence Agency had left him desensitized to tragedy and chaos—that was, until Jesus woke within him a long-ignored yearning for justice and restoration. He prayed for well-being, for God's spirit of peace, for strength and confidence in the midst of uncertainty.

And the terrorist? What about him? Cross grumbled under his breath at the prodding of his heart to offer supplication on the man's behalf. He closed his eyes and pushed the temptation to refuse from his mind. Then, out loud, he prayed for the bomber.

A sharp, musical tone blared from his phone's speaker, startling him. He snatched it from the pew seat and answered without looking at the screen.

"Christine," he said as he stood.

"No, John. I'm sorry. It's Gary," the head deacon and volunteer worship director of the church replied in his deep but smooth voice.

"Gary, yes, it's fine. I didn't look at the number. I've been waiting for her to call."

"Deb texted me when she saw the news. That's why I was calling. I didn't know if, well, if you'd heard from Christine. I know it's a big city, but . . ." His words trailed, dread and hope mixing in the silence left behind.

Cross hesitated with his reply, the involuntary desire to lie lingering in his heart even after being forced to confess his past deeds to the congregation. He glanced at the pulpit, the image of Yunus Anar holding him at knifepoint as clear as if it were happening again. The echo of men, women, and children stifling their cries haunted him every night.

He cleared his throat, banished the images, and enunciated his words. "I believe Christine was involved, yes, but she's texted me and let me know she's OK. She's with the police right now. They're taking a statement. Unfortunately, that's all I know."

"Are you still at the hospital?"

"No, I left after I couldn't get ahold of her. I don't know why. I guess I just thought I needed to go somewhere. Do something. I'm at the church. I've been praying."

"Me too. Praying, that is."

Cross took a deep breath. "Thanks" was all he could offer in return.

There was a brief pause, then Gary said, "I bet it's hard."

"What is?"

"Not being there."

"Actually, Christine's pretty good at taking care of herself. She's been through a lot, but I've never met anyone with as strong a spirit."

"Oh yeah, I believe it. But I meant . . ." The line went silent again.

Cross adjusted the position of the phone against his ear. Before he could double-check the screen to see if the call had dropped, Gary's voice came back.

"Never mind. How are the Potters?"

Strange. It was unlike Gary to refrain from speaking his mind. Cross could recall any number of deacon meetings where the sandy-haired baby boomer spoke a lot of truth with just enough grace. And yet there was no lack of respect for Cross, for Gary's words were always measured and never malicious.

"They're great," Cross said. "Nick's dad texted and let me know the delivery went well and the baby is healthy, all things considered. They'll be in the NICU for a few days just to make sure."

"What was Bri, thirty-seven weeks?"

"Thirty-five. She's doing well too."

"That's great news."

Another moment of silence. Gary was holding back. Cross just didn't know why. "Gary, is there something on your mind?" he prodded.

"Nothing. Just thinking it'd be great if you could get out to New York." No dead air this time. "Let's make it a point to grab lunch soon. No particular reason, just to check in."

Cross was sure there was a reason, but he didn't feel like interrogating his friend. With his luck, Christine's call would interrupt them right as Gary was ready to confess.

"All right," he said. "We'll get lunch soon. I promise."

"Give Christine our love when she calls. I'll see you on Sunday."

"I will. Thanks, Gary."

Cross dropped the phone from his ear and imagined what concern Gary might bring over an informal lunch meeting. A flood of possible scenarios tore through his mind. Rural Grove Baptist, with its small contingent of faithful agrarian attenders, was the only evangelical church context Cross knew. Yet in his meticulous research concerning ministerial responsibilities, there was no shortage of chapters in leadership books and articles on pastoral blogs detailing the darker side of church management.

Taking a cue from those harrowing tales, Cross made it a point as the de facto head of the congregation to focus much less on implementing structural changes and much more on serving and caring for the individual members day in and day out. He didn't have much of an opinion on the administration in any case. The weekly pressure of delivering a sermon consumed all the confidence he could muster.

Perhaps that was the issue. What little progress he had made with his online theological classes prior to the events in DC remained stagnant now that he divided his time between Virginia and New York. He regretted the pause in his training but hadn't considered the ramifications of a season away from the rigor of coursework. Until today.

That could be it. Or something else. He searched his mind for an image or sound from the past few months that might reveal a possible blemish in his ministerial record worthy of a reprimanding lunch appointment. His ability to remember minute details served him in both his former and current life. The possibility remained that his interpretation of an encounter with a congregant or a statement from the pulpit differed from what another might assume.

Cross frowned. If he were honest with himself, it was probably both an encounter and a theological error in a sermon. The latter he could have avoided, had he furthered his religious education.

The ring from his phone shook him loose from the deep dive into his thoughts. How long had it been ringing? He glanced at the screen and immediately swiped to answer as he brought it to his ear.

"Thank God," he said. "I know you already said it, but are you OK?"

He heard a subtle chuckle followed by Christine's static-filled voice. "I'm fine. Really. I just finished giving my statement, but I'm still at the precinct."

Cross winced at the poor connection. She ignored his advice to switch carriers despite the obvious lack of consistent coverage. Brand loyalty, or some other excuse.

"I'm having a little trouble hearing you."

"Is that better?" she asked after a brief rustling of the phone on her end.

"Yes." It wasn't.

"I know you've got a lot of questions, and I want to tell you everything. It'll have to be tonight. I'm sure you can guess, but the network's already sent a car. They're eager to dominate the afternoon with all the insider information."

"I believe it. I'm just glad you're not hurt. Is there anything I can do?"

"Actually, yes, there is." Christine paused. "I just got off the phone with Dad."

The only image Cross called to mind of Christine's father was a literal picture he'd seen one night over coffee as she regaled him with stories from her childhood. Her parents separated when she was young, and her father moved to Springfield, Missouri, but they'd maintained as strong of a relationship through the years as they could despite the distance. As a teen, she'd even spent a summer with him, her stepmother, and her stepbrother.

Cross visualized the photo of a young Christine with a broad smile crossing arms with her dad, Charles was his name, and her younger stepbrother. What was his name again? Paul? Cross shook his head. He always remembered the small details. Always.

The thought of his intelligence skills atrophying bothered him. Maybe there was something he'd done to warrant discipline from Gary, and he just didn't remember it.

"John?"

"Yeah, sorry. I'm here. You were saying you spoke to Charles?"

"He called, obviously. Saw it on the news. I couldn't take the call, so he left a message. It's been a while since we last talked. And, well, I . . . I can't even believe I'm going to say this. But, well . . ."

She stammered. Shaken. It was unsettling. She wasn't like this. Cross held his breath.

"It's Philip."

The stepbrother. That was his name.

"He's been arrested. In Texas." She paused, then Cross detected an audible gulp. "For murder."

CHAPTER FIVE

CHRISTINE FILLED HIM in on the scant amount of detail she'd acquired from the brief voicemail from Charles. The call quality improved as she exited the precinct and entered the awaiting taxi. It seemed her stepbrother was arrested two days earlier on a murder charge. Charles hadn't made any suggestions, but Cross knew Christine: she'd escape the city as soon as she could.

"Can you call him back? I would, but between the police and—" A deeper, muffled voice interrupted hers. "I'm sorry. Steve insisted he ride along, and he's rudely interrupting with his plans for my afternoon."

Cross hadn't had a chance to meet Christine's philander of a boss yet. Which was a good thing for all parties involved. Cross swallowed his annoyance. "It's OK. I know you have to go. Don't worry. I'll call Charles right now and see what more I can find out. Let's talk as soon as you can."

"We'll at least video chat if I can't find a way to ditch these interviews and hop a late flight to Richmond."

Cross smirked as he imagined the glare of jealousy on Jacobs's face. "If only. I'll talk to you soon."

"Love you."

He didn't have to pry the words from her this time. Was it another dig at Jacobs? Or perhaps a genuine sentiment provoked by the harrowing experience on the subway? Cross squeezed his eyes closed and berated himself for questioning her motives. Just because he questioned his standing with the church didn't mean everything in his life was up for debate.

"I love you too," he said, then ended the call.

Cross stood motionless in the middle of the quiet, chilly sanctuary. He never ran the heating system when spending time alone there, considering the use of energy an unnecessary waste on his behalf.

How had they made it this far? Exploring a long-distance relationship had seemed like the natural next step for them. The beginning months were fun, sure. And there was no question the attraction was mutual. But the distance didn't make things easy, and now Cross was unsure. Of everything.

And he didn't like it.

Fortunately, an opportunity to ignore his conflicting emotions lay before him. And it was an activity he was good at: interrogation. Thankfully, he had no need of the techniques he'd used, and regretted, in the past. This time he would have a willing participant in the questioning.

A notification on his phone drew him to the screen. A text from Christine with a string of numbers separated by dashes appeared. That was it. Just Charles's phone number. A few months ago there would've been more. At least an emoji or two. A message devoid of emotion or subtext. He swallowed hard, locked the screen, and headed for the exit.

A sharp wind met him at the doorway as he stepped outside. Early spring in Virginia was fickle, and this particular week seemed in no hurry to welcome warmer temperatures. Even the mostly clear sky appeared less blue, more sour gray.

Cross locked the doors and pulled his jacket together at the neck. He didn't mind the cold, but he didn't care for it either. As he walked toward the modest parsonage he resided in, he couldn't help but steal a glance over his shoulder at the portrait of Rural Grove behind him.

There, behind the faded white structure with a simple cross at the point of a steeple, was the metal outline of a planned but ultimately abandoned expansion of the building, the relic of an embattled former pastor. Cross couldn't gaze at it without reliving the dark moments of his encounter with Yunus Anar. The roar of thunder and rain, the flash of lightning, the crunch of flesh and bone as they fought, and Christine's voice all rang in his memory.

John, don't do it! This isn't you! Not who you really are.

The one bold decision he longed to make for the congregation was the removal of the unsightly thing. Though it reminded him of that night, it also reminded him of his commitment to the new man he'd become in his conversion to Christianity. The old was gone, just like Paul had written in the Bible. Unfortunately, with a hefty loan hanging over their heads, the church found itself tied to the thing. So it remained. A ridiculous yet somehow beautiful monument.

As he looked back at the parsonage, Cross spotted a second vehicle hiding behind his sedan. He slowed, but only for a moment. His spirit lifted as he picked up his pace.

The front door to the house opened as he crossed the small two-lane highway separating the parsonage from the church parking lot. Lori Johnson stepped onto the small concrete landing and shut the door behind her.

"I hope you left something delicious behind," Cross called out.

Lori gasped and grabbed at her wool sweater with both hands. "John Cross, are you trying to give this old lady a heart attack?"

"I can't believe you would accuse me of such a thing." Cross opened his arms and gave her a firm hug. He placed his hands on her shoulders as he stepped out of the hug and broadened his smile. "And cut it out with the 'old lady' talk. You're healthier than I am and twice as strong."

"Now I know you're lying." It was true: she knew when he was lying. She always had.

She stepped off the landing, and together they walked slowly to her car.

"I just came by to let you know I was praying for Christine. I was watching all about the horrible bomb scare in New York. Her name came up, and I thought you might need company."

Cross gave her another hug around her shoulders as they walked.

"Thank you, Lori. That means a lot. I just got off the phone with her. She wasn't hurt, and they're already getting her ready to do a round of interviews."

"Praise the Lord," Lori said with a sigh of relief. "Of course, I already knew she was fine. That girl can certainly handle herself."

"You don't need to tell me."

"Are you going up there?"

"I wish. She might try to make it down here before the weekend."

They both fell silent as they reached the driver's-side door of Lori's car. She hesitated with the handle, then looked into Cross's eyes. He almost laughed out loud as he suddenly suspected she might read his mind.

"John, you can't be too thrilled with the fact that this happened and you weren't there."

Cross felt his heart rate rise a slight degree. He shrugged. "I wouldn't have been there anyway. She was on her lunch break."

Lori's cheeks dimpled and her eyes softened. She patted him on his chest with her free hand. "You're a good man, John Cross. God is going to use you in big ways."

"I hope so. I really care about you. All of you."

"I know." She dropped her gaze as she opened the door to her car. He held it for her as she sat on the driver's seat. She cranked the car on, and he shut the door. As he stood smiling at her, she rolled down the window.

"Oh, and one more thing," she said, the playfulness returning to her voice. "There is something delicious for you inside."

He grinned. "Drive safe, young lady."

Lori glared with a raised eyebrow before winking and rolling up the window as she backed out of the narrow gravel driveway. Cross waved as she exited onto the highway and sped off.

The car disappeared around a curve heading into a thick patch of trees. Lori's words replayed in his mind. In retrospect, he felt she was hiding something. Just like Gary. What did Lori know? And why didn't she say anything?

Cross took a deep breath and scolded himself. Now he was just being paranoid. He took in the crisp air as he stared into the horizon and prayed for the Lord to settle his heart.

Turning, he marched up to the door and into his home. He passed through the living room, ignoring the light switches, and made a direct path to the kitchen. To Lori's word, a covered translucent plastic container sat on the counter. Looked like stir fry. A sweet note on the lid confirmed his suspicion.

He tucked the container into the refrigerator next to a half-consumed dish of Barbara Templeton's "award-winning" meatloaf. The appliance never seemed to catch a break when it came to housing complimentary meals from the mature ladies of the congregation.

With his dinner secure, Cross pulled his phone out from his jacket pocket and tapped the highlighted collection of digits in the text from Christine. He held the phone up to his ear and rested his back against the door to the fridge.

It took more than three rings before the call connected. Cross expected to hear a recorded message prompting him to leave a voicemail, but instead a throaty voice with the hint of a midland accent said, "Hello?"

"Yeah, hi, is this Charles Lewis?"

"That's me. Who's this?"

Cross felt his heart leap. He'd been fortunate enough to meet and converse with Christine's mother on one occasion when they'd both traveled to New York City during Christine's birthday weekend, but this was the first time he'd spoken to Christine's father. Cross pictured an aged version of the man from the photo he'd seen.

"Good afternoon, sir. My name is John Cross."

"Cross? John Cross?"

"Yes, sir."

"I know who you are, and stop calling me sir. What am I, a knight or something?"

"I apologize, Mr. Lewis." Cross lowered the phone for a moment and mentally kicked himself for sounding so formal. He brought the phone up and continued, "Sorry, Charles. I'm a little off today. As you can imagine."

"I take it you've heard from Chrissy?"

Cross stifled a laugh. He hadn't heard that nickname before, and he couldn't wait to let Christine know he knew about it.

"Only briefly. She's on her way to be interviewed by the network about what happened and didn't have much time to talk. She asked me call you."

"She said she would. Said you would know a thing or two about what's going on down here."

What had she said exactly? Surely nothing about his history. "Well, I talk to a lot of people during the week, you could say almost counsel. She probably thought I'd ask good questions."

"That's right." Charles laughed. "You're a preacher. She told me that. Well, that's good. We're definitely going to need some prayer, Preacher."

That was going to be his nickname now, wasn't it? Charles apparently enjoyed handing them out. All things considered, it wasn't the worst epithet Cross had ever been given.

"Charles, I didn't get much more information than Christine's stepbrother has been arrested. Can you fill me in?"

"Well, you need to know that there's not much more I myself know. I can tell you what's been reported, and I can tell you what Philip told me, which wasn't a lot. That's why I asked Christine to come as soon as she could."

Knowing Christine, she didn't need to be asked. Cross imagined she was already searching flight schedules from her phone while having makeup applied before her live interview.

Charles continued, "Philip's been living in Dallas the past few years, working for a technology company. I don't remember the name off the top of my head. Seems last week a coworker of his was found dead in the alley of a downtown nightclub. Place was called Angel Dust, or Angela's, or something. I'm not really good with names."

Hence the propensity for nicknames.

"I'm telling you, not a day later they put Philip in cuffs and locked him up. No bail. The news article I read said they had video evidence Philip killed the man. And then—I'm not making this up—Philip used his one phone call to call me. He would've called Christine himself but hadn't memorized her number. He knew mine by heart. I haven't changed it since I first got a cell phone."

"So," Cross interrupted, "they have video of Philip committing the murder?"

"It appears that way, but Philip told me he hadn't been feeling well the day it happened and went home. Next thing he knows, it's the day after and he's waking up to police busting through his front door. He swears he's innocent."

In Cross's experience, they rarely were. Distrust had served him well in his former life. The gospel shifted his perspective of others, sure, but he still operated by the refrain "everyone lies." They lied to others, or themselves, or in extreme cases, both. He still believed that was true, though grappled with such a cynical outlook given his position of pastoral leadership. Wasn't he supposed to always see the good in others?

Sometimes he doubted how much good there actually was. And it didn't help that his former CIA boss and close friend, Al Simpson, had betrayed him to Yunus Anar last year. Close friend? More like family. If Simpson had made the decision to give in to his evil desires, so could Philip.

The line fell silent for a moment, then Cross asked, "Is he?"

Charles replied with a subtle sigh. "Philip's not always been the straightest arrow. Got that trait from his grandfather on his mom's side. When Tracy passed—" The voice quivered, but only for a syllable. "It didn't help. But he's turned it around the last few years. The boy might've bent the rules a little, but he's no killer."

If there was ever a man to make that judgment, it was John Cross.

CHAPTER SIX

CHRISTINE STOOD STILL, her back straight and shoulders locked. Her last check in the mirror of the green room confirmed her red portfolio dress fit perfectly, but just to be sure she maintained a rigid posture in the hike across the floor to Studio 37. Her next opportunity to survey the state of her appearance would unfortunately be right as the cameras turned on her once she was seated across the desk from Daniel Meyers.

She checked her watch, taking care to only move her forearm at the elbow and tilt her head just enough to catch a glimpse of the narrow face. The silky voice of Meyers droned on as he filled his viewers in on all the latest details concerning the attempted suicide bombing. His opening segment would end in less than a minute, then he'd pitch to the break. That was her cue.

As the final seconds ticked away, Christine closed her eyes, took deep breaths, and prayed. The flutter of her heart, affected by exhilaration rather than anxiety, subsided. She imagined herself in Meyers's place, albeit with a different network logo behind her, and her heart threatened to race again.

Meyers called her name, and she turned to the bright pair of monitors to her left. He stared at her from the screen and finished his sentence. "One of our own national correspondents, in an incredible turn of events, was present on the subway car during the attempted attack. Christine joins me next in studio for an exclusive on what happened on the inside."

The catchy theme song for the show played from a speaker overhead as Meyers pretended to examine a sheet of paper on the slick tempered-glass desk. A beleaguered female producer barked orders into her headset as cameras shifted and production assistants tried not to get fired. A makeup artist stepped onto the elevated stage and touched up Meyers's cheeks.

Someone touched Christine's elbow and nodded toward the desk. There might have been words, but Christine didn't listen. She marched toward Meyers, the heel of her pumps clicking in a commanding rhythm.

She sat in the low-back chair on the opposite curve of the desk from the anchor, his face still obscured by a makeup brush.

The producer stepped up and flashed a pair of fingers in Christine's face. "Two minutes."

Christine nodded, then noticed her image in a monitor pointed toward the desk. She found the camera framing her up from across the studio and stared into its black eye. She felt a surge of delight as she considered what it would be like to have one pointed at her every night.

Shifting her eyes to the monitor, she examined her dress for rumples. Pristine. And the red color popped on the screen just like she'd hoped.

"Beautiful."

Christine let an audible gasp escape as her eyes widened at the sharp sound of Meyers's voice interrupting her concentration. She turned in the chair to face him and exchanged her startled expression for an incurious smirk.

He mimicked her examination of the dress, an unnerving glisten in his eye. "Absolutely stunning. You're going to knock them out tonight."

The makeup girl did her job well. Age lines hid under a thick layer of foundation. A short-cropped haircut concealed the man's thinning hairline. On camera he looked polished and youthful.

But up close and personal, Meyers still reeked of privilege and audacity.

Christine angled an eyebrow. "I haven't told anybody this, but I was the one who stopped the attack."

The smile faded as Meyers swore. "No wonder they grounded you from a foreign beat. Let me guess. PTSD from that time you almost got your head cut off?"

Christine leaned toward him. "You know how I did it?"

The producer started loudly counting down from ten behind the camera.

"I broke his thumb right at the base where it connects to his hand." Christine stared into Meyers's widening eyes, then winked and sat straight up in her chair.

"Five, four." The producer went silent and called the final three numbers with her fingers in the air. The theme music swelled from the speakers, and the show's graphics package filled the monitors.

Meyers cleared his throat as he faced a camera highlighted by a bright-red light atop its hood. The graphics faded into a medium shot of him behind the desk.

"More details have been shared concerning the attempted bombing of New York City subway passengers earlier today," he read off the teleprompter. "Authorities have yet to release the name of the suspected attacker, but, amazingly, NABC's very own reporter Christine Lewis was present in the subway car when an off-duty police officer apprehended the man and prevented the detonation. As you may recall, it was a mere ten months ago that Christine was dramatically rescued from a Jordanian prison by the United States military, then was instrumental in leading authorities to a subsequent chemical attack that had been planned on the nation's capital. Christine joins me live in studio to give us a report from the inside of this near-tragic event."

Out of the corner of her eye, Christine saw the cut to a wider angle that framed both of them perfectly in the shot on the monitor. She beamed at the appropriate camera.

"Christine," Meyers said as he turned to face her. "Welcome, and I speak for all of us here at NABC when I say we are incredibly grateful that you and the other passengers from the subway this morning are alive and well."

The camera cut to a single shot of her.

"Thank you, Daniel. I'm still having a hard time believing it happened, but I want to thank God for his protection of all of us this morning."

Before the camera could cut to the two-shot, Christine detected a slight eye roll from Meyers. "I know there's some things you can't tell us yet about the event, given the investigation currently underway by the NYPD, but describe the sequence of events starting from when you entered the subway."

Christine described the official version of her experience on the train. "Official" meaning the version she and Rabinoff landed on while at the precinct. She insisted he take the credit for identifying the bomber and for getting the jump on the man. The less questions she had to answer about her recent "training," courtesy of her ex–CIA assassin boyfriend, of course, the better. She hadn't even filled Rabinoff in on everything. Given her previous experience with a near-execution at the hand of extremists in a foreign country, he easily believed she took up self-defense classes to help with the post-traumatic stress.

Though not entirely honest, it wasn't entirely a lie either. Yet another balancing act between the self-serving habits of her former life and the higher calling of her newfound faith.

Meyers, for his part, asked engaging questions and feigned interest and surprise for the viewing audience. "As I said at the top of the segment, we're so relived you're OK, and that the brave men and women of the NYPD kept our city safe from this potential tragedy. Thank you for coming on."

Christine flashed him a warm smile and nodded. "Thank you for having me."

Turning to the camera, Meyers straightened his shoulders and used a commanding tone. "President Gray took time out of his busy schedule on his cross-country trip touting his newly revealed energy and environment plan to make a statement about today's attack. We have his remarks, and more about the national response, coming up after the break."

The camera held the shot, and a short string of music accompanied the fade to the show's logo. "Glad I'll never have to talk to you again," Meyers said without looking at her. He muttered what sounded like a slur under his breath just before the makeup artist reached him.

The feeling was mutual, though Christine kept it to herself. The producer appeared and waved her down from the platform. She obliged quickly, with less concern over tousling her dress. A production assistant handed her the only thing she'd carried with her to the studio: her phone.

She pressed the Home button, and the screen flashed on. Resting between a bevy of notifications was a text from John.

"Sounds like Philip is in real trouble. Call me as soon as you can."

Christine slipped out of her heels, scooped them from the floor, and walked swiftly out of the studio to the green room.

"Great job tonight. You were beautiful." She liked hearing the compliment from John much more than Meyers. John's words brought a smile to her face, though Christine wanted nothing more than to dispense with the pleasantries and hear about Philip.

"Thank you," she responded. "But remind me to fill you in on my impression of Daniel Meyers."

"Not a good one, I take it. Maybe later. I know you're anxious to hear about Philip."

So anxious, she'd stayed in the building and called John from her enclosed office adjacent to the bull pen. Jacobs called it a promotion when he gave her the office, though she suspected it was more of a romantic gesture. She stared out the window at the bright, hazy lights of the city against a backdrop of black night, as she recounted the events of the morning. The muffled voices on the other side of the glass office door reminded her the newsroom never slept. She knew the same would be true for her.

With no more questions of his for her to answer, her mind centered on Philip. "Tell me everything."

John cleared his throat. She imagined him studying a notepad of scribbles, though she knew he took all notes in his mind. "Well, Philip has worked for a technology company called Hale Industries, based in Dallas, Texas, for the past three years."

Christine recalled Philip's move, but the details of his employment were vague, a common trait of his. She'd always figured it was another app start-up or tech firm.

John continued, "Last week, a coworker of his named Mano Amaya was found dead in the alley of a nightclub called De Angelis. Philip was implicated in the murder and arrested the following day."

"Implicated?" Christine interrupted. "How so? Eyewitness?"

"Worse. Video evidence."

Christine closed her eyes and drew a deep breath. Her nightmare was true. Philip got himself too deep into something, and now he would pay the price.

"Christine?"

"I'm OK." For now. Maybe not later. She swallowed the bile inching up her throat and turned from the window to face the front of her office. "Did Dad say anything else?"

"Only that Philip claims he's innocent. And wants you to come help him prove it. But you already know that. Have you bought your ticket yet?"

She hated when he did that. But there wasn't any reason to play games. "I couldn't get out tonight, so I booked the 6:25 a.m. flight out of LaGuardia on American."

"Christine, listen."

And there it was. He would speak his mind. She respected his right to say it but didn't like the air of authority he sometimes carried when presenting his case. A week in Texas solving a murder mystery seemed more and more like the break that she needed from the rut she'd fallen into.

"Go ahead, John. Say it."

"I'm glad you're going."

Well, that wasn't what she expected. She narrowed her eyes and stared out the window of her office door at two men debating copy on a word processor.

"I'm sure Philip is scared. And I know you'll do everything you can to help him. I just . . ." John's voice trailed off.

He didn't have to say any more. She knew what it was. And if she were honest, she'd have to agree: Philip was most likely a murderer. Her trip wouldn't be helping him prove his innocence. It'd be confirming what she already feared. And then facing her father with the truth.

She hung her head as John finished his thought. "Just be careful. I'll be praying for you. Text me when you land."

"I will." Christine lifted her head, and she frowned. "John?"

"Yes."

"I need to do this on my own. Don't even think about coming."

"I'd be lying if I said I didn't."

"It may be complicated, but it's my family. And I don't need it any more complicated. You know what that's like, right?"

John hesitated, weighing the implications beneath her words. She knew he did, and not just with her. "OK. But I won't, on one condition."

Didn't she just say no complications? Christine held in a sigh. "What is it?"

"You promise me you'll only talk to Philip and any relevant investigators, then leave. No solving this case on your own. The police will do their job."

Christine faced a choice: confess her intentions or lie to her boyfriend. Before she met John, the lie would've been easy. Now she couldn't force herself to do it. "I'll dig around, and I'll be careful. But if I think he's innocent, I can't promise I won't stay." John attempted to protest, but she stood her ground. "If I do stay, I'll call you immediately and let you know."

Silence. Maybe she'd been too assertive. He had every right to be concerned for her safety after the day she'd just had. But he wasn't in charge of her life, though it dawned on her he might just want to be.

All the nights learning his trade instead of catching the latest superhero flick. He'd dictated the rules of their experimental relationship. What say did she have in the matter? None that came to mind.

She liked superheroes. What kind of movies did he like?

"All right," he said, finally. "If you think something's up, call me. Then we can talk about what to do next."

Her turn to make the rules. "John, I'm serious. Do not follow me."

He conceded her request. They exchanged affectionate sentiments, then hung up. Christine stood motionless in the center of her office, the city lights out the window, her desk lamp, and the overhead fluorescents in the bull pen casting long shadows about the room. She took a deep breath to settle her heart and fought the urge to cry.

John Cross was a liar.

But so was she.

CHAPTER SEVEN

SHE DIDN'T SLEEP. Instead, Christine hired a car and went home to shower and pack. She arrived at the airport three hours before departure. It took as long, if not longer, to go through security as usual, but her early arrival meant she had time to grab the largest cup of coffee she could buy.

While waiting for the flight to board, she studied every news article and broadcast she could find online about the murder. The airline employees did their jobs efficiently, and before long she was forced to put her investigation on hold while the plane sped down the runway, lifted off the ground, and sliced through thick gray clouds with a southwest heading.

It cost to connect her phone to the wireless internet network, a price she gladly paid as soon as they reached cruising altitude. Notifications filled her screen, one text in particular making her grin from ear to ear: "Ready to call a strike on Meyers's penthouse. Just say the word. –g"

They rarely got to see each other but texted enough for Christine to know Guin Sullivan meant every word. The CIA officer, a crucial partner in the Washington incident, was now one of her best friends and would no doubt deliver payback to the television anchor if Christine didn't stop her.

Christine shot off a snarky reply, then dug into her research. She thanked God her seatmates chose sleep over conversation. She dreaded the pressure to make polite chitchat, especially considering the rapidly expanding list of questions that filled her mind.

They were forty-five minutes out from their destination when the heavy man next to her in the window seat excused himself to the restroom. Christine and the groggy woman next to her stepped into the aisle to let him pass, then both sulked to their seats to wait for him to come back and force them up again.

He returned, and they awkwardly danced around each other a second time. Christine clicked her seat belt together as the flight attendant announced their descent. She scanned the last article she found until the internet connection died. The woman next to her, an African American with graying hair, perked up and attempted to converse. Christine wanted to engage but found her mind wandering. The lady was pleasant, and she mentioned something about visiting grandchildren. Was that it? Christine lost track of the conversation and felt guilty.

The plane touched down at Dallas/Fort Worth International Airport and taxied to the terminal. Conversation lapsed as everyone aboard unbuckled, stood, and pulled luggage from overhead compartments. Christine attempted to engage the woman while they waited, but the opportunity was gone. She mentally kicked herself for neglecting a chance to bring up spiritual matters, a discipline she was still learning.

As she stepped off the plane, Christine was struck by the warmth that greeted her. She'd expected the temperature to be higher than New York City, but not the added measure of humidity. She regretted packing mostly long-sleeve shirts. At the first opportunity inside the airport, she shed her overcoat and threw it over her forearm as she marched to the exit.

The car she'd arranged to pick her up arrived late. The driver apologized profusely, blaming pileup on the highway, no doubt hoping for mercy on an online review. Christine wasn't the type to rate drivers and didn't care about his tardiness. Her appointment to meet with Philip was delayed by bureaucratic red tape, so there was time to kill.

Still, she didn't plan on staying idle. The first stop on her investigative tour of the city was the scene of the crime, followed by a quick meeting with a local reporter she'd contacted on the plane. The only one who'd returned her messages.

"I can't wait to meet you," the reply text had concluded. Apparently local NABC affiliate reporter Jeremy Blankenship was a fan. Which could be good. Or bad. It was only a matter of hours before she found out.

The driver navigated the maze of lanes exiting the terminal, then through the massive airport complex. Christine was confident it was the biggest airport she'd ever seen, having seen her fair share.

Her driver, Paolo, kept asking probing questions, and it distracted her from additional research on her phone. He perked up when she mentioned her job with NABC, and he pressured her to reveal insider information about the president and his administration.

"He's on his way here, you know," Paolo said, beaming. "Well, not really on his way right now. But we're one of the stops on his energy tour. He's going to see the new Logan Group headquarters opening in Addison with one of our senators."

Christine thought about her seatmate on the plane and decided to engage. "From what I know, the locals never seem to care when a president stops in their town. Traffic alone becomes a nightmare."

"Oh, not me. I love it."

"Does it bring in more business?"

"Some, but I just love how it highlights the city. More than just sports teams, you know?"

That was right. Christine recalled Dallas being one of the few cities in the country to host a team from all four of the major sports leagues. "Not a sports fan?" she asked.

Paolo laughed. "No, no, no, I love my Cowboys and Mavs. Could take or leave the Rangers and couldn't tell you anything about the Stars. I just think there's so much more our city has to offer. There are so many wonderful things to see. I hope you get a chance to enjoy the city, after your work, of course."

Christine's flight was one way. She assumed, after a satisfactory investigation, her next stop would be Springfield to visit her father and deliver the bad news in person. Being a tourist in Dallas was not a proposition on this trip.

"How long have you lived in Dallas, Paolo?"

"Born and raised." His words echoed with pride.

"Is all your family here too?"

"Most. Some have moved away."

Christine hesitated, but Paolo didn't offer a new topic, so she made her move. "Do you go to a church in the area?"

Paolo eyed her in his rearview mirror as they slowly merged into traffic congestion. He returned his gaze to the road as a broad smile spread across his face. "I do. And I'm sorry, Ms. Lewis. I have to admit I did not expect you to be religious."

"Oh, really? How so?"

"Well, you know, you're a journalist and all."

Christine offered her own smile. "Just because I asked if you attend church doesn't necessarily mean I'm religious myself."

Paolo chuckled, and his cheeks darkened a shade redder. "Oh, true, well . . ." He stumbled over incoherent syllables.

"But." She laughed. "I actually am a Christian."

His eyes wide, Paolo grinned back. "Wonderful! I'm so sorry, I guess I should still ask for forgiveness for judging you so harshly."

"It's not a problem, Paolo. I can understand why you thought I might not be." Christine enjoyed toying with the man a bit too much. "So where *do* you go to church?"

Paolo told Christine about his and his family's history with St. Monica Catholic Church in the north area of the city. Christine loved hearing his stories, and before she knew it, they reached the De Angelis nightclub at the corner of Commerce Street and South Pearl Expressway. Paolo jumped from the car and met Christine at her door with her carry-on bag in his hand.

"Ms. Lewis, it has been great to get to know you. I hope you find what you're looking for in Dallas."

Christine accepted the bag from him and shut her door. "Thank you, Paolo. I hope so too."

Paolo wiggled his eyebrows, saluted her, then scurried to the driver's side. He checked his phone—likely for a new fare—then waved at her as he pulled away. Christine returned the gesture and watched as he merged into traffic heading south.

Christine scanned the horizon from right to left and marveled at the wide, vibrant blue sky hanging overhead. No matter the time of day, a New York sky always seemed gray. To her left were Texas-size skyscrapers. In reality no bigger than any from her hometown, yet somehow standing taller.

She turned to the entrance to De Angelis. The nightclub occupied more than half of a two-story building, sharing the space with a small law office to the right. The law office's faded red brick and green trim clashed with the black brick and floor-to-ceiling windows of De Angelis. The name of the nightclub was emblazoned in bold gold lettering across the overhang above the entrance.

Christine was struck by the openness of the lot. She pictured more of a New York club scene in her mind, not the updated Old West–town street she now faced. A parking lot beside the nightclub separated the building from another that even appeared like it was from that era. This didn't seem like the place to commit a murder.

Although now all she could imagine was Philip in a quick-draw Old West duel.

De Angelis was open, but Christine thought better of asking questions of the employees. The chance of any of them having been present the evening of the incident was slim enough, and they were most likely tired of answering the same questions over and over.

Blankenship's job was to answer her questions. Christine only wanted to gain her bearings on the scene of the incident before they met. And who knew—maybe she'd see something the police missed.

She shouldered her bag and rounded the corner into the parking lot. Behind the club rose the steel beams of some urban-development project mid-construction. And in between the new structure and De Angelis lay a narrow alley.

The cracked concrete formed a small gully running the length of the alley and ending at an industrial-size waste container. Loose electrical wires swayed in the light breeze just off the club, and a metal fire escape sat suspended ten feet off the ground above the back door to the law office.

Christine stood at the corner of the club and examined the scene at a distance. Not exactly the ideal place to commit a crime, at least during the day. Even with the steel beams obscuring part of the area, the alley still felt too open. There was even a second parking lot off to the left of the new construction.

Her eyes scanned De Angelis. Sunlight glinted off a giant black eye encased in a shiny white orb attached to the top of an electrical pole to her right. The camera stared down the alley, a barely perceptible red light pulsating in the top left corner of its eye.

So Philip murdered a coworker near a busy parking lot and in full view of a security camera. Christine shook her head. She hadn't considered just how stupid her stepbrother might be. Depending on the inebriated state of the patrons of De Angelis, he might have had less witnesses had he murdered the man *inside* the club.

A dark-gray door opened out from inside a small recess, and a thin, unshaven man appeared carrying two large plastic bags of waste. He left the door open as he marched down the alley toward the container at the end and tossed them inside. He turned and stared at the ground as he retreated.

"Excuse me."

At her words, the man nearly tripped on the chipped asphalt. He looked up at Christine and frowned.

She walked toward him. "Do you work here? At De Angelis?"

"If I did, I'd say you're trespassing on private property." The man sounded as if one side of his mouth was stapled shut. "The entrance is around front."

"I'm a reporter with NABC. I'm doing a follow-up on the Mano Amaya murder that happened here last week. I just have a few questions, if you don't mind."

"I do mind." The man reached for the handle of the open door just as Christine reached him. "I've got nothing to say."

Years of experience taught Christine to ignore such a definitive answer. She pointed up at the camera. "How long has that camera been there? It looks new. And expensive."

The man paused at the door. "You have a real listening problem, don't you? I said I've got nothing to say. And you need to leave before I call the police." He ended the conversation with a swift slam of the door, leaving Christine alone in the alley.

Christine frowned. Not that she expected a warm welcome, but why the ill temper? She left the parking lot and headed west along the sidewalk toward the high-rise skyline of the city. She memorized the eight-tenths-of-a-mile trail to her next destination, plotted by the map app on her phone, then deposited it in her shoulder bag.

As she walked, questions filled her mind. Assuming Philip was a murderer, why commit the act where he did? And when he did it? Was he really that stupid? That was the part she didn't get. Philip was unpredictable, even reckless at times, but not unintelligent. In fact, Christine always assumed he would succeed at whatever he did with his life.

But truth be told, they hadn't really kept up. Maybe she never really knew him. Maybe he murdered Amaya. And maybe he wanted to get caught. Or was too intoxicated to realize what he was doing.

All the evidence seemed to confirm the police report. And yet Christine had learned through the years to trust her instincts when it came to a story. As she cut through Main Street Garden Park to St. Paul Street, she tried and failed to shake the nagging sense in her mind.

The sense that maybe Philip was telling the truth.

CHAPTER EIGHT

CHRISTINE AGREED TO meet Jeremy Blankenship at Klyde Warren Park for lunch—his suggestion—even though the nightclub was nearly a mile away. Not far enough to warrant hailing a ride, but not close enough to make it a short walk. Still, the time passed by before she noticed as she continued to mull over Philip's situation and expand her list of questions.

Her route was pleasant, especially given the fact that she'd removed her jacket and enjoyed the warmth of sunlight against her bare arms. Traversing downtown Dallas reminded her of New York, but without the obnoxious crowds.

Halfway to the park, Christine passed by the impressive plaza of the First Baptist Church of Dallas. The family center to her right connected to the main building on the left via a suspended pedestrian bridge. Beyond the bridge, the main building curved behind a plaza featuring a fountain as its centerpiece. From the fountain rose a spire topped by a large metal cross. Emblazoned on the base of the fountain was John 4:14: "Whosoever drinketh of the water that I shall give him shall never thirst; but the water that I shall give him shall be in him a well of water springing up to everlasting life."

Christine elected against sightseeing and considered the words as she kept moving. She struggled to place the passage in her mind. Her familiarity with the Bible was young, though the book of John was one of her first forays into its rich wisdom. Most likely the words of Christ, she used context clues to narrow her memory.

Water . . . thirst . . . well.

Well.

Of course! The woman at the well. Christine was filled with joy as she recalled the story of Christ approaching the Samaritan woman drawing water from a well. He masterfully wove the act into an illustration about the life given by him through the Spirit, much like the life given by water, but on an eternal scale. Jesus's brilliance in teaching by illustration and parable only deepened Christine's desire to learn from him and follow his example.

For the next ten minutes, the vexing questions surrounding Philip's incarceration faded to the background as she thought through her favorite parables from the Gospels. The images gave way to thoughts of New York and her Bible study group—they gathered around a table with Park Han, the group's insightful facilitator, in the middle. Her gray head swayed back and forth as she did laps through the pages of her well-worn Bible.

The air seemed even warmer. The tall golden brick wall of the Dallas Museum of Art ended, and the sidewalk merged into the drive exiting the museum. Ahead of her, a beautiful grove of trees fought distant high-rise buildings for attention. At the next intersection, Christine spied her destination: Klyde Warren Park.

A break in traffic allowed her and a mixed crowd of pedestrians to cross Woodall Rogers Freeway to the park. Young couples with toddlers headed to an impressive playground space featuring water fountains and climbing structures, while retirees and business professionals mingled around green metal tables and chairs along a strip of brown gravel next to the road. Parked alongside the sidewalk were an array of brightly painted food trucks.

Christine veered off the main thoroughfare into the park and weaved her way through the table seating while silently ticking off the names of each truck she passed. Blankenship instructed her to meet him at a specific one, the name of which escaped her at the moment. She was confident she would recognize it.

The first two trucks weren't it—one featuring shaved ice, the other promising delicious pizza. Then she spied the bold white letters along the top edge of the third black truck: THE BUTCHER'S SON. That was what he'd said.

Sure enough, Christine scanned the tables just beyond the food truck and spotted Jeremy Blankenship studying his phone screen. A mess of brown wavy hair retreated from his speckled forehead. He wore a pair of ill-fitting glasses on his stout face, and his chin and ears seemed to disappear into his thick neck. He wore the standard journalist uniform of a wrinkled blue oxford shirt and khaki pants.

Blankenship might not know it, but he'd be just as at home in New York as he was in Texas.

He looked up from his phone as she neared and recognized her instantly. Jumping from his chair, Blankenship beamed and shouted, "Christine!" His exclamation startled an elderly woman walking nearby, and he offered an awkward apology.

Christine reached him as he turned his attention back to her, his smile broader. "Jeremy, hi," Christine said as she reached her hand toward him.

He grabbed her hand with both of his and gave it a hearty shake. "I can't believe we're actually getting to meet, especially after everything that happened yesterday." His lips drooped, but he kept his grip on her hand. "I saw your interview last night, and I know you said you were OK, but I really hope you're OK."

She chuckled at his rapid dialogue. If she were honest, Christine would have to admit she expected someone with more drawl. "Yes, I'm really OK. It was scary, but the NYPD are incredibly good at what they do. Are you planning on holding my hand the whole time?"

Blankenship blanched as he released her hand. "I'm so sorry!" He blushed, then lowered his head in surrender. "I'm just overly excited to meet you. Now I'm probably making it weird. Please don't leave."

"That depends on what we're eating for lunch." Christine playfully propped her fists against her hips and tilted her head toward The Butcher's Son.

Blankenship's charm returned to his face, and he motioned for her to step over to the food truck. "I hope you're hungry. I'm sure you're probably used to food trucks in the Big Apple, but I'm willing to bet you've never had anything like The Butcher's Son before. They have a lot of different sandwich options, all amazing, but, and trust me, you're going to want to try their small plate, what they call the German Connection."

Christine raised an eyebrow as she watched him. He really liked to talk.

"It's a famous German dish called currywurst—basically bratwurst that's been flash fried and topped with curry sauce. The Butcher's Son sauce is homemade and amazing. Even the side of tots that comes with the plate is incredible. I'm not saying you have to get it—it's just what I always order."

There was no line to wait in, and the attendant at the counter was ready for their order as soon as Blankenship stepped to the window. "A German Connection please." He tipped his nose down and looked at Christine over the rim of his glasses.

She grinned. "Sounds great to me."

He turned to the attendant. "Make that two. And two bottled waters." As their order was rung up, Blankenship pulled out his wallet and shook an open palm toward Christine. "Please," he said, "let me. It's not every day someone from the mother ship makes it down here, much less meets with someone like me."

Christine obliged, and Blankenship settled the check. They backed away from the food truck to wait for their food, and Christine saw an opening to talk.

"Jeremy, thank you so much for meeting with me. I realize you've probably got a lot on your plate, and this may seem strange given the details of the story."

Blankenship took advantage of her pause to breathe and interrupted. "Oh, it's no problem at all. Our offices are down Saint Jacinto, not a bad walk, especially on a day like today. I have to admit your interest in the Amaya murder case did seem a little strange at first, but I'll be honest—it didn't take me long to figure it out. Judging by his age, I'd say brother?"

Christine blinked and opened her mouth to speak but couldn't think of anything to say. Just as a potential sentence formed in her mind, the attendant at the food truck called out, "Jeremy!"

Blankenship trotted to the truck, grabbed two large Styrofoam containers and two bottled waters, and joined Christine at a table shaded by a tree. She dropped her bag to the ground next to her chair and formed a prayer of thanks in her heart for the food as Blankenship adjusted his chair and opened the container to reveal his food.

"Oh yeah. This is the good stuff."

Christine found her wits, and after opening her own container and helping herself to a fried potato, she shot him an amused glance. "Stepbrother. I guess the last name made it a little obvious."

"Yeah, that was the initial hint, but it is a fairly common surname—half a million with it in the US, believe it or not, so I didn't want to presume. I don't know how they do it in Empire City, but I like to dig, and I mean really dig. Have you tried the bratwurst yet? I'm telling you, it's the stuff dreams are made of."

She really liked Blankenship. And he wasn't wrong. The currywurst was amazing.

"Philip wasn't exactly active on social media, at least not nowadays. What I could trace led me to who I assumed was his father, who either has an unhealthy infatuation with you or was related. No photos or comments of any kind, but he sure liked to share links to articles and videos featuring former-foreign-now-national NABC correspondent Christine Lewis. I took a guess you wouldn't fly out here unless it was a close family member, so that ruled out 'removed distant cousin.'"

Somehow Blankenship managed to talk and eat at the same time. Christine was still digging into her meal when she realized he was closing the container and wiping his mouth with a thin paper napkin.

He leaned back in his chair and sighed. "So what do you know and what would you like to know?"

Christine took a drink from her bottled water and leaned forward to place her elbows on the table. "I know Philip was caught on camera murdering Mano Amaya behind De Angelis nightclub last Thursday night, and I know Dallas police picked him up at his apartment the next morning. They found a mixture of alcohol and narcotics in his bloodstream, the murder weapon with his fingerprints on it ditched in a trash container next to the apartment building, and a string of threatening text messages to Amaya on his phone. I know he's incarcerated at the North Tower Detention Facility, his bail is set at three hundred thousand dollars, and Philip claims he's innocent."

Blankenship glanced up into the tree as he cleaned his teeth with his tongue behind his closed lips. Finally, he looked back at her and nodded. "That's about it, all right. I'm sorry, Christine. I realize he's family, but I'm not sure what more I can tell you. It's a pretty open and shut case."

"Here's what I'm hoping you can help me with, Jeremy. From the outside the story looks tight. But there's one question I can't find the answer to in any of the articles I've read, even yours. And yours are meticulous. That's a compliment."

Blankenship's reddish skin turned a shade darker. He averted his gaze for a moment, then met her eyes again and leaned onto the table himself. "OK then, what is it?"

"Why?"

Blankenship burst out laughing. Christine crossed her arms.

"I'm sorry," he said as he composed himself and raised his hands in surrender. "It's crazy how, if you think about it, it's just a one-word question, and yet, I mean, that's really *the* question, isn't it? That's what we're after as journalists. Not just the who, what, where, how, but the why. You answer that, and, well, you've done something."

"OK then." Christine tightened the cross in her arms. "Answer it. Why? Why did Philip kill Amaya?"

Blankenship spread his arms out to either side, a goofy grin on his face, his eyebrows meeting high wrinkles on his forehead. "Beats me. I have to say, if I'm being honest, and I am, I really thought you might actually tell me. That's the one thing I can't figure out. And I've tried. The text messages suggested an unhealthy work rivalry. Some of my colleagues even tried to read subtext of an infatuation into them on

Philip's part. I don't buy it. This is my thing. I love writing about crime. And this case, this case is too . . ." His voice trailed off as he glanced over his shoulder.

Christine unfolded her arms. "Too what? Complicated?"

Blankenship met her eyes and whispered, "Perfect."

Christine considered pulling her jacket out of her overnight bag as a cold draft gently shook the branches of the tree overhead. She didn't want to break her concentration on Blankenship's words, so she let the bag remain at her feet.

"It's almost as if it was planned. Like he wanted to get caught. He knifed Amaya behind the bar in full view of the camera. The police knew right where to find him. The threatening text messages hadn't been deleted." Blankenship ticked off invisible checkboxes in the air. "Even the knife was found in the outside dumpster of his apartment complex. There were two witnesses from the bar who claimed to have seen the two men arguing. Open. Shut."

"Wow." Christine took a deep breath. "I get it. I'm not here to try to prove Philip's innocence. I just want to know what happened to someone I thought I knew. I want to know why."

"That's what I'm trying to tell you. It's like nobody cares to answer that question because all the evidence is there. Even I was ready to give it up."

Was? Christine cocked an eyebrow. "Sounds like there's an 'except' coming."

Blankenship took the first breath Christine remembered hearing from him. "Except," he said, slower this time, and nodded. "There's one thing that bugs me about the whole thing: the knife. The police report says they found the knife in the dumpster, but Philip was arrested the following morning after trash pickup normally occurs. That means Philip didn't dispose of the knife until mere hours before his arrest. Everybody assumed he didn't return to his apartment until then, probably roaming the city that night thinking about what he'd done. But he carries the bloody knife around the whole night? And doesn't think to get rid of it until he's home?"

"He wasn't sober, so anything's possible." Christine realized she was arguing against Philip's innocence, and her heart sank.

"OK, assume he's an idiot, pardon me, but that's not the only thing that bugs me. I've written about a lot of murders—I used to work in Baltimore when I first got started. Did I tell you that? Anyway, number two highest murder rate behind Saint Louis. So there was a lot of crime to write about. And here's the thing: if somebody used a knife, it usually meant it was personal. Not many workplace murders happen involving a knife. I'm talking more jealous husband kind of stuff."

"A rivalry can get personal."

"A rivalry with someone you've only worked with for three months? Tell me, Christine, who have you worked with for that long who makes you feel like driving a knife into their chest?"

"I read Amaya had been working with Hale Industries for more than two years."

"With the company for two years. Transferred to the same department as Philip around the first of the year. The two men hadn't been working together that long. They seemed to hit it off—plenty of witnesses saw them spending more time outside of work together, but that's it. Three months with the guy, then—" Blankenship mimed being stabbed in the heart, then dropped his hands as his cheeks reddened. "I'm sorry. I wasn't thinking. I didn't mean to—"

"It's OK, Jeremy. It's family, yes, but I've had my fair share of violence."

"Oh yeah." Blankenship's eyes widened. "Washington. That was . . ." He punctuated his thought with a whistle. "I realize you've got a schedule, but I was hoping maybe you wouldn't mind if I sent you an email with some questions about that."

Christine's mouth dropped open, then she laughed and shifted in her seat. "Why would you have questions about that? They could make a movie out of all the interviews I did. There isn't much more to tell."

"Maybe." Blankenship shrugged. "I was just curious if you know anything about the carjacking of a black Jeep Wrangler around the same time the police were in pursuit of the bombers. The owner claimed a blond woman and a dark-haired man stole his car at gunpoint. I can't find any records other than the initial 911 call log. Guy's car gets stolen, then nothing. I know it doesn't sound like much, but I couldn't shake the pit in my gut, so I called him. Now he's saying he made a mistake! So, what, did he make it up?" Blankenship shook his head. "No ma'am, that's a crime. He should've gone to jail. Somebody should've gone to jail."

"That much interest in local Washington, DC, crime here in Dallas?"

Blankenship dropped his gaze as his skin turned a shade redder. "I was really interested in that day. Watched every one of your interviews. It really would make a great movie. But I have this thing where I can't stop until I've dug to the bottom of whatever thing I become fascinated by. I'm sorry, but you didn't happen to rob a man of his car while you were helping the authorities, did you?"

"I'm going to pretend like you didn't just ask me if I was complicit in a crime."

He snorted, then watched a group of young adults tossing a Frisbee on the green lawn separating the food trucks from the playground. Christine let the silence hang in the air, desperate to hide any hint of the truth from her face. Blankenship turned back and nodded. "You're right. I'm sorry. My imagination got carried away. I like to watch a lot of television in my spare time, which isn't really an excuse, now that I think about it. I'd still like to stay in touch, if you don't mind. I would love to pick your brain on a story sometime."

Christine acquiesced and confirmed her email address and cell number with him, making sure she also had his in case she had more questions about Philip's case he might be able to answer. Blankenship was a good reporter. Too good. She didn't want to lose the chance to benefit from his knowledge and experience, regardless of how close he might get to what really happened with John.

"Thanks for your time, Jeremy."

"I assume you're headed to the prison next."

She nodded.

"Listen, Christine, I know I said some things didn't add up, but it's really hard not to take the facts at face value. I don't know how close you and Philip were, and honestly, from what I've seen, you could've been closer to him than you've been to anyone else in your life and still not really know the man. You can never really know anybody, not really. There's stuff buried deep inside all of us that we hide. A lot of times, for life. And when that stuff comes out, well, let's just say I've never seen it be anything but really bad."

Christine simply nodded as she stood and slung the strap of her bag over her shoulder. "I'll be in touch. And thanks for lunch. You were right, the food is amazing."

Blankenship offered her a casual salute and a grin, then dug his phone out of his pocket as she turned to leave. She'd already arranged for a car to pick her up nearby, and according to the app there was just enough time to cross the park and meet her ride when it pulled up to the upscale restaurant located at the northwest corner of Klyde Warren.

Maybe Blankenship was right. As much as she wanted to believe Philip was innocent, and as much as there were still unanswered questions in her mind, there was no denying the mountain of evidence stacked against him. She admitted to herself that as much as she tried to convince herself of the opposite, she and Philip were only as close as two stepsiblings could be after a handful of childhood summers spent under the same roof.

Most of what she believed to be true about Philip's character and beliefs came from intermittent conversations with her father. Could she trust his judgment? Christine pondered what she even believed about her own father and whether she could be certain of who he really was.

As she rounded the sidewalk bisecting the park's lawn and neared the restaurant, she scrolled through the list of questions in her mind, filling in the gaps with the information Blankenship provided. He brought up interesting points about the knife, though not strong evidence proving Philip's innocence. The question of why still lingered,

Blankenship's answers unsatisfactory, but she believed the only one who could truly resolve that question was Philip.

Christine passed by the floor-to-ceiling glass walls of Savor Gastropub and onto the sidewalk running parallel to a drop-off lane alongside the length of the restaurant. She spotted the cherry-red sedan picking her up and froze in her tracks. An unkind word passed across her mind and nearly leapt from her mouth.

Standing next to the car in dark jeans, tight polo shirt, and a smirk was John Cross.

CHAPTER NINE

IT LOOKED LIKE he was right. She wasn't happy to see him. Not that Cross felt any different.

Christine marched up to him as the driver of the sedan popped the trunk open. "You need to know there's a lot of words I'm choosing not to use right now," she said as he reached for her overnight bag and tossed it into the trunk.

"I know," he replied. "And I'm proud of you for that."

She slammed the trunk lid closed as hard as she could. They both suddenly realized the driver, a young, petite Ethiopian woman, stood nearby with wide eyes.

Christine offered the woman a cheerful expression. "Hi, Liya. I'm Christine. Thanks for picking me up. I'm ready."

"I'm coming as well," Cross said.

Christine narrowed her eyes in his direction and scowled. "No, he isn't."

"Yes, I am." This was already shaping up to be their biggest fight as a couple, with a restaurant full of people as witnesses, thanks to the all glass walls. "Look, we can stand here and argue about it, but you've got an appointment to keep, and I'm going to be there with you whether you let me tag along or I have to find my own ride."

She breathed a deep, frustrated sigh of forfeit and threw her hands into the air as she rolled her eyes. "Fine. Get in."

Cross flashed a grin at Liya and opened the passenger-side back door. "We're ready."

Christine slid in and across the seat. He joined her as Liya took her place. She put the car into gear and signaled her intent to merge into traffic heading north on Woodall Rogers Freeway.

"I can't believe you lied to me, John."

"In fairness, you lied too."

Liya glanced at them in the rearview mirror and timidly asked, "North Tower Detention Facility, correct?"

"Yes, that's right." Christine's brief smile faded as quickly as it had formed as she turned back to Cross. "Help me understand how exactly I lied to you."

Cross shifted under his seat belt and stole a glance out the window. He suspected there would be conflict but didn't care for the taste of it. He swallowed the lump of regret in his throat. "Well, for starters you said you were only going to talk to Philip, not poke around the crime scene."

"I said I was going to dig."

"That's what I was afraid of." His reasons were flimsy, so Cross abandoned the argument. "Look, you're right. I lied. I'm sorry. Too much has happened for me to just sit by and let you dig around by yourself."

It was Christine's turn to avoid eye contact. In the silence, Cross observed Liya following signs onto the access ramp to I-35E. He knew the detention facility wasn't far, less than a four-minute drive. It wasn't the first visit he'd ever made to Texas, though thankfully the city didn't harbor any dark memories of his checkered years with the Central Intelligence Agency.

"I realize yesterday was hard."

Even though he wanted to wrap her in his arms, Cross kept his focus on the road ahead of them.

"But you don't always have to be there to protect me. You can't be. Besides, what was the point of all those training date nights if you don't trust me to take care of myself?"

Cross extended his hand, hoping to grasp hers, but she crossed her arms, forcing him to flash his palm at her like some lame school safety officer. "It's not you I don't trust."

Christine laughed. "John, did you think I was going to find my way to the front door of the real killer's house? So far, all I've figured out is there's no way Philip didn't do this."

"You don't think it's odd that a mediocre nightclub in the heart of Dallas has a custom military-grade surveillance system? Commercial businesses don't get access to that kind of state-of-the-art equipment."

She narrowed her eyes in suspicion but didn't acknowledge the realization he had followed her earlier. Truth be told, he'd just missed her at De Angelis, but he'd taken the time to scout the location himself, confident he wouldn't miss her at Klyde Warren. She knew he could track her. Had, in fact, tracked her before to surprise her with a romantic dinner in New York.

"Odd, maybe," she admitted. "But not necessarily out of the realm of possibility. Maybe the owner is the paranoid type."

"What did your reporter friend tell you?"

"He has a name, but I'm sure you already know what it is."

Of course, but he enjoyed the banter. He wouldn't have needed to ask about their conversation if he'd still had access to the full range of reconnaissance equipment he'd used in the field.

"Jeremy is a nice guy, by the way. A little talkative, but nice. And he's a fan of your work."

Cross felt his cheeks warm, and he cocked an eyebrow at her.

She smirked. "Asked me if I knew anything about a couple hijacking a Jeep Wrangler in Washington last year. I promised him I'd send him all the details over email."

She wasn't serious. Was she? "If you don't mind, leave out the part where it took me two shots to hit the tire."

"I was thinking I might write you out of it, actually. Give all the best parts to myself."

There was still an edge, but at least now he was in on the joke.

"Did you get to anything besides the stolen Jeep?"

"He didn't have much to add, except some of his own unanswered questions about the case. He thought the discovery of the knife seemed out of place. And the fact that Philip even used a knife."

"Too personal."

"Yeah."

Cross looked into Christine's eyes and detected a hint of admiration. At least, that was what he hoped it was. Maybe the thrill of investigating together would smooth over the brewing sense of tension in their relationship.

"Blankenship sounds as smart as he is nice."

Christine appeared amused. He winked, then smiled back.

She turned to watch Liya navigate onto the exit ramp toward Riverfront Boulevard. "I'm still mad at you. And it's still creepy that you can track my phone."

She might have a point.

They rode the final minute in silence. Liya let the car roll to a stop behind a low-riding truck in a short cul-de-sac at the base of a wide multi-level set of stairs ascending to the front entrance of the Frank Crowley Courts Building. Cross retrieved Christine's bag as she thanked Liya.

The sedan merged onto Riverfront Boulevard as Cross handed Christine her overnight bag. They climbed the steps side by side toward the brick-and-glass building.

"By the way," Christine said. "How did you get away? I thought you had a Bible study to lead tonight. Does anyone know you're here?"

"Gary does. It's not the best excuse, but there's a pastors' conference happening in town this evening, and I convinced him I got a last-minute ticket that I couldn't turn down."

Christine paused on a step and frowned. "First you lie to me, now Gary?"

Cross spread his arms. "It wasn't a lie. There's actually a pastors' conference happening, I actually did get a last-minute ticket, and I have every intention of attending. It doesn't get started until later this afternoon, so I figured I had time to be here with you."

Christine studied his face. Her frown deepened, then she resumed her march up the stairs as she grumbled, "It's still deceitful."

Probably. That made the score two lies in as many days. And what was a better mark of a good evangelical pastor than lying? Cross's shoulders sank as he fell in line behind her.

At the top of their ascent, a wall of glass framed by a thick arch welcomed them into the first building of a massive courts and detention complex known as the Lew Sterrett Justice Center. Cross had done his research on the plane, and the complex consisted of the Courts Building and three detention centers: the North Tower, the West Tower, and Suzanne Lee Kays Detention Facility. Philip was in the North Tower, with over three thousand other maximum-security inmates.

He held the door open, and Christine led the way inside. With the assistance of a jovial police officer standing in the lobby, they navigated their way through the building, out across a pavilion separating the detention facilities, and finally into the visitor's entrance of the North Tower. Inside, Christine announced herself, and they waited for her contact within the prison to meet them.

"All right," she said. "Let's be clear. I'm in charge of the questioning. I don't mind if you have questions, but there's no need to use any of your enhanced interrogation techniques on my stepbrother."

Cross snorted. "I don't think you have anything to worry about, unless you know where I can get my hands on some bungee cords."

"That's not funny, John."

"It's kind of funny." He offered her his best reassuring smile. "I'm just trying to lighten the mood. This isn't going to be easy."

Christine's eyebrows drooped. He knew he didn't have to tell her. They'd both traveled all this way for this moment, and the odds were stacked against Christine's hope of an innocent verdict for Philip.

Cross checked his watch. He did have every intention of attending the conference, but he also didn't intend on leaving Christine alone with the despair of discovering a loved one was a cold-blooded killer. With any luck, he could convince her to travel to Springfield to be with her father after the visitation with Philip.

A short, sturdy woman dressed in dark-blue fatigues approached them with her hand outstretched. The gold star of the Dallas County Sheriff's Department was embroidered above the left pocket of her shirt, the name "Rodriguez" stitched above the right pocket.

"Ms. Lewis, I'm Officer Becky Rodriguez. I'll be assisting you with your visit today." Rodriguez's brunet hair was pulled into a tight pony-tail, and although she had attractive dimples at the corners of her lips, Cross didn't doubt her toughness. The Dallas County Jail system was one of the toughest in the country.

Christine shook Rodriguez's hand. "Thank you for allowing me to meet with Philip, especially considering you don't normally allow visitation on Wednesdays."

"Well, ma'am, I don't know who you're friends with, but they pulled the right strings and now we're here." Rodriguez eyed Cross. "I'm sorry, I'm not sure I was expecting someone to be with you."

Christine looked over at Cross and opened her mouth to talk. Before she could, Cross extended his hand and let confidence and charm radiate from his face. "John Jameson, producer. I was a last-minute add. I hope that's OK. Our office should've called earlier to let you know."

Rodriguez didn't seem convinced of his ruse but shook his hand and nodded. "I'll double-check. And I'll also need to see both of your IDs, plus you'll need to leave your bag here, ma'am."

Christine passed over the shoulder bag, then dug her ID out of her pocket. Cross mimicked her, and together they handed their IDs to Rodriguez. The officer thanked them, then turned and walked to the welcome desk to confirm the validity of their identification.

"John Jameson? That's the best you could do?" Christine asked, her tone soft and directed toward Cross's ear.

He shrugged. "Don't look at me. Guin picked it out."

Cross instantly regretted dropping the name of his former CIA coworker. He didn't have to see Christine's face to know it contorted into a frustrated state. The two women were friends, as much as they could be living in two different cities with two different career paths, but Cross still suspected a rivalry between them. At least, Christine never seemed eager to talk about Guin with him, so he never brought it up.

Frankly, last night was the first he'd spoken to Guin since they'd parted ways in Washington last year. And she didn't even bother to bring the ID to him at the airport, bestowing that honor on Eric

Paulson, another friend with the CIA. It'd been good to see Paulson, though the two of them communicated with more regular frequency.

Cross looked over at Christine, but instead of jealousy he read fondness in her eyes. "If you got Guin involved, then at least I know it was done right."

He might not be as good at judging relational signals as he thought.

"Guin said to tell you hi, by the way."

"Hi, Guin." One of her eyebrows rose as she smirked. "We should try to see her more often."

How to accomplish that when he and Christine couldn't see each other often enough was beyond him.

Rodriguez rejoined them and returned their IDs. "Thanks. Obviously we want to confirm you are who you say you are before we go any further. And yes, Mr. Jameson, your office did call ahead a few hours ago and confirm your attendance. This way, please."

Cross and Christine traded knowing glances, then stepped in line behind Rodriguez as she turned and led them through an electronically secured door. They passed through a maze of security checkpoints, all identical green steel doors leading to identical white block hallways. Finally, they turned a short corner and stopped at a gray door with a large windowpane in its top half.

Rodriguez buzzed the front desk with an intercom box on the wall in the hallway, and within seconds the electronic lock on the door clicked. She opened the door and ushered Cross and Christine inside.

The same white block comprised all four walls in the room, with a matching door across from the one they had entered. Another intercom box was secured into the wall above a short, rectangular metal table. Two metal chairs faced each other on either side of the table.

Cross motioned for Christine to sit as Rodriguez unclipped the radio on her belt and delivered a command into the microphone.

Then to Cross and Christine she said, "I'm afraid I'm going to require you to refrain from making physical contact with the inmate."

Less than a minute later, the opposite door opened, and an adult male with medium-length wavy black hair, a dark short-clipped beard, and round black-rimmed glasses was led through the door by a male uniformed officer. Philip wore a white-and-gray-striped jumpsuit with matching handcuffs binding his wrists. His eyes welled with tears as he stared at Christine.

"Sit down, please," the male officer ordered in a deep bass voice.

Philip complied and choked back sobs as he attempted to reach across the table for Christine only to be reminded of the restrictions.

Though her back stiffened, Christine held herself together at the sight of her incarcerated stepbrother. Cross considered placing a hand on her shoulder to steady her resolve, then recalled his own subterfuge with his identity and decided to play the part of an indifferent boss.

"Chrissy," Philip managed to utter. He cleared his throat and nose, then formed his words in a stronger voice. "Thank you for coming. I know you didn't have to, but I didn't know who else to ask for. And if there's anyone who can help me, it's you."

Christine sniffled, and she struggled to form her own words. "Philip, I don't know what to say. I don't know how I can help you, but I want to try." She coughed, then steadied herself with her hands on the table. "How have you been? Are you OK in here?"

"It's not great—I'm not going to lie. I've avoided any major fights, but my luck's going to run out soon." Philip glanced at the male guard, who seemed to stare right through him, then scanned past Rodriguez and discovered Cross. He narrowed his eyes and nodded in Cross's direction. "Who's he?"

"Oh, this is John Jameson, my producer. When I told him your story, he insisted on being here and hearing it firsthand."

Philip's nostrils flared as he examined Cross's demeanor.

"It's OK," Christine assured him. "You can trust him."

The guarantee relaxed him. "Chrissy, I don't know what they've told you, but I didn't kill Mano. I swear to you, I'm innocent."

Christine sighed and hung her head.

Philip leaned over the table, careful not to get too close, and reiterated, "I'm innocent. I swear."

Christine looked back up at him. "I want to hear everything. But

I'm having a hard time understanding how you can say that based on the evidence I've seen. There's video evidence, Philip. *Video.* Your fingerprints on the knife, the text messages . . ."

Philip raised his cuffed hands in surrender. "OK, OK. I get it. By all accounts, I murdered Mano Amaya. Except I'm telling you I didn't." He dropped his hands and rapped on the table with his right index finger. "But I know who did."

"What?" Christine's mouth hung open.

Cross took the opportunity to interject into the conversation. "What do you mean you know who did? I'm under the impression you claim you weren't at the nightclub."

Philip rolled his eyes at Cross. "I wasn't there, so I can't tell you who exactly did it, but I know who ordered it."

"Who ordered it? What are you talking about?" Christine asked.

"This was all a setup. They knew Mano was going to tell everything, so they got rid of him and made it look like I did it."

Cross stepped forward and leaned onto the table with his fists. "Who, Philip?"

Philip looked at both of the detention officers up against the side wall of the room, then leaned in close and lowered his voice. "The higher-ups. At Hale. They did this." He glanced at the officers and narrowed his eyes as he studied their expressions. With his voice even lower and his eyes locked, he added, "I think it goes all the way to the top."

Cross made eye contact with a bewildered Christine, then glanced back at Philip and matched the volume of the prisoner's voice. "Are you saying your bosses at Hale Industries framed you for Mano's murder? Why would they do that?"

"Because we were close." Philip hesitated. "I mean, Mano was close. Close to figuring out the truth behind the Ares Project. It's hard to explain, but there was something wrong. He found out about it, and I don't know how they figured it out, but, well, they must've."

Cross waved his hand to cut off Philip's stammering. "OK, slow down. You're going to have to give us more detail."

Christine jumped in. "Why haven't you told anyone else about this?"

"I have! They won't listen. Everyone thinks I'm crazy, and, well, you've seen the evidence. They have everything they need to lock me up for good."

"Philip." Cross increased the level of sobriety in his tone. "If we're going to have any chance at helping you, you're going to have to give us some more to go on. What kind of evidence do you have that company leadership was involved?"

Philip's mouth opened, but he didn't say anything. He glanced from Cross to Christine. Cross didn't need words. He straightened, crossed his arms, and took a breath.

"What about the problem with this project that you're talking about?" Christine pressed. "It must be serious enough to kill over. What was it? And do you have evidence of at least that?"

Philip laughed and hung his head.

"Oh, Phil." Christine shook her head. "We want to believe you— we really do. But you need to give us more to work with than just accusations."

Philip looked back at his stepsister. "I get it. How it looks. Like I'm making up whatever story I can to try to get out of this mess." The corners of his eyes glistened with swelling tears. "Christine, I swear to you. I didn't do this."

The door behind Cross buzzed and swung open. A bald African American man in a rumpled gray suit stormed into the room. "Philip, don't say another word."

Philip groaned.

Cross stood his ground and blocked the man's path to the table. "And who might you be?"

"Excuse me," the man said as he pushed his way around.

Cross relaxed and let him win this round.

"I'm Brian Stack, Public Defender's Office. This is my client, and I did not authorize this interview."

"You can hardly call it an interview," Christine said. "I'm his step-sister, and I'm the only family who's been able to get here to see Philip since he was arrested. You're not legally allowed to prevent us from speaking to each other."

Philip opened his mouth and raised his cuffed hands toward Stack, but the lawyer cut off his attempt to form words. "I don't care. You're a reporter, and I don't need you publishing anything that might impede my ability to represent my client during his trial." Stack spun to the detention officers on the wall and raised his voice. "This interview is over. Please escort my client to his cell and these two out of the building."

The thickset male officer rolled his eyes toward Rodriguez for confirmation. She nodded and replied, "Yes, Mr. Stack. I understand you'd like to end the interview. But I'll let my officers know when they need to return someone to their cell."

Stack pressed his hands on his suit and nodded. He glared at Cross, then Christine. "Fine. Ms. Lewis, let's leave it up to Philip." Stack turned and glared at Philip.

Philip opened his mouth to speak, but no words escaped. His eyes bounced between Christine, Cross, Stack, and finally the table. He nodded as he mumbled, "I'm ready to go."

Stack's lips curled up on one side as he crossed his arms. The male officer stepped around Stack and motioned for Philip to stand.

As Philip obliged, he made brief eye contact with Cross. If his eyes could speak, Cross imagined they would say, *Please help.*

Cross nodded at Philip as the officer escorted him out the door. He shifted his eyes to see Stack attempting to stare him down. Cross considered a handful of ways he could take a swing at Stack and make it look innocent but was quickly reminded of his determined distaste of violence. He repented of his thoughts and backed away as Christine rose from her chair.

Rodriguez extended her arm and waited for them both to exit the room.

CHAPTER TEN

AT THE BOTTOM of the steps leading down from the Courts Building, Cross waited in silence as Christine booked a car using her phone.

"Where am I dropping you?" she asked, looking up from the screen. "Where's this supposed conference taking place?"

"Boy, are you going to be sorry when you find out I'm actually attending a conference."

Christine narrowed her eyes and squeezed her lips tight.

Cross tried a smile on her to break the tension, but she held her expression. He retained his cheer as he said, "Covenant Community Church in North Dallas, near Lyndon B. Johnson Freeway."

Christine turned back to the app, and Cross thought it best not to distract her. He watched as she typed out the name of the church, made a few selections, and finally confirmed the car and locked the screen.

"It'll be here in three minutes," she announced.

"Thank you," Cross said. "But I could've arranged my own transportation. I'd rather make sure you get to the air—"

"Not a chance." Christine shook her head. "I'm going to make sure you make it to your conference, then once we're both settled into our rooms tonight, we can connect and discuss today."

Cross looked away and took a deep breath. He didn't blame her for being upset, but it was too late. He couldn't change what he'd done. They'd just have to work through it. "Look," he replied as he turned back to make eye contact. "I'm sorry. I was wrong. I shouldn't have forced myself into the meeting, and yeah, I probably shouldn't have forced myself into the conference just to have an excuse to be here, but I was a wreck yesterday." He stepped closer as he stared into her ocean-blue eyes. "The thought of you in danger made me sick to my stomach. I almost collapsed when the news report came over the TV, I was so faint. And so help me God, I'll never let you face something like that alone ever again."

Christine's eyebrows relaxed, and she unclenched her teeth. Her eyes twinkled, then she lifted herself on her toes and kissed him on the mouth. Their lips parted, but she kept her face close and held his gaze for a moment. "I'm sorry too." She dropped back on her heels and relaxed her stance. "I should've thought about how you were feeling. I realize yesterday was hard, but you can't always be there to protect me. And you've done so much to teach me how to take care of myself. I guess I just wish you would trust me."

"I do trust you."

Did he? Alarm bells rang in his mind, though he wasn't sure if he was intentionally lying. He *wanted* to trust her. And for the most part, he did. But he was in Texas after telling her he wouldn't come. Now this warped version of the truth. Was he ever fully honest? *At least on Sundays.*

Or was he?

A flood of questions poured into his mind, each one more terrifying than the last. Questions about his relationship with Christine, about his relationship with the church, about what the future might—

Cross caught himself. Something certainly was different. He never spiraled in his emotions, yet here he was in this very moment unable to grasp not only what was occurring in his own heart but also what Christine might be feeling. He needed a distraction, a different kind of problem with questions he could actually answer.

Christine's mouth was moving, but he hadn't been paying attention. He pushed his thoughts away and tried to ascertain what she was saying.

". . . on an airplane to see Dad."

It wasn't enough. "I'm sorry. I lost that first part. What was it?"

Christine narrowed her eyes. "I was saying you didn't seem too bothered by the fact that I've booked a hotel for the night. I figured you wouldn't want to go to the conference until you saw me off on an airplane to Springfield."

There it was. His path to redemption. Up until this moment, Cross believed in his justification for acting against her wishes. But now he couldn't. The truth would set him free, or at least he hoped. Perhaps if he told her the truth now, she might believe he did trust her after all. But he also knew what telling her the truth meant.

That the conference would have to wait.

Cross sighed and closed his eyes. He nodded, then opened his eyes and noticed a car pulling up alongside them. Christine acknowledged the driver but stared at Cross, awaiting his response.

"Yeah, I was hoping you would leave. But you can't."

"What do you mean I can't?"

"You can't because Philip is innocent."

Christine's mouth dropped open, and her eyes widened. The driver of the car opened the door and stood from his seat. "Christine Lewis?" he called out in a thick Polish accent.

His words broke her trance, and Christine replied, "Yes. We're coming." She stood still and shook her head in disbelief. "I don't get it. You really think he didn't do it?"

Cross nodded as he grabbed for her overnight bag. "I know what it's like to stare into the face of a murderer. And that isn't Philip. So yeah, I really think he didn't do it." He stepped off the curb and opened the car door to get in.

As the afternoon Dallas Metroplex traffic swelled, the trip to Covenant Community Church took twice as long as one might expect. Christine prodded Cross with questions the entire way, much to either the amusement or terror of their driver, Borys. Borys was tough to read, partially because Cross was distracted by Christine's interrogation and because the older man said little and kept his eyes locked on the bumper of the car ahead of him.

Cross gave Christine every idea he'd formed about Philip's case. From the moment Philip walked into the room, Cross perceived a genuine fear. A real killer hiding his identity might express his or her innocence, perhaps even feel a measure of real guilt, but were rarely perfect in their facade.

Another major tell, in Cross's opinion, was the act itself. "There's no such thing as a senseless killing," he explained, surely to notice a rise from Borys, but no. Nothing. Cross continued with his thought. "A murder like this one should have a certain logic to it: Philip grows weary of Amaya's constant one-upmanship, then after a heated exchange in the nightclub, they fight in the back alley only for Philip to emerge victorious after striking Amaya with a blunt object he found on the ground. That makes sense. But we're forced to believe Philip planned this attack, bringing the knife with him, and forced to believe there was a fierce competition between the two men when the only proof of anything remotely resembling such is electronic in form, making it susceptible to forgery."

Christine mulled over the facts to herself as Borys navigated a highway exchange. Cross checked his watch. Registration would close soon, and then the opening session would begin. They were minutes from the church, but he didn't like cutting it that close.

"What about the video?"

Cross kept silent as he formulated his thoughts. Borys took the exit off the freeway, and Cross spotted the bold lettering spelling out COVENANT against the enormous tan brick building just off the highway to the south

"Well," he finally said, "that's a tough one. I'm not sure what to think about it without seeing it. There's always the possibility that it's been forged as well, though that would be a much more impressive feat. And I'm not sure I'm ready to commit to that kind of conspiracy."

Borys guided the car onto a one-way loop under the Lyndon B. Johnson Freeway, then merged to the right lane of the service road as they approached the entrance to the church grounds.

"John, one more thing."

If he had to guess, what would come next was the question he feared. After a second of hesitation, Christine asked, "Who else knows you're here?"

Cross clenched his jaw to keep from immediately answering with more lies. He hated how easy it was to formulate deceptive responses and wasn't sure how to turn it off. If there was one thing that scared him more than Lori's disapproval of a sermon, it was bringing shame on his position as pastor by involving the church in his deceptions. He cleared his throat. "Before I arranged everything, I called Gary to fill him in and ask him to teach for me last night."

"Does he know I'm here?"

"No."

Her lips pressed into a firm line as she studied his eyes. It was the truth. But it didn't matter. A battle waged in his mind between the regret of his lies and the drive to complete the mission.

The car rolled to a stop under an awning held over the driveway by square brick columns. To Cross's right, conference attendees streamed from a vast parking lot filled with cars, SUVs, passenger vans, and even a bus. To the left, a short flight of stairs led to a row of glass doors surrounded by glass walls. Beyond the nose of the car, a wide paved sidewalk wound its way alongside the drive to a gorgeous patio bordered by an impossibly green lawn. Mahogany Adirondack chairs encircled matching tables across the patio, and a set of stairs tucked in the back looked like it led to a similarly furnished deck. The building curved away, giving it the illusion of an infinite edge. Cross had expected to be impressed by the luxury of a megachurch in the buckle of the Bible Belt, but the online photos hadn't done the location justice. He loved the people of Rural Grove, but it did little to ease the jealousy brewing in his heart. How easy was ministry when even the assistants had assistants?

"Thank you, Borys," Christine said as she opened her door and stepped out of the car.

The man grunted a reply as Cross unbuckled and exited. Christine was already at the bottom of the stairs when he rounded the car and caught up to her. "Wait a minute. I thought that you were going to a hotel."

"I am. After I make sure you're registered and in your—" She stopped short from what Cross assumed was a choice adjective. "Seat. And I wasn't thrilled about paying more money to be driven around town by a Bond villain."

Cross grabbed at her elbow and prevented her from ascending the stairs. "OK, I get it. You're still mad I'm here. But you're just going to have to trust me. What are you going to do, handcuff me to the armrest?"

Christine held her breath, then arched her eyebrows and grinned. "Maybe." She tugged her elbow from his soft grip and fell in line behind an excited group of young adults taking the stairs to the entrance.

Great. His new commitment to honesty was off to a bad start.

Cross followed her up and through the doors.

A mature brunet woman with a vivacious grin waved as she made eye contact. "Welcome to Encounter Conference!"

He responded with a polite smile and nod. She gave a quick synopsis of the directions to the registration table, then repeated her greeting to the attendees entering behind him.

The curtained wall of glass behind him diffused the sunlight and illuminated the vast lobby in a warm glow. Large brown tile spread in a circular formation from a large, ornate baptismal pool decorated with a small stone waterfall and green hedging at the lobby's center point. A low glass barrier and a collection of seating encircled the pool, and it was illuminated from above by a skylight. To the left, a line of people formed at dark wooden doors cut into a curved stone wall, and to the right a crowd mingled around the counter of a full-service coffee bar.

Display booths advertising ministry products lined the walls of the lobby, except for a section of floor space past the baptismal pool dedicated to the conference registration tables. Cross spotted Christine working her way toward the tables and craning her neck to see over and around the multitude of pastors and lay leaders.

What could he do to salvage his decision to come? Several possible scenarios presented themselves to him. In any given situation, his CIA-honed instinct was to explore all possible outcomes of any decision, weigh the positive and negative, then choose the response most likely to achieve his goal.

So what was his goal? On the airplane, it was to protect Christine at all costs. Now, it was to protect his relationship with her at all costs. He needed to move with care, the ice already dangerously thin.

"Christine!" he called out, just loud enough for her to hear without drawing any unwanted attention to himself.

She spun in his direction as he trotted up to her. "How about I get us some coffee while you check me in?" Maybe encouraging her to see him through to a seat in the auditorium would prove his honest intentions. "If that's OK."

Christine studied his face, then nodded. "You know what I like." She turned away from him and stepped toward the nearest table to speak with a bald, bearded man wearing a lanyard sporting a badge that read "How can I help?"

Cross headed to the coffee bar and stepped up behind a woman in a flower-print dress and wide-brimmed hat. Tempted to watch Christine, he instead studied the menu board, organized his order, and calculated the total cost. If he looked back, he'd only be tempted to read their lips. He smiled as he was reminded of the story of Lot's wife in the Old Testament.

He didn't expect to be turned into a pillar of salt but didn't want to take any chances at a national church leadership conference. His mind shifted to the schedule of events at the church, and excitement swelled in his heart as he considered the opportunity to grow as a church leader. In an honest moment of self-reflection, he found his drive for local church ministry lacking, and concluded his split focus between Rural Grove and Christine lay at the root. This conference might just be the spark he needed to rekindle the passion he felt when he'd first agreed to become pastor of the small congregation.

The dimpled college-age woman at the register took his order with a playful smile. He thanked her, then tucked himself around the edge of the counter to wait for the pair of drinks. The crowd thinned as attendees headed for the worship center.

"Flat white and coffee black," the goateed barista announced as he passed two white cups wrapped in brown sleeves across the counter.

Cross picked up the cups, thanked the man, and headed to the table. Christine turned to meet him as he approached, a black tote bag in her hand.

"This is cute," she said as she riffled through the tote. "Looks like there's all sorts of swag in here. A pen, a notebook, oh, and . . ." She produced a lanyard matching the volunteers', with a different-styled badge at the end, the name JOHN CROSS stamped on it in stylish black letters. "This should make you feel like you're back with the CIA." Her eyes widened, and she glanced nervously around the crowd, but no one was paying attention.

Cross snorted. "I didn't wear a badge that often." As he offered her the flat white in exchange for the tote and lanyard, he heard and felt the drumbeat kicking off the opening session of the conference in the worship center across the lobby. How loud was the drum in that room? He was simultaneously amused and intrigued.

At least the start of the conference wouldn't bore him to tears while he determined his next course of action. He knew all too well that Christine wouldn't leave well enough alone. In fact he suspected she already planned on further investigation into Philip's claims. If Philip was innocent, and Cross was inclined to think he might be, that meant there was another guilty party. A guilty party willing to go to great lengths to hide their motive. He trusted Christine to be careful but couldn't rest until he could rejoin her this evening.

Christine sipped her coffee, closed her eyes, and pressed her lips together in a smile as she swallowed. "I didn't realize how much I needed that. I'm not going to lie—the coffee on the plane this morning wasn't great." She opened her eyes as she took another, longer drink.

A door to the worship center opened as a late arrival rushed inside to find an open seat. Music filled the lobby. Christine stole a glance across the building, then dug into her pocket for her phone.

"All right," she said as she unlocked the screen. "You've got to get in there, and I was up early, so I think now would be a great time for me to head to a hotel."

"I'm booked at Hyatt Regency North Dallas. You could go there for now and arrange for another after the conference." It might be suggesting too much, assuming she was still fuming at him, but the idea carried merit.

Christine sighed as she looked up from the phone. "You already know I haven't booked anything."

Cross drew a deep breath, stopped, and then simply nodded. It hadn't been a question.

"Thanks." She rubbed her forehead, likely trying to get rid of a headache he assumed he'd helped create. "But I think I'm going to look for something closer to downtown in case I get another chance to speak to Philip."

He nodded in agreement. Best not to press further. At least he'd avoided a dressing down for tracking her every move. He didn't blame her. She had every right to be upset that he treated her like an asset on an intelligence operation.

She buried her nose into her phone as she scrolled through available options. On instinct, she nibbled at the nail on the pinkie finger of her right hand, a common occurrence when she was deep in thought. He'd studied her tells early on and loved every single one of them. He couldn't help but imagine every possible way in which Christine could encounter danger, and Cross feared what he might do if she were ever harmed.

Cross cleared his throat as he raised the cup to his lips for another drink. Empty. That was right—he'd already finished it. Faster than usual. He wiped his brow with a couple of fingers, expecting to find sweat, but they remained dry. Why was it so hot?

He tossed the cup into a nearby waste bin and shouldered the tote. "While you're finding a hotel, I'm going to visit the restroom," he announced. "Don't leave until I get back. I want to say goodbye."

Christine looked up from her phone and, eyeing him, nodded. "Sure."

Cross left her side and headed for the restrooms, the route already mapped out in his mind from subconsciously registering every directional sign in the lobby.

As he marched around a curved wall and down a connected hallway, his pocket buzzed. He dug out his phone and, recognizing the number, accepted the call and held the phone to his ear. "Gary," he said as he headed to a recess in the wall with solid brown facing doors. He chose the door with the universal sign for the men's room as he listened to Gary's distorted voice through the receiver.

"John, I hope I'm not interrupting the conference."

"No, no, you're fine," Cross mumbled as he walked through the door with his chin as low as his shoulders.

"Glad you made it safe. How's the weather?"

A man in black jeans and matching leather jacket stood drying his hands at the sink. He fixed the swoop in his bangs, adjusted his square rimmed glasses, then slipped past on his way out the door, leaving Cross alone.

"The weather's fine. Warm."

"I have to say I'm envious. Not a big fan of the big temperature swings we get back here. I'd like to get hot and just stay hot. Did you make it to the church?"

"I . . . yeah, I did."

Gary paused, then asked, "John, is everything OK?"

Cross dropped the tote onto the counter as he stepped up to the sink and turned on the faucet. He splashed some water on his face, then grabbed a paper towel and dabbed his eyes.

"John?"

"Yeah, I'm still here. Gary, look, there's something I've got to tell you."

"I'm listening."

Cross drew a deep breath, then hung his head. "I lied about coming to Dallas for the conference. I mean, the conference is going on, and I'm actually here now, but that's not the real reason I came. Christine's here."

Gary remained silent.

"She has a stepbrother who's in jail for murder, and she's here investigating his case." Cross condensed Philip's story into bite-size chunks, a few slow breaths the only sign Gary was still on the line. "I followed her too. I don't know why. I guess to keep an eye on her or something. I guess you can take the man out of the CIA but not the CIA out of the man, so to speak. I should have just told you. I don't know why I didn't."

The line crackled a moment in silence before Gary replied. "Yes, you should've. If you'd just said something, I would've told you to go anyway."

Cross, dumbfounded, glanced up at his reflection in the mirror. "What do you mean?"

"You need to be there with her. I can't imagine what she's been through the last twenty-four hours. You didn't have to come up with this charade to convince me."

"Well, the truth is, she didn't want me to come."

Gary snorted. "I can't help you with that. But if there's one thing I do know, it's that you are where you need to be."

Cross pinched his eyebrows together. Gary didn't mean the conference, he was sure. There was a deeper meaning to his words. "Gary, what's going on?"

The door to the bathroom opened, and a stocky man in a tan Harrington jacket and gray collared shirt entered. He eyed Cross, then headed for a urinal. Cross noted the man's tight-cropped curly hair and squeaky-clean square chin, then shook his head as he turned his attention back to the phone. Not everything was a mission. He believed that. Didn't he?

"I've been wanting to talk to you about this for a while now. I just want to make sure you're, well, where God wants you to be."

Where God wants me to be? The wheels in Cross's mind picked up speed. What did Gary mean? Spiritually? Emotionally? Physically? Cross leaned against the counter as feelings, thoughts buried deep in his heart fought for air.

Gary was saying something else, but Cross couldn't hear it. Doubts and hopes intermingled, and he wanted nothing more than to open up and expose the hidden truth of who he was. But he couldn't. Something wouldn't let him.

Something wrong.

His instincts fought back and pushed his emotions aside. Gary's words faded from his ears. Cross's CIA training kicked into gear, all his motor functions subordinate to its commands. Accounting for every detail in the room, a subtle blur of unexpected motion in the corner of his eye rang alarm bells.

Suddenly, he pushed off the counter and dropped the phone as the man in the tan jacket rushed from behind and threw his shoulder into Cross's chest.

Unable to dodge the attack, Cross absorbed the blow and fell against the counter. The man swung his clenched fist in an arch toward Cross's face. Cross parried the punch, shoved the man's arm across his body, and punched his midsection.

The man yelped. He sneered as he grabbed a handful of Cross's polo shirt and pulled. Cross felt his feet briefly leave the floor as the man slung him from the sink and into the stall door.

Cross crumpled to the ground beside the toilet, stunned. The man stepped toward him but paused as the sound of footsteps alerted him.

The door to the restroom swung open, and a young man wearing a flat-billed cap entered. He came to a halt as he made eye contact with the big man.

In a deep, gravelly voice, the big man ordered, "Get out."

Cross's eyes cleared as the young man tilted his head to one side and said, "Excuse me?"

"I said get out!" The furious shout drove the timid young man from the room.

The big man was still eyeing the closing door as Cross jumped to his feet. With speed on his side, Cross closed the distance and kicked out with his foot as the man turned back to the stall. He connected with the man's chest and sent him backward into the counter.

His fists flying, Cross attacked. He aimed for all the critical areas, but the man's adept blocking prevented any serious injury. A misjudged throw of his balled fist opened Cross's side, and the man took advantage. Cross gritted his teeth as his rib cage throbbed in pain.

The man slapped another punch away, then grabbed Cross's arm in one hand and his throat in another and shoved Cross backward.

Cross grabbed the man's torso, bent his knees, then pushed off the ground, using the man's momentum to flip himself in the air and somersault them both. The man landed on his back, his diaphragm spasmed, and he gasped for breath.

Cross righted himself and backed up against the counter, his fists poised for combat, his heart rate regulated, his mind clear. The big man stood fully upright and cracked a muscle in his neck. He reached a hand into his jacket and charged.

Cross tightened his fists as the man pulled a knife from underneath his jacket and plunged the tip toward Cross's heart.

CHAPTER ELEVEN

THE THUMPING BEAT of the drum set inside the worship center grew louder, and Christine envied John having the opportunity to experience a level of music and teaching she'd only seen online. Concert-level worship venues existed in New York, but over the months since her conversion to Christianity, she'd preferred the experience of a smaller, less polished congregation, most likely due to her love of the community of Rural Grove. She might not have moved her residence to the church's home-town of Mechanicsville, Virginia, but her Sundays at a small church plant called Grace Church in the Bronx made her feel like she was there.

There was no desire on her part to leave Grace, given the connections she'd made in the weekly women's Bible study. But the music and excitement in the worship center made her linger. Maybe she'd visit one of the megachurches in the city, just to take it in.

Or maybe she'd stay at the conference for the opening session. Her finger hovered over the button to confirm booking a car to the hotel. Was she feeling a spiritual prompt to stay? The idea created conflict in her heart. She wanted to stay for the experience but struggled with wanting to be somewhere by herself to process everything that had happened in the past twenty-four hours. The bomber. Philip. John's deception topping it all off.

His disregard for her wishes she could forgive. Keeping his true in-tentions from Gary was another matter. As she pondered her dilemma, she found it funny how her immediate concern was more another's feelings than her own. Not at all her experience in the few relationships in her life before Christ. She relived several moments of selfish indignation toward previous boyfriends and cringed.

Pushing the memories from her mind, Christine decided to stay. She took the last sip of the flat white, then tossed the cup away. Walking around the baptismal pool, she headed toward the restroom to position herself nearby and wait for John.

Passing the entrance to the worship center, she recognized the familiar tune as a favorite at Grace Church. The lyrics filled her mind, and she found herself mouthing along with the muffled voices singing.

A hand suddenly grabbed her bicep from behind. Christine started, then turned to see who was there.

"Keep walking. Don't turn around," whispered a hoarse voice near her ear.

The man stepped alongside her and matched her pace. From the corner of her eye, she noticed pricks of red hair smattered along his pale chin. She strained her neck to try to see more of his features, when he lifted his black jacket and nodded toward his waistband. Chills traveled up and down her spine as Christine recognized the dark shape of a handgun stuffed into the man's belt.

"I said don't turn around."

Christine stared ahead as the man led her down the hallway toward the restrooms. She regulated her breathing, and her heartbeat slowed. Whoever the man was and whatever he wanted with her, he was about to have a rude awakening when John came out of the men's room.

She just hoped he came out before they left the building.

The few conference staff and attendees who were still mingling in the lobby disappeared from her view as she and the man entered the hallway. She assumed he wouldn't attempt to shoot her in public, so she slowed her pace.

The man grunted and pulled on her arm to keep her moving. "Don't think I won't," he half snarled, half spit in her ear. His inflection suggested enjoyment in the idea.

They passed the entrance to the restroom and kept walking toward a set of double doors at the end of the hallway. The music from the worship center vibrated against the wall to Christine's left, and her heart skipped a beat as she realized there were a thousand people in the next room with no clue of what was happening to her.

One of the double doors opened, and the man squeezed Christine's arm tight as they both froze in place. A squat Latino man in a pinstripe suit and gaudy tie stepped through the doorway and let the door close behind him. He stood in front of the double doors, as if to guard them, and stared down Christine's captor.

"Howdy," a voice called from behind them.

The pale man spun Christine around with him as he turned to confront the voice. Near the entrance to the restroom stood a tall bronzed man in a sharp gray suit and crisp white dress shirt. Christine quickly scanned him from the top of his wavy brown hair to the bottom of his oiled cowboy boots. Handsome, muscular, and confident.

She could get used to Texas pastors.

He held his hands rigid by his side as he started a slow jaunt toward them. "You folks seem lost, and it wouldn't be very neighborly of me to just let you wander around like this." His voice was deep and twangy, but not absurdly so.

The pale man inched his hand toward his waist, and the move caused the man in the gray suit to stop in his tracks.

"Hold on there, partner," he said as he lifted the flap of his gray suit jacket to one side, revealing a gold badge clipped on to his belt. "I'd prefer if this didn't get ugly."

Not a pastor. Thank God.

The pale man uttered a curse under his breath and let his hand go limp by his side.

"Now," the officer, federal agent, or whoever he was, commanded as he took another step in their direction. "Let go of the lady, and keep your hands where I can see them."

Christine felt the hand around her bicep tighten. The pale man lowered his stubbled chin and narrowed his blazing eyes at the man in the gray suit. A thin smile spread across his lips.

The tension in the air was severed at the sound of a thunderous crack from behind the man in the gray suit. Startled, he turned and stared in wide-eyed amazement as the door to the men's bathroom broke free from its hinges and flew into the hallway. It crashed to the ground with two men on top of it, their limbs entangled and thrashing violently. A knife bounced free from the struggle of both their hands to claim it and slid across the tiled floor to the middle of the hallway.

Christine's mouth fell open at the sight of John wrestling with the other man on top of the door. She tried to call out his name but suddenly felt her body pulled like a magnet away from the pale man and tossed toward the man in the gray suit.

She realized too late the pale man had used the distraction to make his move and catapult her from his side. With ease he sent her tumbling, and try as she might she couldn't catch her feet on the floor.

The man in the gray suit turned, and his eyes widened farther as she fell toward him. He reached out to try to catch her, but the pale man rushed him at the same time. Christine's knees buckled, and she rolled onto the floor. Above her, the pale man wrapped his arms around the man in the gray suit and roared as he dug in his heels and swung the stunned officer into the wall with a crash.

Christine propped herself up and glanced down the hallway. The Latino man in the pinstripe suit rushed toward them. She turned and noticed John lunging for the knife. His reach fell short as his opponent, a burly man in a tan jacket, wrapped his arms around John's waist and pulled.

The pale man attempted to shove the man in the gray suit into the wall, but the officer countered with an elbow to the pale man's ribs. He groaned in pain as the officer wrapped his arms around the pale man's neck and flipped him over his shoulder to the floor.

Both the pale man and the man in the tan jacket scrambled on their hands and knees toward the knife.

Christine jumped to her feet and ran to the knife before either of them. She kicked it hard and sent it sliding fast across the floor and out into the lobby. It disappeared over the edge of a short set of steps, clanging against the tile and drawing the curiosity of an exhibitor playing on his phone at his company booth. He glanced at the knife, then up at Christine.

She opened her mouth to say something, though not sure what, but a flash of color out of the corner of her eye drew her attention away. She turned to see the man in the tan jacket jump to his feet and, enraged, place both his hands on her shoulders and push her backward.

Christine braced for injury as she flew through the air. Instead, she collided with a wide, soft object and rode whatever it was to the ground. She bounced on the object and rolled off to one side, a male voice crying out as she did.

The Latino in the pinstripe suit lay on the ground next to her. He gasped for air, then rose to a knee and extended his hands to help her up as well. "OK?" he asked in a thick Hispanic accent.

She nodded. Reaching for his outstretched hand, she glanced back and witnessed the pale man kicking the man in the gray suit backward. The pale man pulled a bizarre-looking handgun with a high rectangular barrel from his waistband and aimed in her direction.

"Watch out!" she exclaimed as she grabbed the Latino man's open hand.

He noticed the gun too and nearly pulled her arm out of its socket as he swung her behind him.

A sharp pop rang through the air, and the Latino man released his grip on Christine as his arm jerked away and his body spun around. A fine mist of blood speckled Christine's hand and arm, and she turned her head and closed her eyes on instinct as the man's body crumpled onto the floor.

Christine braced for more gunfire, but instead she heard the grunting, whipping, and punching of a fistfight.

She forced her eyes open and crawled over to the Latino man. He gritted his teeth and drew quick, heavy breaths. "OK, OK," he repeated. "Go, go!" He let go of his arm for a second to wave her off down the hallway, and Christine saw the bloody tear along his bicep in the fabric of his pinstripe suit. He grabbed at the arm and squeezed his eyes shut, biting down on his teeth even tighter.

There was no way she was going to run.

Christine glanced in the direction of the fight. The man in the gray suit was twisting the handgun out of the pale man's hand. John ducked a swipe from the man in the tan jacket, then countered with a kick, then a punch. Behind the men, the smattering of people left in the lobby ran for cover. The music pulsated on.

Madness.

Thinking, Christine turned to the Latino man and frisked the inside of his jacket.

His eyes popped open, and he said, with a slur, "No. What are you—"

Her hands wrapped around the butt of the gun in his shoulder holster. She felt for the thick clasp holding it in and, finding it, unlocked it with her thumb. She pulled the gun out from under the jacket, to his clear amazement.

Without hesitation Christine turned and stood at the same time. She swung her arm, and just as she released the gun from her hand, she shouted, "John!"

John caught her gaze, then spied the gun spiraling through the air toward him. He kneed tan jacket man in the gut and pushed him to the ground as the man doubled over. In one motion, he caught the gun by the grip, dropped to his knee, and straightened his arm out over his attacker's back.

Christine followed his aim and saw the man in the gray suit pinned against the wall, his arms hanging limp, the pale man about to strike with his own weapon.

John fired, and this time the sound of the gun blast shocked Christine's eardrums.

The pale man screamed as the gun exploded from his hand. He released the man in the gray suit as his arms flailed backward. Gaining control of his arms, the pale man grabbed at his right hand. Blood oozed between his fingers.

Christine turned in time to see the man in the tan jacket right himself, knock the gun away, and headbutt John. John fell backward, dazed, and Christine tried to think of another way to help before it was too late.

To her astonishment, the man in the tan jacket left John alone and ran to his comrade. He grabbed the pale man by the jacket, and as he pulled him toward the lobby, she heard him utter an expletive-filled command for the pale man to run.

Christine ran to John's side and helped him to his feet. He winced as he massaged the bruise on his forehead.

"They're getting away," she said.

He nodded, then motioned to the two men sprawled on the floor. "Stay here with them." John picked up the Latino man's gun and took off after their assailants.

The man in the gray suit appeared beside her, his own weapon drawn. "Good advice," he said as he unlocked the safety on the handgun and followed John's path.

CHAPTER TWELVE

CHRISTINE RAN TO the Latino man and helped him into a seated position.

"I'm OK," he assured her. "Just a scratch."

She noted the absence of any further discoloration on the arm of his suit jacket and accepted his diagnosis as truth. With her help, he stood, cradling his left arm in a gentle embrace.

"Who are you?" Before the man could answer, Christine heard the sound of rushing footsteps and turned to see John jogging up to them. "John!"

He ran up to her and hugged her tightly. As he pulled away to examine her for injury, she noticed the myriad of bruises and cuts scattered about his face. "I'm fine," she assured him. "You're not."

He flashed a wry smile. "A couple of aspirin and I'll be good as new."

"What happened?"

"They got away. Jumped into a black utility vehicle and sped off. Armstrong called it in, so we'll see if the police can catch up."

Christine studied his eyes and tilted her head. "Armstrong?"

"The one in the gray suit." He nodded toward the Latino man. "They're some kind of law enforcement."

"Where's Armstrong now?"

"He's gathering the witnesses and trying to defuse the situation. Apparently there were a lot of 911 calls."

No kidding. Christine wondered what would happen to the conference once word of a gunfight got out. She suddenly perceived the rhythmic drone of music wafting from inside the worship center. The band was still performing. A quieter song, but still.

The man John called Armstrong appeared in her vision, approaching them from the lobby.

"There." Christine pointed.

John turned and acknowledged the man as he approached. The Latino man brushed by them and met Armstrong where the hallway and lobby joined. They conversed in a whisper for only a moment, then Armstrong studied the man's injury. He nodded and dismissed the Latino man, who left for the gathering of witnesses near the coffee bar.

Armstrong whistled as he stepped up to John and Christine and placed his hands on his hips. "Well, that was something else, wasn't it?"

One way to put it.

He dropped his smile and narrowed his eyes toward Christine. "You're not hurt, are you?"

She shook her head.

He nodded toward John. "You look a little roughed up."

"I promise the other guy looks worse," John replied.

While Armstrong studied John's appearance, Christine studied his. Armstrong's handsome features were tarnished by a few bloody scratches along his cheek, the only signs of injury. She presumed his tan skin was the result of genetics, not sun.

Armstrong, apparently satisfied in his examination, nodded at John. "You handled yourself pretty good. Military?"

John hesitated, then said, "I put in my time."

"Wish I could say the same, but the army didn't take too kindly to my chronic asthma." Armstrong straightened his arms and dusted the sleeves of his jacket.

"I'm sorry," Christine interjected. "Who are you exactly?"

"Oh, I apologize. I haven't formally introduced myself." He extended his right hand while using his left to reveal the badge under his jacket. "Special Agent Augustus Lee Armstrong, DPS, Criminal Investigations Division."

Christine raised an eyebrow in response to his confident declaration of his full name as she shook his hand. His grip was strong but his skin soft.

As if reading her mind, his broad smile somehow grew as he said, "I feel like the middle name never gets the same attention as the first, but it's just as good. In fact, you can call me Lee. Most everyone does. Everyone but my mother."

John nodded toward the man's badge. "DPS?"

"Department of Public Safety. Criminal Investigations works in tandem with local authorities on high-profile crimes. I work out of the Garland branch in this area."

At the thumping of boots against the tiled lobby floor, all three of them turned to watch a squad of Dallas police officers enter the church and head for the group of witnesses under the watch of Armstrong's Latino partner.

Armstrong extended his hand to guide them down the hallway toward the double doors at the end. "I directed the ambulance around back. Dallas PD has the scene under control, so we'll get you all checked out behind the building so it's a little more discreet."

As they fell in step behind Armstrong, John grabbed Christine's hand and squeezed it. "Nice toss, by the way."

He let go as she responded, "I would've shot him myself, but I didn't want to show off."

John's smile lingered, then dropped as he caught up to Armstrong. "What are they going to do about the conference?"

Armstrong cleared his throat. "Well, only the people in the lobby witnessed what happened. We won't interrupt the session—don't want to cause a panic. Word will get out quick after, only because PD's going to stay and ensure the safety of everyone inside, but the official story is a domestic dispute that turned violent among people not affiliated with the conference."

Christine considered his statement, then cut off any further discussion with a wave of her hand. "Wait. I don't understand. What is all of this about, anyway? Why did they come after us?"

She caught a disturbed glance from John and realized her mistake. A possible answer to her question was the men weren't after all of them. Just him. Like before. A cold chill raised the hair on her arms as she replayed memories of Yunus Anar's men kidnapping her from the hospital, then holding the congregation of Rural Grove hostage at gunpoint.

They reached the double doors and entered a dark hallway. Armstrong picked up his pace to reach the exit door and pushed it open. He held it in place and waited for Christine and John to walk through to the outside.

"That, Ms. Lewis," he replied, "is what I'm hoping you can tell me."

How did he know her name?

Before Christine could question him further, a pair of emergency medical technicians met them at the door. John protested assistance, but they ignored him and guided him by the arms to a waiting ambulance, its emergency lights still visibly bright against an already bright sunlit sky.

With John seated in the back of the ambulance and being tended to by the female technician, the male technician asked for an assessment of injuries from the others. A quick examination of the cuts and bruises on Armstrong convinced him to pull out antiseptic ointment and skin-closure strips.

John, sporting a couple of the white strips himself, rejoined them. Armstrong opened his mouth to speak, but the sound of the door opening distracted him. Another paramedic walked out of the church with the Latino man, his pinstripe suit jacket carried in his good arm and his shirtsleeve cut at the top of his bicep. His wound was already sealed with gauze and tape.

As the two men walked up, Armstrong pointed to his partner. "This is Segundo Flores. He and I are working the Philip Lewis case."

Christine tensed, and she shot a worried glance toward John. He was looking at her, grinning. "So," he said to Armstrong, "I guess that answers my question about why you guys were here in the first place."

Christine dug her hands into her hips. "And how you knew my name." A thought crossed her mind, and she narrowed her eyes at Armstrong. "Wait. Did you follow us here from the prison?"

Flores rolled his eyes at Armstrong as the paramedic by his side ushered him around the group and into the ambulance. Flores let loose more Spanish vocabulary than Christine could decipher with a meager two years of studying the language in high school. But from his tone, he didn't sound too happy.

Armstrong laughed and responded in kind, "amigo" the only recognizable word. She knew that one, at least.

Flores responded with a grunt of disapproval. Armstrong chuckled, then turned to Christine and shrugged. "You can't fault me for doing my job, Ms. Lewis. The journalist sister of an imprisoned murderer and her producer show up unexpectedly to visit the murderer, so the prison calls my office and gives us your names. We made it to the North Tower just before you left and wanted to see what other stops you had in mind. Lucky we followed you too. But if you don't mind, I'd like to ask you two a few questions, starting with who those men were and why they were after you."

Christine hesitated, hoping John could answer. She looked into the ambulance. Flores sat on one side of the ambulance, the medical technician securing his arm in a black sling.

"We've never seen those men before in our lives," John replied to Armstrong, a little too thick of a denial in Christine's opinion.

"Well, what about why? Did either of you owe Philip money?"

Christine shifted her eyes back to Armstrong and pinched her eyebrows. "What do you mean? Are you saying Philip sent those men?"

"Yes, that seems the most likely scenario at the moment. You show up to visit your brother—"

"Stepbrother."

"Pardon me . . . stepbrother, right after he's been charged with murder and his bail set very high, then are attacked by two men immediately following the visit. My guess is he got word to outside friends who hired those men to abduct you and force you to pay his bail."

"He's my stepbrother, Mr. Armstrong, not a comic book super-villain."

"What did he say to you during your visit, Ms. Lewis?"

"He told us he's innocent."

"And you believe him?"

Christine didn't reply. She studied Armstrong's patient face, then glanced at John.

"We think there's more to this case than meets the eye, yes," John said for her.

Armstrong took a deep breath, then stole a visual check on his partner in the ambulance. He licked his teeth with his tongue, then smacked his lips. Taking another deep breath, he turned back to them. "Well, then I don't know what to tell you. It's a mess, for sure. And I'm going to have a tough time tracking down these guys if you two refuse to provide me all the information I need."

It was John's turn to fold his arms. "We're not lying to you. We've never seen those men, and we don't think Philip had anything to do with this."

Armstrong narrowed his eyes. "See, the problem is, I think you *are* lying. At least about why those men attacked you. You may not know who they are, but I've got a feeling this isn't your first time at this kind of a rodeo."

Christine was sure the two men's chests were puffed out as they stared each other down.

"See, there's just too many unanswered questions for my taste," Armstrong finally said. "For instance, why come here to the church? What do two news network people have to do with a church conference?"

Bridling an anxious gasp, Christine kept her eyes steady and breathing controlled. "We were connecting with a friend who's in town for the conference." And now she was a liar too. Christine's stomach turned over twice, and she fought against the urge to gag or cough—she didn't know which. What was this life? All the lying, all the chaos. It wasn't for her. Not now. Not ever. How had John done this for so long?

Armstrong kept his eyes trained on Christine. "So if you don't think it was Philip, then what else could it be?" He shifted his eyes from Christine to John. "Any enemies interested in revenge?"

The question nearly invited a laugh from Christine. If only he knew. She bit her tongue and let John answer.

"None in Dallas." John gave a sly grin.

Was he testing Armstrong's pride? Christine found herself annoyed at both men. She suspected the conversation was on the verge of shifting from interrogation to a competition in masculinity. Which might not be a bad thing, provided it distracted Armstrong from digging further into John's identity.

Suddenly, Flores stepped down from the ambulance. Christine was momentarily startled. She'd forgotten about him.

"Agent Armstrong," John said, "do you plan to keep us here all night or detain us somewhere else? That is, if you have something to charge us with."

Flores rattled off a couple of sentences in Spanish, clearly aimed in Armstrong's direction. Armstrong eyed John, then straightened his jacket and nodded. "You're right, Mr. Jameson. I can't keep you here all night, and I don't plan on charging you with any crimes. Yet."

John exhaled an irritated breath.

Armstrong dismissed the paramedics, then directed Flores to return to the building. "One more thing," he said to them as he handed John a business card. "Give me a call before you decide to leave town."

John fanned the card and smirked. "Or maybe you can just surprise us at the airport."

Armstrong arched his eyebrows as the corners of his lips rose, then he turned on his heels and walked into the church, leaving Christine and John standing in the parking lot.

Christine's gut told her it wouldn't be the last time they'd see the two men. She wasn't as sure they'd be on the same side.

CHAPTER THIRTEEN

CROSS ENTERED HIS room at the Hilton Park Cities and tossed his duffel bag onto the floor. He ignored the ninth-floor view as he drew the curtains closed. He stepped backward from the window until his legs brushed up against the king-size bed, then let his body collapse and fall into the soft, fabric-covered foam.

He was trained to catch sleep where he could and instantly dozed off. Like clockwork he woke up ten minutes later and rose from the bed.

The shower lasted shorter than the nap. He dressed in jeans and a long-sleeved black Henley, then went to grab for his wallet, watch, and . . .

Phone.

In the aftermath of the attack, he'd forgotten about the burner he'd dropped in the bathroom. Armstrong's men whisked them away from the scene and deposited them at the hotel after Cross concluded that his original booking at the Hyatt Regency was compromised.

DPS wouldn't gather much intel about him from the device, with the exception of his call history. Cross snatched the receiver from the wired phone on the desk and followed the instructions to dial out.

After two rings, Gary answered.

"Gary, it's John."

"John, good grief. What happened? Are you OK?"

"I'm fine. I'm sorry about earlier. Long story short, Christine was with me at the church and, well, we were attacked."

Gary couldn't help but let loose a choice word and immediately apologized.

Cross filled in the details, including the fact that DPS was now involved. "Gary, I can't believe I'm going to say this, but if they call, I'm going to have to ask you to claim to know me as John Jameson, a producer with NABC."

"Of course, yes."

Really? Cross paused, then pressed the phone closer. "Gary, I just asked you to lie for me. You don't owe me that, and I shouldn't have asked. I don't even know why I did. I just, I can't . . ." He couldn't do it. Try as he might, he couldn't form the words.

"John, I understand. Look, earlier, what I was trying to say—"

"Gary, I'm sorry. This has all been a mistake. I shouldn't have called."

"No, hold on. We didn't finish our conversation earlier, and I have something I need to say. I think you need to consider the fact that maybe God is calling you away from Rural Grove."

The statement hit Cross so hard he felt like he might double over from the pain. He released a burst of air from his lungs and dropped his blank gaze to the ground.

Gary drew a deep breath. "And that's OK."

Cross searched for words but found none sufficient. He only stared at the patterned carpet of the hotel room.

Gary's voice was as clear as if he stood in the room. "Sometimes, the Lord puts us in a place for a reason, and I have no doubt he wanted you to be with us these past two years. But then sometimes he'll ask us to go to another place, and I don't want you to think that means you did anything wrong or that we don't love having you as our pastor."

Cross tried to swallow, but his mouth was too dry. "If you love having me as your pastor, why are you telling me this?"

"It's just something I've sensed for several months. I'm not sure if Mechanicsville is the place where you can best be used by God. And that's it ultimately. Isn't it? The best place we can ever be is in the center of God's will for our lives."

"If it's not Rural Grove, then where do you think I need to be?"

"Right there. Not Dallas, but there helping Christine. There, Washington, anywhere you need to be to do what you do best. Protecting others. Stopping evil."

Cross snorted. "I'm not a superhero, Gary."

"You know what I mean. If you didn't choose to go to Washington that day, there would've been a terrorist attack. If you hadn't forced your way into the conference, Christine might've been killed. John, you've been a good pastor. We love you, and you'll always be a part of Rural Grove. But I'd have trouble sleeping at night if I knew there was a chance for you to stop something bad from happening but you weren't there."

"I'm never going to put myself in a situation again where I might have to . . ." Cross's words trailed, the guilt of every assassination he'd committed on CIA orders forcing its way to the center of his heart.

"I'm not saying you have to kill anyone. I'm saying you were made for something other than being a small-town pastor. You've gotten us back to a healthy place as a church. And that's more than any one of us ever expected. We'll be fine." The line went silent for only a moment. "For what it's worth, this is just what I've been feeling recently. And I spent a lot of time in prayer over it before I decided to say anything. Take everything I've just said as counsel. Pray about it yourself. I could be wrong, and that's OK too. I guess what I'm saying is that for now, don't worry about the conference. Take care of Christine."

"OK" was all Cross could muster in return.

"Be safe, John. I'll be praying for you. Good night."

The line went dead, but the phone remained frozen in his hand. He considered redialing, a thousand responses to Gary's declaration ready to spew forth, but fought back against the temptation. Finally returning the receiver to its place, he flicked off the light, opened the door, and headed to the elevator.

Maybe Gary was right about him. Maybe his place in the world was exactly where he didn't want to be.

If anything, Cross had a feeling he was about to find out.

CHAPTER FOURTEEN

CHRISTINE GRABBED HER blazer and headed to the door as she heard the familiar cadence of the second knock she and John had worked out in advance. She slipped an arm into the coat and opened the door. She turned away and looked into the full-length mirror against the wall as she pulled her hair out from under the blazer and let it cascade over the collar.

"There's a coffee shop a few blocks away. I thought we might go there," John's voice called from the open doorway.

Turning back to the door, Christine nodded at John in approval, then noticed his grim expression. "Is everything OK?"

He shook his head, as if to loosen his thoughts, then smiled wearily. "Yeah. Just tired. Don't forget your laptop."

Christine reached for her shoulder bag resting on a bench seat under the mirror and held it up for John to see. She forced a grin to hide the brewing discontentment with their situation, then flipped the lights of her room off as she stepped into the hallway and securely locked the door behind her.

After a quick stop at a drugstore for John to purchase a new burner phone, they made their way to a coffee shop he'd picked out in advance. The walk was long, but the early Texas night was temperate, though Christine imagined not without her blazer. She appreciated John's insistence that they conduct their meeting in a nearby establishment rather than in either of their hotel rooms. He took great care to ensure they were never together in a private location alone, to protect the integrity of their relationship. She always stayed with Lori when she visited Mechanicsville, and he would book economy hotels when visiting New York City. Tonight, though, there would've been zero chance of any impropriety.

And not just because of Philip.

They entered the shop and fell in line behind an indecisive older woman torn between blended coffee or herbal tea.

"I got this," John insisted. "Find us a quiet spot."

Christine left his side and found an open bench seat behind two small round tables tucked into a corner. Above the bench seat, a chalkboard design promoted COFFEA ARABICA. "Harder to grow, better to drink," it read. She admired the coffee plant chalk drawings as she took the padded chair across from the bench and set her laptop on the table.

A quick online search took her to the business website of Hale Electronics. A full-motion video played under a headline reading, "The Next Generation Is Now." The video featured a black quadruped robot, resembling a dog, walking alongside a Caucasian man in a blue jacket down a hallway. The man's gray hair was cropped short, and Christine noticed his handsome smile as he admired the robot's smooth gait. His jacket bore the same insignia as the top banner of the website, the letter *H* with elongated stems. A blue button below the headline promised more information about "Project Bast."

John appeared by her side bearing two paper cups sheathed in brown sleeves and topped with white caps. He dropped one on the table next to her but kept his in hand as he settled onto the bench seat against the wall.

"I had them add an extra shot to yours," he quipped as he lifted the lid off his cup and blew the steam rising from the black liquid.

Christine smirked, not taking the bait. He liked his coffee as bitter as they would make it, but not her. She preferred a more caramel color to her coffee. She took a sip from the cup and enjoyed the warm combination of espresso and hazelnut as it coated her throat.

"It looks like Hale Industries does exactly what you would think they do," she said as she took another sip. She rotated the screen so John could see. "They build robots."

"Wow," John replied as he watched the introductory video on the home page. "That's impressive. Also a little creepy."

"Tell me about it."

John scanned the copy on the page. "'Project Bast,'" he read aloud. "Sounds like they enjoy naming their robots after mythological gods."

"Except, isn't Bast Egyptian? Philip mentioned Ares, which is Greek. Pick an ancient civilization and stick to it."

John took control of the trackpad and expanded the site's menu. "No mention of Ares. Interesting."

Christine leaned in to look for herself and arched an eyebrow. There were only three projects named after ancient gods in the menu: Bast, Chiron, and Heimdall. Egyptian, Greek, and Norse. She clicked the "About Us" option, then nursed her drink while she waited for the page to load.

A paragraph of detail about the company appeared alongside a full portrait image of the gray-haired man from the video, only this time he wore a suit and cheesed toward the camera, his arms folded. Under the photo was a caption that said, "Anthony Hale, Founder."

"Nice suit," John commented as he stared at the screen.

Christine ignored him as she read the accompanying paragraph. It boasted of the company's roots in the engineering department of the University of California–Berkeley, and it spouted more than a few cliché business phrases and words intended to inspire. Christine grew bored of the marketing copy and returned to the site's menu. She clicked through to "Project Chiron," another quadruped. This one was larger than Bast, and its detail page featured Chiron's ability to transport heavy loads over rugged terrain.

With nothing else to see, Christine used an online search engine to try to find anything related to Project Ares. Her request was denied, the search engine instead offering sites related to either Ares or the company but not both.

"I'm not seeing anything online," she announced.

"Found it," John countered, to her surprise.

She widened her eyes and dropped her mouth as he held up his phone for her to see his discovery. On the screen was an article from a site featuring military news, the headline blaring in bold, black letters, "US Army Narrows Down Robot Project to Two Companies."

She frowned as she skimmed the first paragraph of the article. "It doesn't say anything about Ares."

John nodded. "Yes, but Hale was one of two companies on the short list to develop a ground assault–robot prototype for the military. That explains why there's no information about the project on their site."

"Assuming they won the bid."

"True. That article is from two years ago, and I can't find any follow-up. Still, it's a lead."

"You think you should call Guin?"

John stared at his phone momentarily. What was going on in his mind? Christine never felt threatened by Guin, though she sensed a chemistry between the two. She always thought she shared similar chemistry with him.

Until just now.

Christine imagined Guin joining John on the bench, the two of them oblivious to her presence. They would find a joke immediately, then try to one up each other in witticisms. Christine didn't care for the idea of them together, if she were honest, but it wasn't as painful as she expected. She loved Guin. And wanted both of them to be happy.

Did she and John belong together? Christine suddenly felt a wave of emotion overcome her as her mind voiced the one thought she refused to have. Before she could consider it another second, John looked up from the phone with bright eyes.

"I've got a better idea. An old friend from the army. I just found his contact info, and I think he might be able to help."

He wasn't thinking about Guin at all. An invisible hand wrapped tightly around her heart as Christine mentally punished herself for accusing him otherwise. The question, though, still lingered. She ignored it and cradled the warm coffee cup between her hands as she watched John keying in digits on his phone screen.

"His name's Louis Costa. We were in basic training together. He went on a handful of combat tours after I left to join the CIA. Works for TRADOC now, Training and Doctrine Command. Their primary responsibility is recruiting, but he's pretty high up, so he might know how to find the information we're looking for."

After hitting the Call button, John brought the phone up to his ear and gulped his black coffee. Christine pulled up the article on Hale's bid to win the military contract and started skimming.

"Louis? It's John Cross. Remember me?"

Christine heard a loud guffaw from the phone's speaker and couldn't help but smile as Costa fired off a rapid, garbled string of pleasantries and reminisces. John struggled to keep up with his own responses.

"I know . . . I know. It has been a long time. I've been great. Yes, they treated me very well. Actually, I'm not with Special Activities anymore. I'm doing some contract work with Homeland Security."

John looked up from the phone with a sheepish grin. Christine understood his conflicting emotions over lying but also knew it was necessary to maintain anonymity between his old and new lives.

"I'm working on an analysis of artificial intelligence for the Field Operations division of I and A, and I'm struggling to compile a comprehensive list of outside contractors. I know this is a little out of the ordinary, but I thought I would cut straight to the source and see if you had any information on a particular contactor. Hale Industries."

John paused to allow Costa a moment to consider his request. Christine prayed the man could access the information they needed, and at such an inconvenient time.

"I'm presenting in front of the undersecretary in two days. It's this whole thing on robotics in the field, and this is the last bit of info I need."

Another pause in the conversation. Worry crept into Christine's heart.

"Oh man, you don't know what this means to me." John winked

at her. "Yes, Hale Industries. There's a particular contract I haven't been able to gain access to for some reason, maybe clearance issues. It's called . . ." John hesitated, then let out a breath. "Project Ares."

Christine strained to hear Costa's reply. John listened intently, his eyes locked on the texture of the wooden table. She called the look on his face his "downloading" expression, having seen him take mental notes of a conversation many times. She trusted he could repeat every word Costa said in an incredibly precise manner.

"Oh really? Man, that's great. That's exactly what I need for my presentation. Thank you so much for your time, and sorry to bother you after hours. Let's get together soon when you get back. This is my cell, so feel free to call. Talk to you soon."

John hung up and placed the phone on the table. He folded his hands and stared at Christine. "It wasn't much, but the good news is we now know what Project Ares is."

Christine spread her hands in impatience.

He took a sip of coffee, then repeated the information from Costa. "Hale won the bid to develop an artificial-intelligence combat-support robot for the army. They've been working on it for the past two years under the name Ares, and here's the unbelievable part—they're holding a demonstration for a select group of department representatives tomorrow morning at the company headquarters downtown. Apparently it's the third such demonstration, and the department heads can't stop talking about it."

Christine glanced from John to the article she'd scanned when he and Costa had talked on the phone. She rotated the screen again and pointed at a block of text. "John, that contract was worth one hundred and fifty million dollars. You said people murder for money, and last I checked, that's quite a lot of it."

"Sure, but there's still the question of why. What are they covering up? If Louis is correct, the technology is game changing. Sounds like Hale is poised to get a whole lot more than a hundred and fifty million dollars."

"If the technology is so advanced"—Christine leaned in closer and lowered her voice—"maybe they're offering it to other buyers to drive up the price tag."

John narrowed his eyes and stared off as he contemplated Christine's theory. "Use the military's investment to develop the technology, then sell on the black market to the highest bidder. Maybe, though I can't imagine the US government unable to beat another organization's bid. It's like they can't spend money fast enough."

Christine wasn't convinced she was wrong. Money was a good reason to murder, sure, but she suspected treason might be an even bigger reason. In her theory, if Mano knew the company's intentions to offer their product to a third party unbeknownst to the military, it could be a compelling reason for someone to want him dead.

She folded her arms and took a deep breath. "So what now?"

John beamed as he grabbed his phone. "Now?" he said as he unlocked the screen. "Now we call Guin."

CHAPTER FIFTEEN

CROSS ADJUSTED THE thick-rimmed glasses sitting on his nose, then tugged at the bottom edge of the blue blazer to smooth out the rumples gained during his ride in the black SUV. The morning sunlight glistened off the gold jacket buttons of the immaculately pressed uniform.

As he stood at the entrance to the sprawling business campus at 5400 Legacy Drive in Plano, over twenty miles from downtown Dallas, he couldn't help but straighten his back and lift his chin. The uniform salvaged lost memories—some he was proud of, others not. The CIA hadn't recruited him because of his friendly nature during his tours of duty.

He slipped the dark-green service cap on his head and waved to the driver. The black SUV pulled away, leaving Cross standing alone at the large glass front of the complex's southern wing. The southern and northern sections of the campus were bifurcated by a jetty between the two structures that created a ceiling over the cobblestone double driveway.

He heard a whistle followed by Christine's distorted voice. "This is amazing," she said, the sound traveling up his jawbone and directly into his brain's auditory nerves. He tongued the microphone attached to the tooth in the back of his mouth. The high-tech piece of equipment was affectionately called a *molar mic*. He was still getting used to processing the sound, the mic transmitting it via his jawbone, but was impressed with the clarity of her voice in his head.

"I still can't believe the picture I'm getting from that tiny camera."

Cross let out a subtle laugh as he imagined her enthusiasm over seeing his vantage point from the image transmitted to her laptop screen from the camera embedded in the frame of his glasses. His call to Guin the night before resulted in an early morning rendezvous at Addison Airport, halfway between their hotel and the business complex. There, he and Christine greeted a small jet carrying the army greens along with a bag of "accessories," as Guin put it in her note: the molar mic, the glasses, and more gadgetry to assist in their unofficial undercover operation.

She also wrote, "Don't call me again," but he didn't think she meant it.

Guin provided all the appropriate credentials to guarantee his entry into the demonstration, this time the silver badge above the right-hand breast pocket of his blazer emblazoned with his new last name, "Sykes."

To give Christine the full experience, Cross turned from the southern entrance to look at the giant bronze statue of an eagle stationed between the dual driveway. The offices of Hale Industries were located only in the southern wing, the opposite side of the complex partially filled with smaller businesses renting office space. According to their research, Hale renovated his entire wing to accommodate the specific technical needs of their project development.

And Cross was about to have a front-row seat to the fruits of the company's labor.

He checked his watch.

"You're early," Christine noted.

"Not by military standards," he replied, then turned and marched toward the glass double doors. In one swift motion he grabbed a handle, swung the door open, and stepped inside.

The gray tile and white walls of the interior lobby shone with prestige as the morning sunlight beamed through rows of floor-to-ceiling windows on the left. All six floors above were open to the lobby, running the length of the building, a handful of narrow walkways bridging the gaps either side of each floor. The entire structure was capped by an arched ceiling made of glass.

Just ahead, a group of men in identical dark-green jackets and khaki trousers stood in front of a large display of plant life protected from intrusion by a low glass barrier.

"Beautiful." There was a pause, then Christine added, "The lobby, I mean."

No point in rolling his eyes since she couldn't witness it. And he wouldn't return a quip, should the others notice and assume he was crazy.

Each man turned as they noticed his approach. Cross kept his expression stern and saluted. "Gentlemen," he announced. "Major John Sykes, INSCOM, Four Seventieth Brigade." A midlevel position with Intelligence and Security Command was the best Guin could do on short notice. The 470th was located out of Fort Sam Houston, Texas, near San Antonio, and to the best of Guin's knowledge, no one else from that brigade had been invited.

He was greeted with similar salutes from the group, then each man introduced himself, all of similar rank but from varying commands. Acronyms such as FORSCOM, AFC, and USACE were offered, all the while Cross imaging Christine's furious online searches to decipher what each meant. Cross's service had ended over a decade earlier, but the Rolodex of knowledge in his mind opened to cards such as *Army Forces Command* and *Army Corp of Engineers*.

An older, shorter man in a blue beret shook Cross's hand and leaned in as he said, "Sam Houston, right? Ever run into a Captain Hicks with MEDCOM? You'd remember him. Tall fellow."

Cross considered any number of responses, though in truth he already knew the best choice. In his experience, when playing a role in a mission, it was best to keep any lies to a bare minimum. There was no reason to try to invent a story to satisfy casual curiosity. He only needed to give just enough to be sufficiently convincing, which in this case was his uniform, the credentials he carried, and a passing knowledge of army decorum.

He opened his mouth to deny knowledge of the man's friend, but his words were cut short by a loud, masculine voice from behind them.

"Gentlemen!"

Cross glanced around the short man's beret and spotted Anthony Hale approaching them from down the hallway leading deeper into the wing. His polished shoes clicked on the floor as he walked, and he wore a similar suit to the one from his portrait on the website. A woman in a sharp gray dress followed close behind. She carried a clipboard, and a thin white cord snaked its way down from behind her ear and into the back of her dress.

With his arms open as wide as his smile, he rounded the collection of potted plants and lowered the volume of his voice to a comfortable level. "My name is Anthony Hale, founder and CEO of Hale Industries, as I'm sure you can guess. Thank you all for being my guests this morning. Now, if you don't mind, please follow Marissa to the escalator. Ares is waiting for us to arrive so he can show you what he's been up to."

The twinkle in Hale's eye was magnified by the bright sunlight. He shook hands with each of the men as they passed to follow the woman down the hallway. Cross thanked Hale as he shook his hand, then kept a short distance between himself and the group heading to an escalator connecting the lobby to the first floor. He took the brief moment to say, in a low tone imperceptible to anyone but Christine, "Pretty soft hands for a guy who builds robots."

"What was that, Shepherd?"

She'd heard him. He could whisper in the middle of a hurricane, and the molar mic would pick it up. He wasn't about to fall for her trap to repeat the insult louder, her use of his old CIA call sign another clue to her sarcasm. His grin faded as he realized she was going to stick with the name all day.

Might be a good time to assign her the radio moniker "Chrissy."

Marissa stood stoic in the lead as they rode the escalator up. On the way, Hale boasted of his company's purchase of the entire property, the northern wing rented to various technology companies and the southern wing renovated exclusively for his team of researchers to develop technologically advanced systems for use in both private and military contexts.

"We're not just about robots, but next generation robotic intelligence across a spectrum of applications. Our work has evolved over the past twelve months from implementing intelligence systems into things like aircraft and personal transports to fully autonomous machines capable of performing a variety of tasks in hostile environments," he explained as they all stepped from the escalator.

Marissa directed them to the left. A pair of men in dark suits flanked another in a short-sleeved button-down shirt bearing the elongated letter *H* logo.

Cross noted the trace bulge of firearms under the black jackets of each of the two guards. They too wore semi-clear earpieces attached to coiled wires disappearing beneath their collars. If he were a betting man, Cross wouldn't hesitate to put money on the men as members of a private security firm. He knew ex-military muscle with a dash of patriotic indifference when he saw it.

The man in the short-sleeved shirt carried an electronic tablet strapped around his hand. He flashed Marissa an awkward grin as the military personnel lined up.

Hale stepped around them and waved at the man. "This should be obvious, but Dasya will be confirming your identity before we proceed any further."

The short man in the beret eagerly stepped forward and offered his ID badge and thumb. Dasya swiped the badge through a card reader attached to the tablet, then directed the man to place his thump on the screen.

The process was repeated for each man, Cross included. The card reader flashed green as his badge was passed through, then he smirked at one of the black-suited guards as he let the tablet scan his thumbprint.

"Thank you, Major Sykes," Dasya said with a nod.

Cross stepped away to let the next man up.

"Guin is good," he heard Christine say.

It didn't hurt that the CIA retained all his information, including more than just fingerprints. Giving him a false identity was the easy part. Using the false identity to procure secrets without getting caught, now that took skill. Fortunately for him, this mission, if you could call it that, was to get eyes on Hale, the inside of the company facility, and Project Ares. No theft of company secrets necessary.

Unless, of course, the opportunity presented itself.

Satisfied in their credentials, Hale clapped his hands and took the lead toward a set of thick paneled doors locked by an access panel on the adjacent wall. One of the guards produced a key fob and waved it at the panel, access immediately granted. A clink prompted Hale to grab at the handle.

He paused, holding the door open only wide enough to keep it from locking again, and addressed the group. "The second and third floors contain all of our research and development offices and laboratories. Fourth and fifth dedicated to executive, classroom, and employee recreation space. I'm particularly proud of our warehouse and garage space connected to this building and adjacent to our parking structure. There we've built training facilities for our fleet of intelligent combat assets, and I'll give you a tour in due time. Today's demonstration will be taking place in a more secure space, with us observing from a viewing room for obvious safety and security reasons." Hale grinned from ear to ear and cocked an eyebrow. "Are you ready to meet Ares?"

Cross felt the same sense of indifferent reservation he read on the faces of his fellow servicemen. These men were privy to many a secretive and expensive defense research project and were rarely impressed. Make that never impressed. Despite the showmanship of whoever might be attempting to sell the military on the latest and greatest technology.

"Intelligent combat assets?"

It was still weird to hear Christine's voice in his head without the sensation of an earpiece in his auditory canal. She'd have to conjecture the meaning behind Hale's words on her own as Cross held his composure and followed the executive through the door.

Besides, they would both be introduced to Ares in a matter of minutes.

They entered a dimly lit room, with Marissa bringing up the rear.

She closed the door, and Cross noticed the two guards were absent from the room. The walls were bare, apart from a single wide pane of dark glass covering half of the wall to their right.

Hale stood to the left of the window, his brow and nose casting long black shadows on his face from the recessed light in the ceiling above him. "Two years ago, the United States military awarded Hale Industries a contract to develop unmanned intelligent combat units that could be used in the field to minimize loss of human soldiers during violent conflicts. I stand before you today to announce that we not only succeeded in our mission but have reached technological heights years beyond our competitors." He lowered his chin, his eyes disappearing into the black void created by the shadow from the light. "I give you . . . Ares."

Behind him, the room on the opposite side of the glass appeared as overhead lights powered on. Audible gasps filled the viewing room as they all spotted the figure standing in the middle of an unfinished concrete floor. Cross held back his own audible exhale of air, though no less stunned at the sight of the humanoid robot holding what appeared to be a modified M27 Infantry Automatic Rifle.

The initial shock wore off, and the servicemen exchanged cryptic glances. If his own thoughts were any indication, Cross assumed they'd all expected to see something more in line with other unmanned combat units he'd seen before. Usually, military robots took the form of miniature armored vehicles on tracks, with mounted guns or rockets. Not this.

"Is he kidding? That thing looks like RoboCop."

Cross pressed his lips together and narrowed his eyes as he compared Ares to Christine's reference, ultimately deciding that no, the thing did not resemble RoboCop. Its torso was box shaped and covered in a Kevlar vest lined with stuffed pouches. Limbs full of sharp edges, metal plates, and small round indentions of screws were connected to its body by large box plates extending upward at the shoulders. The gun appeared attached at the end of its right arm, no visible evidence of articulating fingers. The left hand was hidden behind the barrel. Its legs were thick and square, with metal plates hiding the wires, gears, and steel bars of its thighs and calves. The plates were reasonably designed into the shape of combat boots at the base of each leg.

With the exception of the black color of the vest and gun, key elements of Ares's metal skin were painted in the official US Army Operational Camouflage Pattern, though the pattern did little to knock the shine off the metal. The most striking feature of Ares's, though, was its head. With a wide neck narrowing only slightly as it rose to a flat top, its dominant feature was a rectangular plate of black glass encased in a metal box extruding from its face. The glass plate reminded Cross of a rectangular version of the sand goggles he'd worn in various missions in the Middle East, sans a cutout for a nose.

Though the room was mostly spare, a collection of human-shaped targets stood at attention directly behind the humanoid robot. The whole room had a hazy feel about it, though Cross wasn't sure if it was the atmosphere of the demonstration room or the effect of the observation window.

Hale was looking at Ares and ignoring the military personnel, a bit dramatic in Cross's opinion. The construction of the mechanized soldier was impressive, but at the moment it stood immobile. Cross wondered who would move first, Ares or its creator.

Without turning, Hale lifted his open hand and gestured toward the window. "We knew this day would come, and it is finally here. Ares is a fully operational, synthetically intelligent, bipedal combat unit capable of engaging hostile forces in environments designed for human beings. While his structural components are built using advanced alloys, we've taken the extra precaution of encasing Ares's sensitive intelligence and motor control system into his Kevlar-protected chest."

Hale finally turned to face the men. His face appeared brighter, and Cross noticed the lights in the room were brighter than before. "We're still working on his head before we're ready to do a complete field demonstration. Right now, the camera system is implemented into the faceplate, but our team agrees we need to continue to refine the vision capabilities, with an emphasis on designing something more aesthetically pleasing." He laughed. "But you don't want me to keep blabbering on about the technical specifications—we've got a printout for that later. You came here to see Ares in action."

The army representatives exchanged eager glances, causing Hale to widen his already disturbing grin. He turned to the window as a buzzer sounded inside the demonstration room. A red light blinked behind Ares, and a metal door on the opposite side of the room opened. A man entered and shut the door behind him. The red light disappeared.

The man stepped between the targets and lifted an arm to wave at the observation window. He wore a black padded suit with the outline of protective plates over vital areas, padding along his arms and legs, and a thick helmet with a large curved plate of glass attached above his brow and covering his face. At various points on his suit were large white squares with patterns of smaller black squares, forming digital barcodes.

"Scott is one of our engineers and will be assisting in our demonstration today," Hale explained. "Ares's advanced computer system is able to detect the visible patches on Scott's suit and identify him as a friendly, though I believe given some time we can program Ares to differentiate targets based on perceptible characteristics without the use of the patches." He nodded toward the window, and Scott offered a lazy salute.

Another buzzer sounded, followed by a thunderous rumble and the deep drone of motors. Ares suddenly moved, straightening itself even more than it already was. With rigid movements of its abdomen and arms, it settled into as relaxed a position as a robot could.

One of the others, a sergeant major, uttered a loud oath. No one else moved. Cross forced himself to take quiet breaths.

Ares bent slightly at its knees and raised its weapon, the other arm connected just under the barrel, a ball rotating on an axis at its wrist instead of fingers. It pivoted on its heels and marched toward the target field. A squat pack with four antennae, each varied in height, was attached to its back.

With precise aim, Ares fired short bursts of live ammunition of the M27, striking the heart and brain regions of the targets. When it reached the target nearest Scott, the left arm of Ares detached from the rifle. A sharp bayonet released from inside its forearm and extended to its full length. The robot raised its arm, then plunged the tip of the bayonet into the neck of the stationary wooden stand cut into the shape of a human combatant.

Another buzzer sounded, then the bayonet retracted, and Ares stood upright facing Scott. The men inside the observation room broke into a round of applause. Cross narrowed his eyes to continue studying Ares's visible components as he slowly clapped his hands.

"Did that just happen?"

He knew how Christine felt. During his CIA days, Cross was privy to a number of classified defense projects related to the integration of advanced technology in the field, even participating in covertly procuring similar designs and plans from other countries. But Ares was unlike anything he'd ever seen.

Hale laughed as the men peppered him with questions. "Gentlemen, all of your questions will be answered in due time. Remember the printout I promised you? But right now I want you to be able to meet Ares in person. My team is going to do a quick system check and secure the demonstration room, then we can enter. Please accompany me to the lobby, where Marissa will have some light refreshments."

As the others lined up at the door to the lobby, Cross took one last look at Ares standing motionless before Scott. The engineer himself stood frozen in place as well, a single stream of sweat just noticeable on his forehead, his eyes bulging as he stared into Ares's faceplate. Scott's eyes darted from the robot to the observation window.

Then the room went dark.

CHAPTER SIXTEEN

CROSS ACCEPTED A paper cup filled with black coffee from Marissa and took heavy gulps of the bitter liquid as he observed Hale gloating about the Ares Project to the colonel from the Corps of Engineers. At the moment, the possibility Hale might be moving to sell Ares to a foreign buyer seemed the most plausible explanation for Amaya's death. If any of the officers present had the authority, he was sure they would've handed Hale a blank check and told him to put any number he wanted on it.

He took another slug of the coffee as Christine's voice traveled into his head from the molar mic. "That was unbelievable. Did you know about something like that?"

Cross turned away from the others and pretended to admire the architecture of the building. With a low tone, he replied, "There were a few civilian projects we monitored, but nothing this advanced."

"It was like something out of a movie. The speed, the accuracy. I mean, I've seen videos online of robots doing backflips and stuff, but I never thought we'd see one perform like that so soon. He said synthetic intelligence. Does that thing think on its own?"

"I don't think so. I'm willing to bet the entire sequence was programmed."

"Still . . ."

"Yeah."

Cross turned back to avoid drawing attention. Marissa whispered into Hale's ear, then he opened his arms to the men and beamed. "Ares is ready for his close-up. If you'll all follow me."

The men deposited their paper cups onto a small table, then tried to beat each other to the demonstration room entrance not too much farther down the hall from the observation room. Hale held the door open, and the men filed through. Cross kept himself in the middle of the pack and, like the others, ignored Hale on his way into the large room, instead craning to catch a peek at the robot inside.

Ares hadn't moved. It stood rigid, it's blank faceplate staring at the back wall. The M27 was nowhere to be found, and Scott stood just off to the side, his safety helmet removed and cradled in one arm. The targets were also unmoved. The haze in the room accentuated the beams of light from overhead fixtures.

Hale called out from behind the men. "You can see we've removed Ares's weapon. I promise you even if he still had it, you would be completely safe, but I'm told my lawyers would prefer we keep the armaments secured when interacting with guests."

A few of the men chuckled. They all stared in wonderment at the robot, circling it but resisting the urge to touch it.

Cross stood in front of Ares and stared into the blank faceplate. He imagined himself in a combat situation, then imagined engaging something like the mechanized figure. Never before had he felt so helpless.

He didn't like it.

"Sykes, right?"

Hale's voice startled Cross from his daydream. He held his composure and glanced over to find Hale standing beside his left shoulder, the executive miming Cross's posture and stare.

"From Fort Sam? You were a late addition."

"Yes, sir," Cross replied. "Chief Warrant Officer Williams sends his regrets."

"I was very sorry to hear of his illness. Thank you for stepping in at the last minute to take his place."

"I just happened to be in the right place at the right time, sir." Cross motioned to the stoic machine. "This is impressive."

"Well, I was hoping for more than just impressive," Hale said with a smirk. "Revolutionary, groundbreaking, world shattering." He paused, then snorted and added, "Actually, I'm not sure there's a synonym strong enough."

"The bid for this project must have been astronomical." Cross held his breath, wondering if the statement was too suggestive.

Hale snorted again, this time to himself, and looked Ares up and down. "He's worth every penny."

The man in the beret bent over to examine the robot's arms.

Hale noticed and stepped away from Cross. "Did you enjoy the bayonet feature?" he called out with a grin. Joining the man in the beret, Hale proceeded to explain the technical aspects of how the bayonet could extend and retract from the arm.

Cross stood motionless but ignored the robot and the men to focus on Scott. One of the military guests joked with him about the kind of courage it took to trust a robot carrying an automatic rifle. Scott's temple was clean of sweat, but Cross took note of the safety helmet quivering in his grip.

"I don't blame him," Christine said. "I wouldn't have trusted that thing to fire a gun in my direction."

Christine's attention to the small detail made him smile. She was smart, but maybe wrong. Cross figured there would be nerves given Scott's role in the presentation. But with the success of the demonstration, he expected to see more relief.

He detected fear.

"Scott!" Hale called out as he waved the engineer over from behind Ares. "Everyone, I'm so sorry, I neglected to formally introduce our lead hardware engineer, Scott Reardon. Didn't he do great today?"

The group applauded Scott as he mustered a smile on his way over to Hale. Cross finally moved from his post, circling Ares to observe the two men interacting. Hale grabbed at Scott's shoulder and pinched as the officers bombarded the engineer with questions. Scott's answers were succinct but deep in technical jargon and statistics.

Hale beamed as the engineer rattled off the specifications of the robot's range of communication, then released his grip and directed Scott out the door with one of the armed security guards. He clapped his hands and announced, "I hate to say it, but we do need to move on so you can tour our testing facilities and laboratories." Someone groaned, causing him to laugh. "I know. I know. I would love to send each of you home with your own Ares, but we need to let him have a break after such a stellar performance."

The men laughed, then filed out the door, sharing excited chatter. Cross took one lingering look at the humanoid machine, then reached his hand up to feel one of the four antennae poking out the top of the square pack secured to its back.

"No, no, Major Sykes."

Cross froze his fingers just next to the antenna and looked over to see Hale staring him down from the door.

"That'll cost you another hundred and fifty million." Hale, an eyebrow lifted in amusement, extended his hand out the door.

Dropping his hand, Cross marched through the exit on the heels of the group of military personnel ushered by Marissa toward the escalators. They all rode to the second level to tour the labs where Ares, and other Hale Industries projects, were developed. The staff present in the offices were cordial but guarded with their answers to various questions posed by the group. Hale repeated his promise of a detailed portfolio of technical specifications that would be handed out at the end of the tour.

They explored the majority of the second floor without a sign of Scott Reardon.

An idea formulated in Cross's mind. On their way to a set of offices dedicated to user experience and interface, he caught Marissa by the elbow and said, "I've got to make a pit stop, but don't worry. I'll catch up." He nodded toward a sign with the familiar silhouettes of a man and a woman.

Marissa responded with a cold smile. "Of course. Jerry will accompany you, as we cannot allow any guests to roam free, due to the sensitive nature of our work. You do understand."

A statement, not a question.

Cross anticipated as much, and he accepted Marissa's condition with enthusiastic amicability. With Jerry in tow, he split off from the group and entered the men's room. Much to his irritation, Jerry followed and posted himself near the door in full view of the restroom.

So much for having a private conversation. There was no way he could talk to Christine with the guard in the same room, even if he whispered. He'd have to think of something else.

"They're taking this thing really seriously, aren't they?"

Cross felt dumb hearing Christine's voice but unable to acknowledge it.

"While you've been getting cozy with Anthony, I've been scouring the web looking for information on his employees."

Sounded like Christine had already thought of his idea.

Cross positioned himself at a urinal and kept his eyes locked on the tile squares of the ceiling. He kept his business to a minimum, then stepped away and up to the counter as the flush triggered automatically.

"A lot of office-management positions listed, and a whole team of people labeled simply 'Roboticist,' whatever that entails. From what I was able to gather earlier, Mano and Philip both worked under Reardon's team. Might explain his nerves, given Mano's murder was just last week."

The water from the faucet flowed with a wave of his hand, and Cross took his time lathering with soap. He looked into the mirrored wall behind the counter and gave a slight shake of his head, then glanced at Jerry and caught him stifling a yawn.

"You think Reardon might know more than he's letting on?"

Cross looked into the mirror and replied with a subtle nod.

"OK, there's only one thing to do. Take out Jerry over there with one of your signature surprise attacks, then extract Scott to the safe house for interrogation."

Cross narrowed his eyes at the mirror, his lips pursed. She was having too much fun with the clandestine nature of his current situation. Not that he couldn't take Jerry. He'd already considered three different ways to neutralize the guard.

He removed his hands from under the flowing water and reached for a paper towel from a stack neatly resting in a wicker basket. He dried his hands, then stepped toward Jerry to toss the towel into a wastebasket.

Deciding against a surprise attack, Cross let Jerry open the door for him. As Cross stepped across the threshold, the presence of a small security camera discreetly tucked into the corner where the wall and ceiling met caught his eye. He kept his glasses pointed at it for a second longer than comfortable, then glanced away as Jerry circled him. "Sir," the guard said with a suspicious frown. "Is there an issue?"

Smiling at the guard, Cross remarked, "Just checking the security for when I come by tonight and try to steal the designs for the robot."

Jerry rolled his eyes, then motioned Cross forward with his arm.

The two men reunited with the rest of the group as they moved from a series of software development offices to a large workroom with unfinished walls and exposed ducts and pipes hanging from the ceiling. Worktables, rolling toolboxes, and shelves filled with mechanical parts lined the walls. The middle of the scuffed concrete floor was littered with wooden crates fortified by metal frames.

Hale continued his lecture. "This is one of our many testing facilities. Here we put all of our robots through a series of exercises designed to find the limits of their mechanics and programming. In the packet we'll be handing out at the end of the tour, we've included a data stick with footage of the various tests Ares has been subjected to, though we withheld the less successful tests for a blooper reel we'll release at a later date."

The man's smarmy stand-up routine was wearing on Cross. He gave his best polite chuckle, then continued to examine every feature of the room, collecting his own footage to comb through with Christine, not that he expected to discover any evidence of a treasonous plot out in the open. Hale mentioned the fifth and sixth floors were executive space, more likely where he might find the truth behind Amaya's demise.

Cross might just have to break in later after all.

Hale announced the end of their tour and that the project information packet was available in the lobby. He bid them goodbye and handed the lead off to Marissa. "I have to give a quick toast to my team on their success today, then crack the whip and get them working late on refining Ares's image recognition." He laughed again, and Cross fought the urge to roll his eyes.

Hale shook each man's hand, then took an escalator up to the next floor. The group followed Marissa to the down escalator. Cross stepped in behind the man in the beret, who turned and widened his eyes.

"That was something else," he said.

"Yeah," Cross replied. "Something."

The man in the beret took the hint and turned away as they descended. At the exit, Marissa accepted a box from a young assistant and handed each man a manila folder marked PROJECT ARES and CONFIDENTIAL. She insisted Hale Industries would be aware if the men made copies of the documents or data stick inside, then wished the men good fortunes.

"See you soon," Christine said into his receiver.

He smirked at the thought of the sentiment being directed at Marissa instead of him.

Cross followed the others to the outside drive, where several black SUVs sat idling. The men piled into their respective cars as Cross's own hired driver pulled up in the rear of the procession.

In the short six-minute drive, Cross unbuttoned his blazer, removed his service cap, and loosened his tie. He enjoyed the feeling of a uniform but enjoyed removing it even more. His video glasses came off next, but the removal of the molar mic would have to wait until he was reunited with Christine.

The driver rolled to a stop on Windsor Avenue just before a crosswalk between two rows of modern commercial real estate. Cross thanked the driver as he exited the right side of the vehicle and stepped out of the road and onto a wide sidewalk of red brick and painted white stripes.

He ignored the SUV pulling away and took brisk steps to the outdoor patio of a coffee shop on the corner of a break in the connected buildings, which led to a parking structure. He spotted Christine at a table on the end of a long, cushioned bench seat shaded by a wide umbrella overhead. She removed a pair of earbuds and stood as he approached her. They hugged, but Christine let go quickly and shrank back into her seat. Cross hesitated, then joined her.

"That was exhilarating," she said as she offered him a half-filled cup of iced coffee.

Cross accepted the drink but paused to remove the molar mic before he took a sip. He handed the drink back after guzzling half of what was left, and remarked, "We might have to get a refill."

"I'll get a refill. You get your own," Christine replied with a wink. She glanced over her shoulder, cleared her throat, then motioned toward the folder in his hand. "Should we take a look?"

He handed it over and shook his head. "You can, but I don't think we need it."

"How so?"

"Did you save the recording?"

Christine glared. "I know how to use a computer."

Cross considered apologizing but decided she was joking. "Pull up the footage."

She unlocked the laptop and opened the video file. Cross accepted her invitation to take control, and he scrubbed through the first section of the captured footage from the hidden camera in his glasses until he found the moment he stood behind Ares in the demonstration room.

Pointing at the screen, he said, "The packet is probably going to tell us that this backpack is what holds the communications and video systems being controlled and monitored by an operator. What do you see at the top?"

Christine arched an eyebrow, then replied, "Four antennae."

He scrubbed the video to the demonstration and paused it when Ares turned to engage the targets. "And now?"

Christine narrowed her eyes at the screen. "Still four antennae. What are you getting at?"

"The one on the end isn't an antenna. It's a two-dollar piece of heat-shrinking tubing you can buy at any hardware store."

Christine sat back in the bench seat. "I don't get it."

"Look again." Cross pulled up a frame from earlier and compared them side by side. He pointed between the two images of the backpack. "There's four antennae visible in both, but the first one is made of different material and is even slightly shorter compared to the others."

"It's not the same robot?"

"Exactly. I'm not sure why, but I think there were two different machines. They switched it out between when we left the observation room and when we got into the demonstration room. They probably figured no one would remember the details when the robot was in motion."

Christine stared at the screen, deep in thought, by the look on her face. Cross removed the two images and returned to the camera footage. "Here's something else." He scrubbed the video again and paused it on a frame showing the security camera just outside the bathroom. "Notice anything?"

Christine blinked, then sat forward and examined the still. She tilted her head, then suddenly her eyes widened, and she swatted his hand away from the trackpad. Switching to her open web browser, she cycled through a collection of tabbed pages until she found the one she was looking for. Opening the page, she turned the monitor back toward Cross.

On the screen was the home page of an industrial-security company called Visco. The header of the website featured the company's logo, block letters inside the outline of a rectangle with curved edges. The same logo featured on the camera inside Hale Electronics.

With her finger calling out the logo on the site, she replied, "Different model, but that's the same company that installed the camera outside De Angelis."

CHAPTER SEVENTEEN

SCOTT REARDON STARED at the black bar pulsating against the stark white background of the word processing software filling his computer monitor. No words came to his mind, only the image of Ares firing the M27 in his general direction repeating over and over again, like a visual record stuck on a loop.

He was supposed to be writing a proposal with solutions to the known issues with the embedded control systems of Ares. A proposal expected by the end of the day. Not enough time to properly evaluate the problem plaguing his development team, but when did Anthony Hale ever give his team enough time to achieve any of their goals?

Reardon took a deep breath and averted his eyes from the screen long enough to pull the half-chewed pen from between his teeth and throw it into a pile of circuit boards. He needed to clear his mind, so he stood and stretched until he heard his joints crack, then buzzed out of the suite of cubicles and stepped into the open walkway.

A few security personnel roamed the fourth floor, and while he offered quick polite waves when they were close, he mostly kept his eyes on the ground and his hands in his pockets. Though the floor was vacant of Hale Industries employees, it didn't mean the offices were empty. These days, everyone chose a low profile.

Reardon bypassed the escalators and headed for the central structure suspended over the driveway below, the space known as the Archway. He raised his gaze as he entered and caught sight of the object of his desire.

The middle of the Archway was open to the three floors above. A large upside-down arch descended from the ceiling on one end and bisected rows of columns as it swooped along the edge of each floor and finally connected at the opposite end of the structure.

The two halves were mirrored in design, with a large open area of seating scattered on the bottom floor. There, in the middle of the brown carpet, sat the beautifully composed sculpture of a compass the size of a subcompact car.

The rose of the compass was engraved in glass in the middle of a large circular frame. Two bands wrapped around it in opposite angles, and the entire sculpture was suspended oblique to the floor by an ornate column on one side and a support post on the other. The entire piece occupied the center of a wide pedestal of bronze, with the compass situated above a circular pane of glass in the middle of the floor, which looked down into the exterior driveway below.

Reardon stopped in front of the compass and put his hands on his face. He pressed his fingers into his forehead, then his palms, and finally slid both hands up and through his tousled black hair. He didn't need a mirror to know that the bags under his eyes were darker than usual.

He dropped his arms and dug his closed fists into his jean pockets. Relaxing his shoulders, he fixed his eyes on the middle of the compass rose and let his mind wander, a learned habit since he'd started working for the company a year before. He loved the Archway and the compass, both representing the hope of escape from a situation that seemed inescapable.

He considered leaving, as he always did when he stared at the sculpture. It wouldn't be possible, not with what he knew, but he considered it anyway. In reality, the only way out was to finish the work.

All of the work, not just the problem with the embedded control systems.

The impossible nature of what they were attempting to accomplish depressed him most days. Today, however, was different. Reardon was resigned to his fate, to the fate of everyone working at Hale Industries.

He and the others would have to keep working until they either failed or, by some miracle of universal goodwill, succeeded.

What was Hale going to do? Have them all—

"Star of the north, whose steadfast ray pierces the sable pall of night," a deep voice called out from just outside Reardon's peripheral vision on the left. The vocal interruption startled Reardon from his daydream, and he pulled his hands from his pockets as he jerked his head up to see who it was.

With the glare from the wall of windows behind him, Anthony Hale strode toward Reardon in a slow, methodical manner, his hands behind his back, his eyes on the compass. He continued reciting as he rounded the compass. "'Forever pointing out the way that leads to freedom's hallowed light: The fugitive lifts up his eye to where thy rays illume the sky.'"

Hale came to a stop to Reardon's right, still examining the compass rose, a deceptive warmth to the slight upward curve of his lips. Reardon kept his hands out of his pockets but fought the incessant twitch of his fingers that only occurred in the presence of his boss.

"'The North Star,'" Hale said without looking over. "By James M. Whitfield. I read it in an article once, and I think about it every time I look at this thing." He dropped his hands and held them up, palms open. "Don't ask me what it's about. I just thought it sounded cool." He chuckled at himself, then relaxed his posture.

A bead of sweat formed against Reardon's temple. He lifted his hand quickly, used his fingers to wipe it away, then relaxed in an effort to minimize Hale's attention toward him.

Hale, either unaware of or uninterested in Reardon's movements, glanced from the compass and down the hall toward the north wing, then back across the compass and over at Reardon. He narrowed his eyes and nodded. "You've had a long day today, Scott. How's the proposal on Ares's explicit interaction control coming?"

Scott swallowed, but the lump in his throat wouldn't budge. He felt his shirt sticking to his underarms. Time was running out. He wasn't sure what to say. Should he lie? Hale knew enough of the technical aspects of robotics engineering to be dangerous, but Reardon could be convincing if he needed to be.

But Hale would find out eventually.

"I'm sorry, sir," Reardon replied. "Programming embedded systems is hard, especially considering the complexity of the desired interaction with Ares. We've tried adding so many features, it keeps breaking the code."

Hale hung his head and dug his hands into the pockets of his suit pants. Turning away from Reardon, he circled the compass in the opposite direction. "You know, my dad used to say if something's easy, it's not something worth doing. Of course, the irony of his sentiment was almost anything I tried was 'too easy' to him. Then one day it dawned on me. He wasn't teaching me a lesson on work ethic, but on value. Well, he didn't know it, but what I learned was everything has a value. To get what you want, you just have to find what that value is and pay it."

Hale rounded the compass to the left of Reardon. His hands were out of his pockets, and he stared intensely into Reardon's eyes.

"Things can have monetary value, sure. Take this building, for instance. I had to put up a lot of money, *a lot*, to acquire it. Those officers in there"—Hale pointed toward the company's offices—"they don't care about money. Uncle Sam's just throwing it out the door. What do you think they value, Scott?"

Hale stopped a few feet away, his eyes wide and aflame, his lips curved upward and parted just enough to reveal white teeth.

Reardon wished he'd been shot dead earlier. He maintained his composure and forced himself to make eye contact with his boss. He took a moment to reply, gathering all his inner strength to keep from breaking apart in the man's presence. Finally, Reardon opened his mouth and pushed out a single word with as much force as he could muster. "Power."

Hale burst out laughing, and Reardon's skin suffocated him.

"I'm sorry," Hale replied as he stifled his laughing with a hand. "No, no, that's a solid guess. Really. Money, power, pretty much it, right?"

He paused, his smile fading, and looked out the window toward the highway beyond. "Love, maybe." His gaze and smile returned. "That's usually where people stop. But value can be found in so, so much more."

Hale started his pacing again, this time circling behind Reardon. "Those men earlier today, they don't value power. They might use the word, but really what they mean is position. What rank am I? Whose office do I work for? Who reports to me? Sure, power can come with certain positions, but some positions may not have a lot of perceived power and yet still be highly valued."

Reardon jumped as Hale grabbed his shoulder.

"Are you following me, Scott?"

Reardon nodded but kept his gaze on the compass. Hale let go of his shoulder and continued to speak as he appeared on Reardon's right side and returned to his original spot.

"Let me put it this way: in that moment, those men weren't thinking about the power they would wield with something like Ares. Let's say we solved all the problems, and they got what they wanted. So what? They don't get to use it. No, today was all about position. Being in the position of believing in something no one else knows about. This morning they were who they were, nothing new. But when they left, they were men who'd seen the future. What we did was worth it to them. And really, it wasn't that hard." Hale flashed a wide smile. "What do you know. Turns out my old man was wrong."

Reardon swallowed for the hundredth time. The lump stayed. He took a labored breath, then raised his hand.

Hale cursed, then said, "You don't have to raise your hand, Scott. This isn't preschool."

He dropped his hand. "Sir, I'm just wondering what this has to do with me."

Hale rolled his eyes, and Reardon kicked himself for referring to Hale so formally. Hale breathed through his nose, then stabbed his index finger in Reardon's direction.

"Now that's a good question. Embedded systems, explicit interaction control, it's complicated—I admit it." Hale dropped his finger and stepped toward Reardon until they were an uncomfortable distance apart. "All we need to do is figure out what solving those problems is worth to you and your team."

Reardon's brain processed the conversation, and after evaluating the risk, he decided to go for broke. "Well," he said as he looked up into Hale's dark eyes, "I think if we added additional engineers and upgraded our computer systems, we might actually be able to work out the kinks faster."

Hale chuckled. "Scott, didn't I just say money wasn't the only valuable thing? Position, time, experience, friendship." He backed away from Reardon and turned to the compass as he ticked off the list using his fingers. Suddenly, he stopped and stared into the compass rose. "Life."

He'd pushed too far; Reardon was sure of it now. *Idiot.* With Hale's back to him, Reardon thought about making a run for the exit. Before his feet could move, Hale turned around, his finger in the air.

"Rest."

Hale took quick steps toward Reardon and reached his hands out. Reardon widened his eyes, and he opened his mouth to scream but stopped short as Hale squeezed his shoulders and smiled.

"I'm such an idiot," Hale said. "I already asked a lot of you today, and now I'm asking even more. You know what, forget the proposal. It can wait until tomorrow. Go home, Scott. Get some rest. I think that's exactly what you need."

Reardon, his mouth agape, nodded in reply. Hale nodded back, slapped him on the shoulders, then walked past him and toward the south wing of the building. The Archway was silent once more.

He didn't know how long he stood staring at the compass in shock, but eventually Reardon regained his senses and forced himself to turn and walk out of the Archway. He deemed it unwise to return to his desk for his laptop, instead heading straight for the escalators.

In record time, Reardon made it to the lobby and south out of the main wing into the parking garage. He found his car and, keeping his speed at a responsible level, headed out the curved driveway, through the security checkpoint, and onto Parkwood Boulevard.

Reardon navigated his way to the Dallas North Tollway and mechanically joined early afternoon commuters heading north into Frisco. By force of habit, he passed the more direct exit off the freeway to his apartment building and instead chose to get off at Main Street. Though he usually took the route to enviously spy on the more luxurious and lively apartments and shops of Frisco Square, he passed by today without a thought toward the life he wished he lived among the thriving community of young adults the area was known for.

He thought of nothing but the look in Hale's eyes the rest of the way to La Cala Apartments. The exterior of the complex was modest, though the same could not be said for the condition of the apartments themselves. His choices were limited, due to the financial strain of a meager salary. The promise of frequent and generous pay raises remained unfulfilled. Besides, the allure of the company from the beginning was its commitment to pushing the envelope in the field of robotics.

Now all Reardon wanted was to never see Hale Industries again. As he parked the car, exited, and headed for his building, he strained his imagination to find a way out without the threat of being found. If only he could build a robotic version of himself. Except human skin would be a lot harder to fake than—

Reardon suddenly stopped at the top of the stairs leading to the second floor of building fourteen. A man in a black T-shirt, dark-wash jeans, and a black jacket stood by the door to Reardon's apartment. The man stared at Reardon, his arms hanging loose by his sides.

He'd expected it, though not so soon. Reardon blinked away threatening tears as he resumed his walk to the door. As he closed the gap, he narrowed his eyes and studied the man's familiar face.

"Do I know you?" Reardon said as he stopped a safe distance from the man.

"We met," came the reply. "Sort of."

He did know the man. He could picture the face, and the voice sounded familiar too. Reardon's eyes widened. "Wait a minute. You were there. At the Ares demonstration today." He pictured the man standing nearby in uniform. There were patches, but Reardon didn't know enough about army ranks to know what it was. There was also a small silver nameplate attached to the man's jacket. What had it said? He reached further into his mind.

Finally, it came to him. "Sykes?"

"Actually," the man said as he stepped toward Reardon and lifted the flap of his jacket to reveal the black stub of a grip protruding from under his belt. "My name's John Cross. We need to talk."

CHAPTER EIGHTEEN

CHRISTINE STOOD AT the bottom of the staircase as the robotics engineer descended with John right behind him.

"Who are you?" Reardon asked as she fell in step next to him.

On their way to the man's apartment, John had insisted she maintain anonymity when speaking to him, so Christine shook her head and replied, "You don't need to know."

Reardon let out a sigh and dropped his shoulders. It was strange to her that he seemed resigned to having been unceremoniously abducted from his home. She wondered if John was forced to convince him with a show of the flashlight handle tucked in his belt behind his jacket. John assured her a flash of the object would convince Reardon he was carrying.

She disapproved of the deception, more so now watching Reardon sulk. To think John was planning on attending a church leadership conference all day. Now he was threatening a private citizen with a fake gun.

It wasn't like she was any better. She was the one who'd thought they might need to prod Reardon along. She was adapting to the amoral lifestyle of a former CIA assassin, and she didn't care for it.

Christine stared straight ahead at Reardon's car as they approached. John asked for the keys, then passed them to Christine and motioned for her to drive. He opened the back door, directed Reardon inside, and slid in next to him.

Add larceny to the list.

After situating herself in the driver's seat of Reardon's modest sedan, Christine started the car and navigated out of the La Cala parking lot. It didn't take them long to arrive at their destination, and as she and John discussed, she parked the car on the third floor of the parking garage in the first open space she could find in a crowded row. They all exited, and Christine led the way to the stairs with Reardon positioned between her and John.

"What exactly are we doing in Frisco Square?" Reardon asked, his eyebrows squeezed together above his nose.

"Quiet," John snapped, playing the part of the bad cop all too well.

Reardon obliged and remained silent as they exited the parking garage and crossed the access road to the Tower. It was one of many developments in the square, with vacant storefront and office spaces eager to be leased by anyone looking to integrate their business into the thriving community. Christine and John had explored one such vacant office space earlier as they'd formulated their plan to question Reardon. With John's talent at breaking and entering, they entered the Tower and locked themselves into the empty second-floor office suite.

With the sun setting and the blinds on the windows closed, both they and the room were cast in a dark pale-blue hue. John motioned for Reardon to stand in the middle of the room, while he positioned himself near the windows. Christine put herself between Reardon and the door, certain she was capable of preventing his escape, a combination of his size and her budding confidence in her own combat skills.

"No chairs?" Reardon asked, his tone less dismal and more annoyed.

"You tired?" John replied, again layering too much brusque into his voice.

Christine rolled her eyes, then realized he couldn't see her across the room in the dark, so she called out, "John." When he glanced over, she put her hands on her hips and cocked her head to communicate displeasure with his approach. Was this what CIA John was like? If it was, she wasn't impressed.

Time to take over.

She moved closer to Reardon and made eye contact. "Scott, I'm sorry for all this, but we didn't want to take any chances of being seen with you."

"Seen with me? What is this? Who are you people?"

"My name's Christine Lewis—"

"Christine," John interjected, but she waved him off.

"I'm Philip Lewis's stepsister."

Reardon's eyes widened, and his mouth dropped open. He lifted his twitching index finger and pointed in Christine's direction. Then he turned and pointed at John, then back to her. "You're not here to kill me." His hand came back up, this time with his palm open to her. "Wait. You're not going to kill me, are you?"

"No, we're not going to kill you. We need to talk. About what happened to Mano Amaya. We know something is going on with the Ares Project, and we think someone high up in the company was involved in murdering Mano and framing Philip."

Reardon, his eyes still wide and mouth agape, slowly dropped his chin and stared at Christine's feet. John stepped away from the window and to Reardon's side.

"Scott, you can trust us," John said, his bad cop routine replaced by a more authentic tenor. "We only want the truth about what happened to Mano Amaya. You're not a bad guy—I could tell. That's why we thought you might be able to help." John crossed his arms and stared at Reardon's dazed face. "Let's start with this: Why was there a different robot when we came into the room this morning?"

Reardon's head jerked up, and he arched an eyebrow. "How did you—" He stopped short of finishing his sentence and just stared at John.

"There were a few subtle differences between the models. For instance, one of the antennae wasn't an antenna at all."

Reardon shook his head, and for a second Christine thought he might smile. "I can't believe you noticed. I mean, I told them I thought it was too much of a risk to cut corners making the decoy, but—" Again, Reardon cut himself off. He glanced over at Christine, the realization of his accidental admission evident in his eyes.

He sighed, then hung his head again. Christine opened her mouth to say something but remained silent when John waved her off with a slight flick of his hand.

Reardon looked back up at her. "Ares doesn't work." He aimed his next statement at John. "The demonstration today was faked."

Christine caught John's glance as she processed the revelation. It looked like Reardon was going to be helpful after all.

The engineer took a deep breath, then straightened himself. "We've actually been working on the project for two years, but we keep running into major issues with making the system completely autonomous. Well, as autonomous as you would want a mechanized killing machine to be. We've done some pretty amazing work, all things considered, but we haven't been given the time or the resources to pull it off. A real Ares is still years down the road, and that's best case for a fully supported development team."

"It looked so real," Christine said.

Reardon narrowed his eyes at her.

"I saw the whole thing through a secret camera in John's glasses."

Stunned, Reardon looked over at John, who flashed a grin and shrugged. Reardon glanced back at Christine. "Well, technically it was real. We reworked Ares's outer shell to make it just big enough to fit someone inside it. Then we hired a thin actor who played the part of the robot during the actual demonstration."

John tilted his head. "There was a man inside that thing?"

Reardon nodded.

Lifting his chin, John shifted his eyes around the room, something Christine always saw him do when forming a theory. "So you swapped out the actor for a nonfunctioning model before we came in," he said. "That way when we were close, there wouldn't be any perceptible movements to give it away."

"The demonstration kept getting pushed the more problems we encountered, but we ran out of time, so we made do with what we could scrape together."

Christine caught John's eyes and held his gaze. "Mano must've intended to expose the truth about the project, and that's why he was killed."

"No," Reardon cut in. "I don't think so."

"How so?" John pressed.

"Mano was an electrical engineer, and he spent most of his time with the Chiron team. He would help when we needed an extra hand, but he wasn't brought in on the team that rigged the demonstration. Anthony kept that circle small, and we didn't even build the decoy until a day or two before Mano was . . ." Reardon swallowed. "Well, you know."

Christine looked away as she pictured Mano Amaya and the large industrial robot billed as Chiron on the Hale Industries website. Mano's absence from the Ares Project only opened a floodgate of questions in her mind.

"So Hale directed you to build the decoy?" John asked.

"Yes. He told us it was the only way to keep the project afloat. I guess we were all convinced it would be real one day anyway, so what did it matter if we tricked the government into giving us more money?"

"I'm guessing he promised the check would be bigger this next time."

Reardon snorted. "After what those men saw today, Anthony said they'd give us billions."

"Well, he's not wrong. That'd be a deal if it meant owning the world's first army of autonomous robotic soldiers."

Christine looked back and waved her hands to interrupt. "Hold on. If Mano didn't know about the dog and pony show today, then why was he killed?"

"I thought Philip killed him."

Christine breathed a frustrated puff of air out of her nostrils. Reardon's story about the fake robot was compelling but offered nothing in respect to Philip's guilt or innocence. She crossed her arms and stared down Reardon. "Philip didn't kill Mano—someone else did because Mano was getting too close. You said he helped out some. Maybe he figured out Ares wasn't working and was going to tell someone." She was grasping at straws, and she hated it.

Reardon shrugged. "Maybe, but not likely. Philip worked on Chiron too, so I just assumed they got into it over something and it pushed Philip over the edge. We were all working nights and weekends, and if I'm honest, we all expected something like that to eventually happen."

John jumped into the exchange before Christine could press for more. "It sounds like the working environment wasn't exactly healthy."

Reardon laughed out loud. "Unhealthy doesn't even begin to describe Hale Industries. We're all underpaid and overworked, and the whole company has to deal with inadequate equipment. It's all frustrating, especially considering all the capital that's been invested."

"The hundred and fifty million from the US government for the Ares Project."

"Yeah, but that's not all. Anthony spends as much time raising capital as he does threatening our jobs if we don't work our—"

Christine cut him off before he could finish. "There's got to be something you can tell us about Mano's death. If Ares was struggling, maybe Chiron was too, and Mano was going to blow the lid on the whole operation." She fought against the urge to cry, though the wetness at the corners of her eyes suggested it wasn't working.

Reardon studied her, glanced at John, then back at her. "I'm sorry, really, I am, but I don't know what to tell you." He shrugged. "Maybe he knew about Ares."

John dropped his arms and stepped closer to Christine. Without touching her, he leaned close to her ear and said softly, "It's OK. We'll keep digging. Just because this guy doesn't know what happened doesn't mean something didn't."

She wanted him to hug her, but she knew he'd refrain from physical contact with Reardon in the room. Instead, she turned her back on both men and pressed her fingers into her eyes to stop the flow of tears. She'd perceived Reardon as the source of all the answers to her questions, the concept now only a misguided delusion. He couldn't help them. And the real possibility of failing to exonerate Philip dawned.

"Actually," Reardon announced from behind her.

She cleared her throat and turned to face him.

"Now that I think about it, there was this one thing." He tapped his temple with an index finger, as if it helped loosen the memory. "I didn't think anything of it at the time, but Mano came in to help with wiring the camera system, and we took a break to grab some coffee. It was just the two of us, and he asked me if I knew anything about what he called the Sixth-Floor Project."

Christine and John exchanged puzzled looks. Christine thought about the layout of the south wing of the building and recalled Hale mentioning the sixth floor held the company's executive offices.

John arched an eyebrow at Reardon. "Did you?"

Reardon shook his head. "I had no idea what he was talking about and haven't heard a thing since. This wasn't that long ago. Only a few weeks." He started picking at his lip as he stared off. "I mean, think about it. Ares is already a train wreck, so who's to say Anthony isn't hiding more? Mano could've stumbled onto something I didn't know about. Something big enough to get him killed."

John snapped his fingers. "What if the United States isn't the only country Hale was offering Ares to? We already thought he might try to take it onto the black market, and the fact that the robot doesn't work wouldn't change that. He's already proven he can convince a roomful of military officers to give him more money. Maybe Amaya discovered Hale was going to go global but didn't know Ares wasn't functional and just assumed treason."

Christine nodded as she followed his train of thought. It sounded plausible. Reardon might only think Hale was dishonest, but the prospect of high crimes could've been enough to convince Mano to reach out to authorities, something Hale couldn't abide. So what they were saying was—

"Wait," she said. "You think Hale is behind Mano's murder."

John processed her statement, then nodded as he replied, "I think we have to assume this goes all the way up. I mean, if the guy was willing to lie to the US Army, he doesn't seem on the up and up." He looked over at Reardon and lifted his open hand. "I mean, you know him better than we do."

Reardon shook his head and breathed deep. "The guy freaks me out, but I'll be honest. I wouldn't have thought he would betray his country." He paused, then moved his head up and down slowly. "That said, I think it's possible."

Suddenly, John grabbed Christine by the hand and pulled. As she fell toward the floor, him falling over her, he yelled, "Get down!"

Glass shattered.

A loud shriek of wind whirred by her ear.

Reardon's body collapsed.

CHAPTER NINETEEN

"Stay down!"

Christine pressed herself as tight as she could to the floor. The room grew still. Cars and pedestrians milled about the square as if nothing were wrong. Reardon lay still, unmoving.

"Is he dead?" she whispered.

John didn't reply. He crawled on his stomach to the engineer, but his body blocked Christine's view of Reardon's status. She looked toward the bay of windows and spotted the web of cracked glass behind torn rows of slats in the blinds, where the bullet had entered.

"Why aren't they shooting?"

"He's got to have a target to shoot at, so the angle must not be good enough to see us on the floor."

A groan distracted them from the window. "Scott? Is he OK?"

"He's hit."

Christine's heart jumped, relief and concern intermingled. "What are we going to do?"

"Shoot back" came Reardon's grumbled reply behind clenched teeth. "With your gun."

"It's not a gun," John admitted. "It's a flashlight."

Reardon moaned, either from pain or disappointment, though Christine assumed from a combination of both.

John scanned the room from his vantage point, then spun on the floor and pointed to the door. "Try to get as close as you can to the door. When I tell you to, jump to your feet, open the door, and run out into the hallway. No matter what happens, stay away from windows."

Christine nodded. John whispered in Reardon's ear, then grabbed him with one hand and pulled the flashlight from his belt with the other. With the bulb pressed into his abdomen, he flicked the flashlight on. A faint glow of yellow encircled the spot on his shirt where he blocked the beam.

Looking back at Christine, John ordered, "When I throw this, go."

He took two deep breaths, then tossed the flashlight into the air across the room. Bullets pierced the far windows in quick succession as the gunman pelted the target.

Christine was out the door in seconds. The hallway light spilled into the office. She pressed herself against the wall, out of view. Reardon fell through the doorway with a grunt, John at his side.

"Go, go, go!"

Christine grabbed at Reardon and pulled him along as they huddled together just outside the doorframe. Bullets impacted the opposite wall of the hallway in a spread pattern.

With the walls between them and the sniper, John stood upright and muscled Reardon into position next to him. Christine grabbed at Reardon's other side and found his blood-soaked hand pressed against his ribs.

"Oh no," she breathed as she supported him on her shoulder.

"I can move."

She didn't believe him.

They moved as fast as possible in tandem down the nearby staircase to the first floor. At the bottom of the staircase, Christine veered left for the lobby exit.

"No," John said. "He'll have a shot. This way."

Following John's direction, the trio turned down the hallway toward the east side of the building. They exited through a side door and out onto the sidewalk.

"Across the street. Hurry."

Easier said than done, given Reardon's condition. As fast as they could, they crossed the street into the shadow of the parking garage. Empty retail space occupied the first floor. All of the night's activity was directed toward the center of the square a few blocks to their right.

John slowed, then looked at Christine. "Help him." He let go of Reardon, paused for a second to ensure she could manage, then picked up his pace to take the lead.

"Car . . ." Reardon said, slurring the word. Christine shifted under the increasing weight of holding him up.

"Not yours," John replied. "They've already found it by now."

They neared the exit for the parking garage. John slowed and held up his hand. Suddenly, he arched his fist back and swung, but pulled the punch a fraction of a second before striking a startled male teenager walking hand in hand with a girl.

John stepped aside to let them pass as the teenager hurled a string of profanities at them. They both shouted insults in Christine's direction as well, unfazed by Reardon's pale, sweating appearance. Christine rolled her eyes and moved past them with Reardon.

The irate teenage boy stopped and started back for John, again spouting uninspired obscenities. His girlfriend begged him to drop it. John ignored the boy and turned to cross the garage exit.

Suddenly, he ducked as an arm swung out from around the corner of the exit. The arm belonged to a thin but muscular man who stepped out from the shadows dressed in black pants, shirt, and jacket. He brought his other arm down in a chop against John's shoulder.

John grunted, then countered with his own punch to the man's abdomen. They traded blows until a kick from John struck the man in the knee and sent him to the ground. John punched him as he fell backward, then kicked once more at the man's face.

The man rolled out of the way before John's foot connected. The attacker jumped to his feet and ran at John. Wrapping his arms around John's waist, he dug in his heels and pushed John into the wall of the building.

John gasped for air as his back slammed into the concrete. He shook his head, then brought both his fists together and drove them flat into the man's back.

The man yelped and released his grip. John pounded him with punch after punch, the man desperately trying to parry. Finally, the man found an opening and swung at John's ribs, but his timing was off, and John effortlessly grabbed him by the arm and bent it backward at the elbow.

Grabbing the man's jacket collar, John planted his feet and spun. The man's body lifted from the ground as he swung around John. John released his hold on the man at the height of his turn, and the man's body flew through the air before landing on the asphalt and rolling to a stop in the middle of the access road.

The teenage boy held his hands up and, his girlfriend cowering behind him, backed away as he said, "It's cool, man." At a comfortable distance, they both turned and ran.

John ran to Christine and helped her shift Reardon again over her shoulder. "There'll be more where he came from. Keep moving. I'll get us a ride out of here and come back for you."

Christine didn't argue. She grabbed ahold of Reardon's belt and walked him toward the street as best she could. John parted ways with them at the entrance of the parking garage, breaking into a run as he headed deep into the structure.

The process of guiding Reardon across the street and down the side-walk of the next block was agonizing. He was losing strength, and she struggled to keep him upright and moving. They passed a covered parking lot on the right, then another combination retail and apart-ment building identical to many that surrounded the square.

Christine felt safe next to the building, though she couldn't shake the feeling that another gunman was around every corner. Reardon tried mumbling something, but he was losing consciousness.

"Come on, Scott. Keep moving." She nudged him to stir his senses.

A row of windows with red frames broke the monotony of brown brick. Imprinted on the windows, and repeated with vertical white letters on a red sign hanging on the corner of the building just ahead, was the name of the establishment: BEST THAI.

Patrons seated in booths against the windows inside studied them curiously as they passed. At the second window to the end, Reardon's feet slipped, and Christine grunted as she strained to keep him from falling over.

"I . . . I can't . . ." He could barely speak the words.

"You can." Christine took deep breaths, then steadied herself in preparation of continuing their hike.

A scream startled her from behind. She turned Reardon and gasped as she watched a figure plummet from the third floor of the parking garage. The man landed with a thud onto the ground and writhed in pain, grasping at his right foot.

John? She prayed it wasn't.

A squeal from car tires cued Christine to keep moving. With Reardon slumped against her, she tried walking to the end of the block, but his legs just wouldn't move. Right at the stop sign for the access road traffic intersecting with Coleman Boulevard, Reardon went limp, and with no other choice, Christine let him drop to his backside on the sidewalk.

Christine took deep breaths and held on to keep him from collapsing completely to the ground. His hand slipped from the gunshot wound, and his eyes fluttered.

"Is he all right?" a voice called out from around the corner of the building.

Christine ignored the question and maintained a pattern of breaths to regulate the flow of adrenaline. She heard an engine roar and looked back to the garage to see a black luxury sedan slide from the exit at full speed. Its wheels smoked as it shot down the access road toward them.

"Ma'am, is he OK?"

The unfamiliar voice behind her was closer this time, and she turned to see a bearded man in glasses bending over to examine Reardon. The man's eyes widened, and he uttered a breathy oath when he spotted the thick patch of blood covering Reardon's side.

The sports car, a four-door BMW, braked to a stop next to them. The driver's-side door opened, and John jumped out and ran around the front of the car.

"No, he isn't," Christine admitted to the stranger.

John knelt down beside Christine. "Back door."

She shifted Reardon over to him, then stood and opened the door to the back seat. John lifted Reardon and, in one motion, carried him into the car and laid him inside.

The screech of car tires caught their attention. Two black sport utility vehicles emerged from the garage.

"Get in with him and stay low!" John shouted. He turned, slid across the hood of the BMW, and jumped in behind the wheel.

Christine scooted in next to Reardon and shut the door as John jammed his foot onto the gas pedal. The car lurched away from the intersection, turning right down Coleman Boulevard.

"You've got to stop the bleeding," John said from the driver's seat.

No kidding.

"Is he still conscious?"

Christine tried to rouse Reardon, then checked his pulse to make sure he was still with them. "He's not responding," she announced. "Heartbeat is weak."

John flipped open the center console and rummaged through it, averting his eyes from the road. Christine raised herself from the seat and peered out the back window long enough to catch sight of the two SUVs taking the turn one at a time onto Coleman at alarming speed.

A high-pitched beep turned her attention to the front. The display in the middle of the dash showed a black-and-white version of the road ahead of them. Two yellow figures stood frozen in the middle of the car's path.

"John!"

The car's automatic braking system kicked in as John looked up from his search. He grabbed the steering wheel and mashed on the brake pedal. Together, he and the car brought their momentum to a halt before they ran over the man and woman in the crosswalk.

John sheepishly waved an apology as they jumped out of his way. Working the gear shift, he brought the car to top speed as they approached the T intersection of Coleman and Frisco Square Boulevard. Twisting the wheel right and alternating between the brake and gas, John drifted the car around the curve and accelerated down the middle of the boulevard.

To their left, the bright lights of the square illuminated Simpson Plaza against the dark-blue hues of night. People filled the grassy field of the plaza and stared in confused irritation at the luxury sedan's smoking tires.

John grabbed into the center console and pulled out a collection of items. He dropped unwanted things into the passenger seat, his left hand locked on to the steering wheel, until he only held a small plastic bottle of hand sanitizer.

He tossed the bottle to Christine. "The alcohol should wake him up."

Christine unscrewed the blue cap and reached to place the bottle under Reardon's nose. Her hand fell from his face as John took a left-hand curve at high speed, the force shoving her backward into the car door.

"Hold on!"

Information she'd needed a few seconds earlier.

Bracing her foot against the front passenger seat, Christine pulled herself over to Reardon and waved the open bottle under his nose.

The car lifted for a brief moment as they rounded the final curve to reverse course on the boulevard and head east down the length of the plaza toward the exit of the square.

Reardon's eyes opened, and he choked as he tried to speak and swallow at the same time.

"He's awake!" Christine yelled over the sound of the car engine.

"Put pressure—"

"On the wound. I got it." She remembered what he'd taught her one night over a French press.

Reardon, stammering, sat up. "What happened?" He winced as he grabbed at his injury. "I've been shot!"

Christine pulled him down onto the seat and shushed him. "We know, Scott. Just hang on." She scanned the back seat of the car and noticed a dark cylinder shape roll along the opposite floorboard. Grabbing it, she held it up to examine it in the light of the square.

An umbrella. Perfect.

She ripped the nylon fabric from the frame of the umbrella, then, fighting Reardon's resistance to her, pulled up his shirt to expose the wound. Blood poured from both entry and exit wounds just inside his abdomen.

Reardon shrieked and clawed at her hands. Christine regretted rousing him before tending to the gunshot wound. "This is going to help. I promise."

She stretched the nylon fabric across the bleeding holes in his side and pressed into it. His eyes rolled into the back of his head, and he bit down hard on his lip but didn't lose consciousness.

Peering over the back seat, Christine spotted the lead black SUV gaining on them from behind. The second car was gone. On their left, the trees of the plaza whizzed by, with panicked pedestrians beyond them, making it difficult to see the entirety of the boulevard.

"The other car," she shouted to John. "It's gone!"

He didn't respond, so she repeated her warning. Turning to face the front of the car, Christine spotted the second black SUV swerving onto the boulevard off Library Street, headed against traffic and straight for them.

"John."

"Yeah."

"John!"

"I know!"

A dark figure leaned out of the passenger-side window, cradling a large weapon of some kind. He pointed it in their direction as the two vehicles sped toward each other.

"Christine," John shouted. "Get down!"

CHAPTER TWENTY

BULLETS IMPACTED THE front of the BMW. Sparks flew across the windshield.

And yet it was still somehow less stressful than standing in front of a congregation of fewer than a hundred people to deliver a sermon.

Right as the sparks arched up at him, Cross jerked the steering wheel and braked hard. The car's hood dipped, its front wheels biting into the asphalt as they turned. The BMW tore through a row of traffic cones blocking empty parking spaces, then hopped the curb and shot between two trees onto the grass lawn at the corner of the Frisco Public Library building.

In his rearview mirror, Cross saw the gunman cease fire as the SUV behind them swerved. The second SUV banked into the empty parking spaces and hopped the curb to follow them.

Cross steered the BMW across the lawn, carving a straight path toward the access road cutting between the library and another parking garage.

Another burst of gunfire shredded a thin tree nearby as he crossed the sidewalk and the curb. With space, he let the BMW drift in a wide arch, then gunned the engine and sped down the access road.

He smacked on the middle of the steering wheel to warn pedestrians ahead. A group of young adults jumped clear of the road as the BMW sped by a circular drive into the library on the right.

Bits of brick exploded off a pair of statues stationed at the crosswalk to the library as more bullets were fired in their direction. The Frisco nightlife erupted in screams.

Cross mowed over a yield sign in the middle of the crosswalk as he took evasive maneuvers. Another sedan appeared in his peripheral vision as it exited the parking garage to his left. Hitting the car his only other choice, he turned into a short parking drive, then onto the sidewalk.

In his side mirror, Cross saw the black SUV chew off the front bumper of the sedan as it tore past the parking garage, its companion SUV bringing up the rear.

The shadow of the tall library building gave way to another dimly lit lawn lined by young trees. The sidewalk ended ahead at the intersection of the access road and Church Street.

It was going to be close.

"Hold on!" Cross shouted as he pressed down on the gas pedal.

The lead SUV pulled parallel to them on the road. A short tree scraped the side of the BMW as it squeezed through an opening and barreled off the lawn and across the wide patch of concrete pavers connecting intersecting sidewalks.

The tires uprooted a square area of shrubs, then bounced as they jumped the curb and onto Church Street, barely cutting in front of the lead SUV.

Car horns screamed at them as cross traffic screeched to a halt.

Cross maneuvered the BMW down the right lane of Church Street, then hopped the curb again onto the green lawn of the quaint church situated at the end of the road.

"What are you doing?" Christine shouted from the back seat.

"Shortcut!"

The two SUVs mimicked Cross's move onto the lawn. Out in the open, it was harder to avoid the gunman. Shards of glass and metal sprayed the back seat as the rear of the car was pelted by bullets.

Within seconds they reached the end of the lawn, and the car shook as its tires rolled over the curb. Cross pushed the BMW's speed even higher, and they took off down Page Street, the SUVs in hot pursuit.

He hoped the 560 horsepower V-8 engine outperformed the two

bulky sport utility vehicles. With enough distance between them, Cross would be a harder target to hit.

Sixty miles per hour and rising.

It was working. Sort of. The SUVs lagged behind, but not by enough. Cross lost speed as he jerked the wheel side to side to minimize the accuracy of the man hanging out the passenger-side window.

A bullet caught the sideview mirror on the passenger side, shattering it. They were terribly exposed, wide green fields on either side of the road awaiting development.

"We can't stay out here!" Christine exclaimed.

Cross glanced over his shoulder to see her hunched over Reardon's body in the back seat, her hands bloody from applying pressure to his wounds with some form of black material. Reardon covered his face with both his arms.

She wasn't wrong. They were in trouble.

God, help.

Just beyond another collection of buildings he saw the faint silhouette of the Dallas North Tollway, the blurred lights of cars traveling north and south at high speed.

"I've got a plan," he announced. "But you're not going to like it."

Picking up speed, Cross weaved around a growing collection of cars traveling along Page Street toward Dallas Parkway, the access road to the tollway. At the intersection, Cross braked and turned the wheel.

The BMW drifted, its tires skidding, and they rounded the curve pointing the wrong direction on the parkway. Cross let the wheel correct itself, then snagged it and hit the gas pedal. The car shot down the parkway headed against traffic.

Oncoming cars dodged out of the way. Angry drivers laid on their horns. The sound of crunching metal accompanied the collision of a truck and a coupe.

"This is your plan?!"

"I said you weren't going to like it!"

A quick check of his rearview mirror confirmed Cross's fear. The two SUVs didn't hesitate in following his path down the parkway. At least the challenge of avoiding a head-on collision provided a respite in the gunfire.

A car horn brought Cross's attention on the road into sharp focus. Headlights from oncoming traffic made it even harder to navigate the chaos. It was too much.

He needed an exit.

The blurred lights of cross traffic ahead indicated an intersection, but Cross's view was swiftly blocked by the large, boxy form of a tractor trailer bearing down on him. Cross banked to the left and shot by the cab of the truck as the driver blared his displeasure.

Jumping the curb to avoid another crash, the BMW tossed dirt and grass behind it as it tore through a field, then into the driveway of a gas station. Cross jammed the steering wheel to the right, and the car begrudgingly obeyed, swerving back onto the parkway and cutting across all four lanes.

The concrete wall of the tollway rose above them to their right. Just ahead, the farthest right lane curved right and disappeared under the highway just before the other three lanes intersected with Cotton Gin Road.

The cross traffic ahead slowed to a stop, clearing their path through the intersection. They had a chance, but he'd have to take the curve blind.

Cross said a prayer, then stomped on the gas pedal.

As the BMW entered the curve, the bright lamps of another car appeared to Cross's right. He ignored it, his eyes locked on the path. Brakes screeched, and the lights swung away without plowing into them.

They barely missed a traffic pole to the left and a concrete column to the right as the BMW leapt over the raised cobblestone median between the turnaround and Cotton Gin Road. Traffic on the road stood frozen to their left, Cross's prayer answered.

After another narrow median, the car crossed the final three lanes and through the median separating Cotton Gin from the second turnaround. Cross yanked hard on the steering wheel right, then left around the curve. The car skidded as it rounded the corner of the turnaround.

Cross let go and let the car correct its drift, then grabbed it once the nose of the BMW pointed straight down the parkway. Oncoming traffic was detained at the traffic light behind them, and the road ahead was clear.

He stepped on the gas, and the car's powerful engine gleefully replied. The turnaround behind them was empty.

Or so he thought.

As Cross looked in the mirror, both SUVs shot out from around the curve. His maneuver gave them some space, but not enough. The pursuing vehicles boasted engines just as, if not more, powerful as the one under the hood of the BMW.

If more, Cross hoped by a trivial amount.

He one-handed the steering wheel and adjusted his rearview mirror to see Christine and Reardon in the back seat. Reardon's chest heaved up and down. Christine held the fabric against his side, blood matted to her hands.

"You OK?"

Christine was breathing just as heavy as Reardon. "Bumpy ride" were the only words she mustered.

"We're not out of the woods yet."

Christine lifted herself for a moment to spy out the window. She dropped down and sucked in more air. Reardon's eyes fluttered open, then he squeezed them tight after a reassuring glance from Christine.

Cross readjusted the rearview mirror and took one last look at their pursuers. The black SUVs ran neck and neck, taking up both lanes of the parkway. The man with the SIG Sauer remained in his seat for the time being.

The entrance to the tollway appeared on the left. A handful of cars clogged the entrance as they merged at low speeds. Cross held his velocity steady.

Just before plowing through the hind end of a coupe, Cross swerved onto the shoulder of the ramp. The right side of the BMW scraped against the concrete barriers, sending sparks into the air. The SUVs muscled traffic to the opposite side as they followed suit.

A large concrete gantry loomed ahead, with cameras mounted in the center. A yellow sign announced, "Keep moving. We'll bill you later."

The BMW roared past a service van under the gantry, and Cross took his chance to cut in between the slow van and an SUV. Red brake lights glinted against the window as the SUV slowed behind a line of cars merging onto the tollway.

The short concrete barrier to Cross's left ended. He gunned the BMW, slipped past the SUV onto a grass-filled median, then dodged a light pole as he drifted onto the tollway. A cascade of horns sounded behind them.

The black SUVs found no trouble copying Cross's tactics. He'd either lost his touch or misjudged Texas drivers. The one thing he didn't care for was the flat, straight roadways of the state.

Traffic wasn't light, but neither was it heavy. While there was no problem navigating around the other cars at high speed, Cross longed for some form of cover.

He rounded a tractor trailer on the right, then used the shoulder to bypass two sedans jockeying for position in the farthest two right lanes. Glancing in the mirror, Cross watched the two SUVs pass the tractor trailer on the left and disappear from his view.

A second later, the lead SUV appeared past the nose of the semi's cab, the gunman's window rolled down and the barrel of the SIG Sauer semiautomatic multi-caliber rifle sticking through the opening.

Cross attempted to map a route through the traffic as far left as he could go. An assortment of vehicles blocked his path. They were sitting ducks.

The man opened fire. His bullets struck a sedan nearby before slicing through the trunk of the BMW. Cross wanted to curse the man for his lack of regard for innocent bystanders, but he breathed through his rage and looked for an opening.

At his first chance, Cross cut across all four lanes and out of the sight line of the rifle. The lead SUV swerved into the second-to-last lane on the right and let his partner pull up alongside him. The back driver's-side window of the second vehicle opened, and another rifle appeared.

Just his luck.

Probably too much to hope for a miraculous intervention by the CIA.

Keeping the car at as high a speed as possible, Cross swung the BMW back and forth between the SUVs. Both gunmen fired in spurts as he came into their view, but his evasive maneuvers kept them from hitting any vital spots on the car.

A pair of cargo trucks provided a respite as he slid by them in between two lanes. The noise from the rifles ceased, and his ears picked up the muffled blare of sirens. As the highway curved to the right, he checked his mirror and spotted the blue lights of Texas State Troopers far behind but gaining on their position.

One of the SUVs appeared from behind the cargo truck to his right, startling Cross. The driver's-side window was open, and a black gloved hand holding a handgun stretched out in the BMW's direction.

Cross jerked the steering wheel to the left and pulled away from the attack. The gun fired, the bullets impacting the BMW's hood.

The other SUV appeared on their left, the gunman in the passenger seat staring down the barrel of his rifle at Cross's head.

Cross tapped his brakes, and the BMW lost power just as the man on the left fired his weapon. His aim was sure, but his target not. The SUV on the right braked and swerved as the burst from the rifle tore into its side.

A metallic shriek accompanied by the hiss of pressurized air emanated from behind. The grill of one of the cargo trucks filled Cross's rearview mirror. He squeezed his grip on the steering wheel, his biceps tightening, and forced the gas pedal into the floorboard.

The smash of colliding glass and metal sounded to their right as the back end of the first SUV was clipped by the bumper of the other cargo truck.

The BMW roared past the second SUV before the man with the rifle composed himself.

"John!"

Cross glanced in the rearview mirror. Christine was pressing a hand into Reardon's side and trying to revive him with the hand sanitizer in the other.

All for naught if Reardon died.

Time to go on offense.

In the mirror, Cross watched the second SUV nose a sedan out of its way. The sedan's headlights arched away as it spun 360 degrees, then collided with another car.

Cross moved the BMW into the same lane as the SUV as it gained on them. Just as it bored down on their bumper, Cross swerved farther left to the shoulder, positioning a hatchback between him and the SUV as they sped under an overpass.

The SUV pulled alongside the hatchback and pushed it toward Cross. The hatchback slammed into the side of their car, smashing it into the concrete barrier on their left. Christine grunted from the back seat as she and Reardon tumbled to the floorboard.

The gunman in the passenger seat sat on the open window of his door and pointed the rifle at them from across the SUV's roof. He fired into the back of the hatchback, causing the terrified driver to slam on his brakes and slip out from between the SUV and the BMW.

Cross braced himself as the SUV careened into them. The impact unsettled the gunman, and he nearly dropped the rifle as he struggled to hold on.

The concrete barrier gave way to an edge of grass along the road. Cross dropped into neutral, tapped the gas, and slowly rotated the steering wheel. Guiding the BMW to the front of the SUV, he allowed the car to turn its side toward the front of the other vehicle.

The BMW drifted perpendicular to the SUV without losing much speed, thanks to the SUV's superior power. The momentum kept them turning until Cross's car rotated completely to the other side of the SUV and traveled backward.

Now in reverse, Cross gave the engine gas and nudged the SUV with his front bumper. The other driver responded as Cross hoped, turning right into them.

Cross let his car drift again, momentum now on his side. Both cars turned in unison, then at the right moment, Cross swung the wheel and shifted into high gear. Pressing on the gas pedal, he swung the BMW facing forward again with the SUV's right side now perpendicular to them.

The front end of the BMW plowed into the side of the SUV, gaining speed and pushing the other vehicle along. The gunman in the passenger seat fell backward from the window, his arms flailing. Somehow, he managed to hold on to the rifle and not fall out of the car.

"Christine, brace yourself!"

Cross pushed the BMW harder and guided the SUV off the left lane and onto the median. The gunman righted himself and glanced over his shoulder. Both vehicles bored down on a row of black crash-cushion barrels lined in front of concrete columns holding up an overpass.

The gunman turned back and raised his rifle.

Cross reached the limit of the BMW's power and, keeping his foot on the accelerator, ducked behind the dash.

Bullets ripped through the front windshield just as the SUV slammed into the barrels.

The cars kept moving as they both tore through the barrels at high speed. The SUV came to a sudden stop and folded in on itself as it slammed into the concrete pillar.

Glass exploded.

The earth spun.

And everything went white.

CHAPTER TWENTY-ONE

THE LOUD RINGING roused him. Cross shook his head, knowing it did little to free his eyes from the fog. Small bits of glass fell from his shoulders as he raised his head from under the steering wheel.

Air bags surrounded him. Two ejected from the front, one from the steering wheel and the other from the dash, while several more hung against every door window, shielding the inside from the blunt of the glass shrapnel.

Cross heard Christine groan. He straightened in his seat and turned to her when something caught his eye.

The BMW faced down the road from the grassy median inside the supports of the overpass. Just beyond the front, Cross saw the smoking wreckage of the SUV pinned against the first column.

The passenger, sans his rifle, was attempting to push himself free from the car, but his legs were pinned. Blood streamed from his hairline.

The second SUV screeched to a stop nearby. Someone jumped out from the back seat and ran up to the trapped man. In the glow of an overhead streetlamp, Cross recognized the pale man with a stubby red beard from the conference.

Red Beard pulled a handgun from his waistband and pointed it at the other man. He squeezed two rounds into the man's head. The man trapped by the SUV fell limp against the door. Red Beard stepped toward the crushed driver's-side door and fired another two rounds into the open window.

Cross grabbed at the release to his seat belt as he thought of a way to fight back. His vision was still hazy, his hearing compromised. He sensed liquid on his face, probably blood, and pain signals overloaded his brain from his extremities.

He, Christine, and Reardon were dead.

Red Beard made eye contact with him, but just stared. Behind him, the roadway was suddenly illuminated in blue light.

The man turned and sprinted to the idling SUV. As the black vehicle pulled away, the crash site was descended upon by half a dozen police vehicles.

Cross unbuckled himself and rotated in his seat. Christine was lifting herself off Reardon and gasping for air. Cross slipped his arm under her abdomen and helped her up onto the back seat.

"Are you hurt?" he asked.

She stared at Reardon, her face frozen in shock. "He's . . . he's . . ." She repeated the contraction in between short inhales of air.

"Breathe, Christine. Breathe."

Cross tried his door handle and found it operational. He stood from the driver's seat and, ignoring the thunderous cacophony of police sirens around him, grabbed for the handle to the back door.

He knelt and caught Reardon's upper body as it fell backward out the door. Cradling the engineer's torso, Cross pressed his fingers into the man's neck and held his breath.

A pulse. Faint but present.

Reardon's chest lifted for a slight second, then dropped.

Cross checked the gunshot wound. The nylon fabric from the umbrella remained stuck to Reardon's bloody side. With care, Cross pulled Reardon's body completely from inside the car and laid him down on the grass.

With Reardon free, Cross returned to the open car door and leaned inside. He grabbed Christine by the hand and pulled her toward him across the seat.

". . . dead . . . he's dead . . ." she stammered as she let him lead her.

Cross used his thumb to staunch a small bloody gash on her temple, then smoothed frayed strands of her blond hair. Using a gentle touch, he turned her chin toward him until they made eye contact.

"Christine, it's OK. He's not dead. He's still breathing."

Christine's mouth hung open, and the corners of her eyes glistened with tears.

The stomping of boots on the grass announced the arrival of a squad of state troopers. Flashlight beams pierced through open gaps in the cracked windows. Radio static and chatter surrounded the car.

"Out of the car, now!" a gruff male voice demanded.

Cross let go of Christine and backed out the open door.

The troopers hurled a litany of commands as he dropped to his knees. Cross kept his hands open, his arms extended in the air, and rotated to face them.

"That man's been shot and needs medical attention now," he shouted as he squinted in the glare of the numerous beams of light pointed at his face.

Someone grabbed his left wrist and twisted. Cross allowed himself to be pushed to the ground, wincing as a knee drove into his back. A tunnel of wind formed over him, the grass flattened, and everything seemed to glow as the bright searchlight of a helicopter hovering overhead illuminated the area in a perfect circle.

He twisted his head against the grass until he spotted a male state trooper attending to Reardon. An emergency medical technician appeared at the trooper's side, carrying a red duffel bag emblazoned with the Star of Life. Cross prayed for Reardon, the EMT, and the troopers as his hands were twisted behind his back and cuffed together.

Finally, a pair of thick hands grabbed his biceps and lifted Cross from the ground. The trooper manhandled him around the BMW, then across the median toward the collection of squad cars, ambulances, and fire trucks. Another EMT rushed past him with a stretcher in hand.

Right at the edge of the asphalt, the trooper spun his body and ordered him to sit, a command Cross was more than willing to oblige. The ringing gone, subsided or at least overpowered by other noises, and his eyes clear, he was anxious for a chance to catch his breath.

Most of the activity was still centered around the BMW, though a second group of troopers was stationed near the SUV. Traffic traveling both directions on the tollway disappeared.

A female trooper led Christine away from the BMW. Cross considered slipping out of the handcuffs so he could run and embrace her but elected to respond with patience. Within seconds, a handcuffed Christine was seated on the ground next to him.

She breathed in a regular, deep pattern, and her eyes remained locked on the BMW.

"Anything broken?"

She shook her head. "You?"

"I'm all right." Cross glanced at the crowd of officers by the wrecked car. "He's going to be OK."

"I know."

They sat in silence. Cross replayed the events of the past two days in his mind. Philip's innocence seemed even more apparent, though Reardon's information did little to answer questions around Amaya's death. What Reardon did reveal painted a different picture of Hale, his company, and the government-funded projects they were working on. Philip's involvement in Amaya's murder was orchestrated to cover up something, that much Cross was near certain of.

"Thank you, by the way."

Her words freed him from the trance of deductive reasoning. "You never have to—"

"Say it. I know." Christine took a deep breath. "I just . . . thank you for coming. If you hadn't been here . . ."

Cross shook his head. "If I hadn't been here, maybe none of this would've happened. You're a great reporter, Christine. You track down leads, piece together clues. That's how it should be done. I . . . I just invite chaos. You would've uncovered the truth a different way, a way that wouldn't involve people getting hurt."

"You're right," Christine said. "Maybe. I don't know. I don't think I could . . ."

Cross held his breath as he waited for the admission.

"That it would've gone any other way. And I wouldn't have wanted anyone else here."

A pair of EMTs appeared from around the BMW, Reardon atop the extended stretcher. With a police escort, they wheeled him across the grass to an ambulance. As they paused to ready themselves for the lift, Cross observed Reardon inhale and exhale in a short, shallow pattern.

"Thank you, Lord," Christine whispered as she closed her eyes and tilted her chin up.

Cross repeated the prayer himself, then looked her in the eyes. "You did great back there."

"We're all alive because of your driving."

They exchanged smiles. Cross glanced over his shoulder at the empty asphalt of the tollway. "Honestly, I didn't think that last move was going to work."

Christine looked out at the troopers buzzing between the SUV and the BMW. "This is going to be the first time I've ever been arrested."

Cross shrugged. "Third or fourth for me," he replied. "Though this is the first time not a part of an official operation."

"What are they going to do with us?"

As Christine asked, one of the troopers broke off from the rest of the group and headed toward them.

"Looks like we're about to find out."

The officer, an African American man, wore the mismatched tan-and-gray shirt and pants of the Texas Highway Patrol. He wore a cowboy hat, also a different shade of tan. The lines along his face suggested he was in his mid-forties to fifties, though Cross couldn't narrow the range without better lighting.

As he approached, the patrolman pulled a notebook and pen from his shirt pocket. "All right, Bonnie and Clyde, my name's Officer Dekens. Somebody better explain what exactly happened here, starting with why there's two dead men with military-grade weapons in the Jeep."

"How's our friend?"

The officer dropped his notebook and pen and stared at Christine with narrow eyes. "He lost a lot of blood, but stable. The umbrella was a good trick."

Cross nodded as Christine glanced at him with a twinkle in her eye. "Now, care to start at the beginning?"

Christine kept her eyes on Cross. He nodded at her, then looked up at Dekens. "I'm afraid it's complicated."

Dekens studied them both, then offered his own smile. "Well, then the good news is you'll have plenty of time to tell me your story."

The sound of approaching vehicles startled Dekens. He turned his back to Cross and Christine to watch a pair of black sedans roll to a stop next to the squad cars. The driver's-side door to the first sedan opened, and a tall man exited, his muscular frame and tailored suit silhouetted against the headlamps of the other vehicles. He strolled toward them, his handsome features and the gray color of his suit now visible.

"Excuse me," Special Agent Lee Armstrong called out to Dekens in his warm Texan drawl. "Thank you for your response to this situation, Officer Dekens, but I'll be taking over the detention of these two individuals. Official state business."

Armstrong revealed his badge from under the flap of his jacket and flashed a Texas-size smile.

Dekens studied the badge, then put his hands on his hips. "Criminal Investigations?" He sniffed loudly. "Just what kind of official state business is going on here?"

"The kind that's also federal," a smooth female voice replied from behind Armstrong. The woman stepped out from the shadows, standing almost as tall as Armstrong, the fitted pantsuit accentuating her impeccable figure. Her layered brunet hair fell loose on either side of a pair of stylish black-framed glasses.

Christine gasped.

Cross smirked.

Guin Sullivan held up a small open wallet displaying a gold badge on one side and an identification card emblazoned with the letters *C*, *I*, and *A* on the other. "And I'm afraid, Officer Dekens, that means we can't answer any of your questions."

The highway patrol officer stood his ground for a moment, then with a heavy sigh stepped aside and waved at Cross and Christine. Armstrong winked as he grinned, then said, "Thank you, kindly."

Guin lowered her badge and stared at Cross and Christine with a stern expression as Dekens brushed past her and Armstrong on his way back to the scene of the wreck.

"Oh, one more thing." Armstrong held his hand open and extended in Dekens's direction.

Dekens rolled his eyes as he reached into his pocket, produced a set of small keys, placed the keys into Armstrong's palm, then resumed his departure.

Armstrong jingled the keys as he walked over. Within seconds, Cross and Christine were free of their handcuffs. Armstrong offered Christine his hand to help her stand.

Cross rubbed his wrists as he took a step toward Guin. "Am I glad to see you."

She tilted her chin up as she squinted and crossed her arms. "Don't get too excited, Cross. I almost let DPS have their way with you. You're lucky she was with you." Guin nodded toward Christine.

As Christine stepped toward them, Guin dropped her arms and smiled. The two women embraced, then Guin inspected the scratches on Christine's face. "Considering the driver, it could've been worse."

Christine gave Cross a smirk. "He did all right."

Armstrong took a step toward the mob of highway patrol officers, held up the handcuffs, and said, "I'll return these to their owners, then I suggest we get a move on."

Guin nodded, then slipped her arm around Christine. "Come on. Let's get you cleaned up. We've got a lot to talk about."

CHAPTER TWENTY-TWO

THEY DIDN'T DISCUSS as much as Christine expected on their way toward Dallas proper. Armstrong's partner, Special Agent Segundo Flores, drove the car, with John in the passenger seat and Guin and Christine occupying the rear. Armstrong's car followed behind them.

Guin kept the banter limited to catching up on Christine's life. John remained silent in the front seat. It bothered Christine but didn't stop her from sharing stories from the last year in New York and asking questions about the apartment Guin shared with a Great Dane named Maks. Christine knew well enough to skip questions about Guin's role at the CIA.

From what John had relayed, after the arrest of his former boss Albert Simpson for his involvement in the chemical-bomb episode, Guin left her administrative role and was now with the Special Activities Division. John didn't elaborate, and Christine was left to imagine Guin's new adventures in the field instead of behind a desk.

Despite his repeated attempts to convince her of how the agency actually operated, Christine preferred her Hollywood version of Guin's new job. It usually involved exotic locations and explosions. John insisted it was more cinder-block buildings and lukewarm coffee. Boring.

"Oh my goodness!" Christine exclaimed with a laugh as Guin displayed a recent photo of Maks on her phone. "He's so big!"

"Can you believe it? Only six months and he's almost to my waist."

"I'll bet he leaves quite an impression on your neighbors."

"He's a big baby, actually. Runs away when he sees other people."

Christine laughed, but felt a pinch in her side. She slid her fingers across her abdomen until she found the offended rib bone. Bruised, not broken, so that was a positive.

"I'm sorry we had to run out so fast, but I promise we've got some good meds at the house."

Guin must've seen her wince. Christine nodded. "It's OK. I'm a little bruised, that's all."

The drone of city night traffic filled the awkward silence as Christine stared past the front seats and dash and out the windshield. The cars never left the tollway after their departure from the wreck site. Flores kept his speed high, but within reason. Even so, with the light traffic, they covered a long distance in a short period of time.

They finally exited the tollway for a quarter-mile jaunt down 635 to the exit for Hillcrest Road. Just as they merged with the access road, Flores cut a quick right across three lanes and sped down a quiet street dissecting a collection of commercial buildings.

"When we get inside, you'll be able to freshen up and receive any necessary medical attention." Guin didn't bother to look up from her phone as she texted furiously.

"I'm looking forward to a bagel and a cup of coffee," John admitted.

Guin glanced at Christine as she replied to John. "Fine, a bagel for the priest, but pizza for the rest of us." She winked.

Christine laughed. She'd have to explain the difference between a priest and a pastor at some point during the evening.

The commercial buildings ended as a neighborhood appeared. Their car slowed, and Flores flipped on his right blinker. As they turned onto the street, Christine caught the reflective green sign announcing TURNER WAY, though the street meant nothing to her.

They passed an eclectic row of homes, most large and well lit, with manicured green lawns and deep driveways. Flores announced his intention to turn left into the drive of a more modest home set far from the road. The black sedan braked to a stop behind a black SUV parked in front of the garage.

Christine followed Flores, John, and Guin's lead as the four exited their car. Armstrong parked on the street and fell in step behind them as they followed a paved path away from the driveway toward the front of the house.

One of the two large glass-paned double-entry doors opened. CIA Officer Eric Paulson stepped across the threshold and, grinning, held his formidable arms open. "Welcome to casa de CIA." The light coming from inside the house highlighted the tightly trimmed blond curls on his head.

"Casa de *la* CIA," Armstrong called out from behind them.

Eric ignored the CID agent and enveloped Christine in a bear hug.

"Hey, Eric," she said with a laugh and a flinch as he pressed her into his barreled chest.

"Oh, I'm sorry," he blurted as he released her and backed away. "I forgot you were just in a car wreck. We've got meds and food inside." He waved them in, giving a lighter squeeze across John's shoulders as they entered.

The interior of the home was an immaculate blend of hardwood floors and tall white walls forming an open-concept floor plan. The entry led into a giant living room with a freestanding brick fireplace as the central focal point. A collection of plush chairs and glass tables occupied one side of the fireplace, a long farmhouse dinner table and chairs on the opposite side.

A half dozen men and women in suits scurried between the dining table and the open kitchen nearby. Laptop computers, stacks of paper, and heavy black cases filled every available surface. Christine's stomach growled when she spotted the pizza boxes crowding the island countertop in the nearby kitchen.

But first, a shower.

Guin gingerly placed her hand on Christine's back. "Follow me. We've got a change of clothes and some Tylenol waiting for you in the master bedroom."

Was she a mind reader?

Christine found John looking at her as Eric prodded him past the kitchen and down a bright hallway. He nodded at her, his eyes twinkling. She returned the gesture, then followed Guin out of the living area.

They worked their way into the back of the house and down a hallway lined with large bay windows overlooking a beautiful tiled pool deck. The pool water glowed blue from submerged bulbs.

Christine whistled. "The CIA doesn't skimp on its safe houses."

Guin shot a peeved glance over her shoulder. "Thanks, taxpayers."

At the end of the hallway, Guin held a door open and beamed as Christine entered the bedroom. "Enjoy the shower and the meds. Just don't get too comfortable, or there won't be any pizza left."

Christine gave a casual salute and a wink, then watched as Guin shut the door. As she turned to enter the adjoining bathroom, she spied the king-size mattress covered in a billowing white bedspread.

Maybe the shower could wait.

Christine closed the door to the bedroom behind her and headed down the hallway, a slice of meat lover's calling her name. Her hunger for food exceeded that of sleep, so she had bypassed the bed for the combination of Tylenol and a hot shower. The dark jeans and black top waiting for her in the bathroom were a simple combination, but the material comfortable and the cut perfect. She'd have to thank Eric later.

She rounded the corner into the living area and gasped as she almost ran into Armstrong walking toward the entry to the home.

"I'm sorry," she said.

"Pardon me. Things are a little hectic here." Armstrong studied her new outfit and flashed his teeth in a smile. "I hope you feel as good as you clean up."

"The medicine helps. I guess we're lucky that car had a million airbags in it."

"Still, your boyfriend took his best shot at that concrete pillar."

Why didn't she like it when he said the "B" word?

She pushed the nagging questions out of her mind and returned Armstrong's smile. "I need to thank you, Agent Armstrong, for saving us from a night behind bars."

"Oh, I never said prison wasn't an option. We'll just have to see how satisfied I am with your answers to all my questions." His smile broadened. "And please, call me Lee." Armstrong patted her on the arm, then left her to meet Flores at the front door.

Christine pointed her stride toward the kitchen. She glanced past the fireplace into the dining area and spotted John studying a laptop screen in front of Guin. He was clean, dashing even, and wore a crisp new dark-blue collared shirt over black pants. He noticed her and offered a warm smile before turning back to the computer.

A friendly CID agent named Perry directed her to the box of meat lover's pizza as he handed her a paper towel as a substitute for a plate. "Mr. Cross told us to save you a slice," Perry admitted.

Christine struggled to maintain a polite composure as she took her first bite. It was the best pizza she'd ever had, though that might be the ravenous nature of her spirit talking.

As she chewed, she noticed Armstrong and Flores deep in conversation. Flores didn't seem happy, his eyes narrow, lips pressed firmly together. After a brief exchange in Spanish, Flores shook his head and waved off Armstrong's final thought with his hand. Opening the front door, the Hispanic agent stormed out and slammed the door behind him.

Christine averted her eyes as Armstrong turned and headed toward the dining table. She engaged Perry in small talk and learned that apart from Guin and Eric, all of the agents were members of the Criminal Investigations Division.

The pizza didn't last long, but it was enough to satiate her appetite. Christine thanked Perry, then grabbed an unopened bottle of water and headed toward Guin and John.

". . . making the payments difficult to trace," Guin said as she scrolled through a spreadsheet filled with data. "To our surprise, we found the name of your defense contractor at the end of the thread. I was in the director's office by noon and on a plane here by one."

John leaned into Christine as she settled in next to him. "It looks like Hale's been funneling money to a group of cyberterrorists based in England. Not a large amount, but enough to get caught in the web of the agency's investigation into the group."

Armstrong crossed his arms and addressed the two of them. "I think it's time for your story, and I mean the real story. Not the line you've been selling about producing a news story on Philip's arrest, Reverend John Cross, if that's your real name. Which is it: Jameson or Cross?" Armstrong smirked as he reached into his jacket pocket and pulled out a lanyard. A laminated plastic card hung at its end, John's name written across it in bold black letters beneath the logo of the Encounter Conference. "You forgot this the other day."

Guin sat back in her chair and breathed through her nose as she glanced up at Christine, then over to John. Eric pretended to thumb through a stack of papers at the other end of the table. John put his hands on his hips, narrowed his eyes at the badge, then gave a self-assured smile.

"All right, Armstrong," he said. "You're right. I'm not a news producer. Believe it or not, I *am* a pastor, but before that I was a . . ." He looked at Christine for a brief moment. "I worked for the CIA. I followed Christine to Dallas to help her investigate Mano Amaya's murder. We think Philip is innocent and Hale had something to do with it."

Armstrong pocketed the lanyard as he considered John's story. "Well, now's the time to try to convince me."

Christine cut John off before he could reply. "Hale staged a fake demonstration of a robotic soldier to a group of military representatives this morning to continue his scheme of embezzling government contracts worth hundreds of millions of dollars. We think Mano found out about it but was killed before he could blow the whistle and that Philip was framed for the murder."

Armstrong stared at Christine, then scanned the group of quiet CID agents. "A *robot* soldier?"

"John was there. At the demonstration. But it was all faked. Scott Reardon admitted it."

"And he told you Philip was innocent?"

Christine felt her cheeks warm. She shook her head. "No, but, I mean, it makes more sense than Philip murdering Amaya out of jealousy. They were friends."

Armstrong laughed. "Friends make the best murderers, Ms. Lewis."

"Call me Christine."

Her comeback made him laugh again. She grinned and crossed her arms. John glanced between them with a frown.

"Well, unfortunately we're going to have to wait to corroborate your testimony with Mr. Reardon. He's in stable condition but unconscious. Agent Flores is on his way there to get a statement when Mr. Reardon wakes up."

Guin leaned toward the laptop. "Maybe we won't have to wait." All eyes trained on her as she keyed in commands and cycled through windows of figures. "This whole thing started with us looking into the cyberattacks originating out of England. Hale's payment traveled the same underground channels a terrorist might use, but the contract we suspect he paid for didn't set off any alarms." She found the spreadsheet she was looking for and pointed at the screen. "There. We think Hale paid to have the metadata of this phone altered. It's a Dallas area code."

John leaned in and placed his hand on the back of Guin's chair. A grin formed as he read the number. "Agent Armstrong," he said without looking up. "How much are you willing to bet that number belongs to Philip Lewis?"

Armstrong replied with a frown as he stroked his chin.

Christine opened her hand and pressed it into John's bicep. "That's it! Hale paid Guin's cyberterrorists to plant the incriminating messages on Philip's phone, implicating him in Mano's murder."

Armstrong finally chimed in. "What about the video of Philip committing the murder?"

Christine felt her heart sink as she recalled the more condemning piece of evidence. Creating fake text messages was one thing, editing security camera footage a whole other. "Maybe they did both?"

Guin shook her head. "So far we've only been able to connect the money with the phone hack. It doesn't look like they did any more than that."

John stood straight and waved his hand. "Hold on. I can't say how they did it, but if Hale is connected to the company that installed the camera system, that would explain how they got their hands on the footage."

"Connected? What makes you think that?"

Christine felt a surge of optimism. "We think the same company installed both the system at Hale's building and the one at De Angelis. The camera in the alley looked brand-new."

Eric reached for another laptop across the table. "Well, then, let's see what I can dig up about that nightclub."

Armstrong opened his mouth, but the sudden ring of a phone from the other end of the table prevented him from uttering a word.

Christine followed everyone else's gaze to see Eric staring at the screen of the phone in his hand. He looked up at her as he rounded the table. "It's yours, Christine. Unknown number from New York."

Christine reached for the phone, then paused as she searched John's and Guin's faces. They both nodded to the phone and remained silent as she accepted the call. "Hello?"

A deep voice bathed in the recognizable accent of a city local replied, "Christine? It's Detective Rabinoff, NYPD. I need your help."

CHAPTER TWENTY-THREE

CHRISTINE EXCUSED HERSELF from the room, leaving Cross and the others to stare at each other in awkward silence. Armstrong rubbed his teeth with his tongue, then looked at Cross as he folded his arms. "CIA, huh?"

"It's classified, Agent Armstrong," Guin interjected.

Cross shrugged at Armstrong, then smiled at Guin. Despite the harrowing events of the past twenty-four hours, he admitted it was comforting to be in the company of old friends.

"All right, Ms. Sullivan," Armstrong said. "Since Mr. Cross's background is off limits, I'm sure you won't mind if he walks us through the events from tonight's performance at the square."

"There's not much to tell," Cross said. "We took Reardon to the square so we could talk to him without being seen, but Hale's men found us anyway. That's when the shooting started."

"Reardon just went with you. To tell you the robot was fake."

Cross opened his mouth but paused to consider his words. There was no point in lying. The truth was they'd kidnapped Reardon, though only by ruse and not true threat to his life. No matter how he described it, Cross knew it wouldn't sound good.

Just as he formed the first word of his thesis in his mind and sent it to his mouth, a sharp ringing from his pocket startled him. Cross dug the phone out and checked the number of the incoming call.

Gary.

"I'm sorry. I have to take this."

Cross flipped open the phone and stepped away from the table as Armstrong threw his hands into the air, rolled his eyes, and grumbled, "I didn't know it was time to break for personal calls."

Guin was saying something back to him, but their voices faded into the background as Cross raised the phone to his ear. "Gary, it's John. Is everything OK?"

"John, hey, yeah, no, everything's fine. I honestly shouldn't have bothered you, but, well, I just wanted to make sure you both were OK. I . . . I've been keeping track of news in Dallas, and there was a report about a major highway accident."

"It was us, but we're both OK."

There was a pause on the other end. "Good. Thank God. And thank you for telling me. I know everything must be complicated."

Cross reached the front entry and, in one motion, opened the door, walked onto the outside step, and closed the door behind him. "Things got messy, but the good news is, we've discovered some evidence that might help us clear Christine's brother. The authorities are involved now, so there's no need to worry. How's Bri and Nick?"

He hoped a change in topic would keep Gary from asking any more about the accident.

"They're doing great. Brought their newborn home today. John, have you thought more about what I said last night?"

The answer was no, but not just given the distraction of espionage and snipers. He didn't want to think about it.

"I haven't, but I plan to."

"Well, I wanted you to know that I meant it. That I still feel right in talking to you about it. I'll keep praying about it, and I want you to pray about it too."

"I will."

"Tell Christine I'm praying for her and that I'm happy to hear the news about Philip. See you back home."

"Sure."

The call ended. Cross dropped his hand and stared out into the dark shadows of the street running by the house. Rural Grove Baptist Church had been his home for the past two years, and there was nowhere else he'd rather be.

Nowhere else.

Nowhere.

Except . . .

Cross shook his head. Focus. He needed to focus on the next thing in front of him, and at the moment it was clearing Philip's name. After that, everything would settle down. It would have to settle down. He dismissed the growing unease in his heart and cleared his mind of stray thoughts as he reentered the house.

Eric and Armstrong were chatting near the laptop. Cross scanned the dining and living areas before spotting Guin in the kitchen. She downed the last gulp of a bottle of mineral water as he approached.

"Pretty good," she said. "I could get used to Texas food."

"Guin, I never said thank you."

"That's right—you didn't."

"Sounds like somebody's promotion's really gone to their head."

Guin tossed the empty glass bottle into a bin by the counter and smirked back at him. "Sounds like somebody's wishing they never left. It's about time you realized you're a better fit for this kind of work instead of the preaching kind."

Cross gaped after her as she returned to the conference happening by the laptop. Did she and Gary already talk? He'd have to find out.

"John," Eric called to him.

Cross rounded the counter and joined in the discussion.

"I got a hit on a sizable loan taken out by De Angelis a couple of months ago for renovations. The loan coincided with their custom security install. Something didn't look right, so I went further and discovered the money was fronted by a shell company. It's not much to go on, but the whole thing was set up through Luxembourg, which is also where our man Hale happens to hold investments."

Armstrong shook his head and curled his upper lip. "That connection is no better than an eyeless needle."

Cross, Guin, and Eric exchanged amused glances. Cross patted Armstrong's broad shoulder. "You're going to have to explain that one."

Christine suddenly appeared in his vision as she entered from the back hallway and marched to the table.

"Everything OK?" he asked as he dropped his hand from Armstrong's shoulder.

"You're never going to believe this. That was the NYPD detective who was with me on the train. They've been investigating the attempted bombing, and he called to see if I could help with a particular problem. The bomber isn't talking, so they thought they might be able to connect him to a larger organization by tracing the materials used in his bomb vest. They almost missed it, but an investigator discovered a serial number on a piece of the detonator casing. They tracked that piece as far as they could, but all that turned up was a symbol on a shipping manifest. Nobody's been able to connect the symbol to any existing terror networks, so Rabinoff thought he'd reach out and see if I recognized it."

Eric spread his hands open and waved her on. "And?"

Christine unlocked her phone and held it up for everyone to see. A photo filled the screen, its edges blurred as the camera drew attention to a black insignia in the center of the frame.

Cross's mouth dropped involuntarily. He blinked multiple times, convinced the mirage would disappear at any moment. It never did. "What . . . How?"

Guin narrowed her eyes and drew a loud, short breath. "Care to explain what I'm looking at?"

"That, Ms. Sullivan," Armstrong said as he pointed at the photo, "is the company logo of Hale Industries."

Eric reached out for Christine's phone, and she released it into his grasp. "Hold on." He studied the image closer. "You mean to tell me this Hale guy was involved in the attempted bombing? That doesn't make any sense."

Cross found a dark knot in the surface of the wood dining table and concentrated on it as he sorted through the theories in his brain. "You're right," he said. "It doesn't." He discarded each theory one by one until only a handful remained. "Unless . . ."

"John?"

Christine's voice shook him free of his trance. Cross looked up to see everyone staring at him.

"Unless what?"

He didn't have a working theory. Yet. Instead of responding to Christine's query, Cross reached across the counter for a bottle of the mineral water. He twisted the cap off. "Why didn't the bomber detonate on the train?"

Guin folded her arms and studied Cross's face. "Because the train wasn't his target."

Cross nodded, then took a sip from the bottle. She was right. The mineral water was excellent. He glanced at the label and confirmed it originated in Texas.

"Target." Armstrong took a turn studying the knot on the table. "Meaning the bomber wasn't there to just blow up anyone." He looked up at Cross. "But someone."

Cross pointed at Armstrong, his confidence in the path of logic growing. "Someone specific. An assassination meant to look like a random terror attack."

Christine waved her hands. "OK, wait. You're saying the bomber was sent to New York by Hale to assassinate someone?"

"How else does a piece of material from Hale's company end up on the explosive belt?"

"Couldn't it have been a random coincidence? The bomber cobbled together the belt out of discarded parts."

Cross shook his head. "No, there's something here. We've already seen the lengths Hale's willing to go to protect his interests. And now we know the Ares Project isn't the only thing he's being secretive about."

Guin, Armstrong, and Eric exchanged quizzical looks.

"Reardon mentioned a secret project Mano Amaya knew about,"

Christine explained. "Something Hale's hiding on the top floor of the building."

Cross stepped back toward the table. Guin slid into the chair and keyed a command into the laptop. "No hits on Hale's name and New York," she announced.

He didn't expect there to be. "Try searching for anything related to a defense robot contract."

Guin shook her head. "Plenty of hits near Boston, but nothing in New York."

Armstrong cleared his throat. "What about the Department of Defense?"

Eric bobbed his head in agreement. "That's a good idea."

Guin typed out the necessary keywords and paused as the results loaded. Her eyes lit up. She turned the screen to face Cross and pointed at the bold headline across the top of the page that read, "Secretary MacAuley to Unveil Next Generation Defense Initiative." She waited for everyone to read the headline, then added, "Secretary MacAuley was scheduled to give his talk at New York University in Greenwich two days ago. There was a rumor he was going to make a special announcement. Then the bomb scare caused them to cancel the event."

Christine let out an audible gasp. "If MacAuley was going to go public with Hale's project, it would've meant more scrutiny. And a lot more risk to continue stealing money from the government."

Cross set the near-empty bottle of mineral water down on the table and put his hands on his hips. "If there's anything I know, it's that people will do just about anything for the right amount of money. The question is, exactly how much is the life of a US cabinet member worth?"

A sly grin formed across Armstrong's face. "I know how we can find out." He pointed past Cross and waved his finger.

Cross glanced over his shoulder, then grinned as he reached for a full bottle of the mineral water. He tossed it across the table into Armstrong's open hand. "Thank you, sir," Armstrong said with an accented emphasis on the words. The CID agent glanced around the room. "Let's go ask him."

Hale wasn't in the mood to ask questions, so he elected to stare out the window at the flat landscape of buildings, highways, and landscaping silhouetted against the night sky above Frisco. His office on the sixth floor offered a view, just not a view worth much in his opinion. He resisted the urge to fantasize of an upper-floor office view of New York or Chicago. He needed to keep his mind on the matter at hand. As Brand continued his report, Hale crossed his arms tighter.

"They secured transportation and attempted to escape, but we pursued until they and Beta Team wrecked. I contained our exposure, but we had to evacuate before I could confirm elimination of the target."

Lucky for him, they'd know soon enough. Hale took a deep breath, cursed, then smiled as he turned to face Brand. "Contained our exposure?" Hale cursed again. "I was hoping you guys were tough when I hired you, but that's pretty dark, even for me."

Brand didn't react. Hale raised an eyebrow. He'd have to try harder to get a rise out of the man. "That's good. Because what's going to happen next is going to take some pretty dark—"

"Sir, I take full responsibility for not fulfilling the contract. We didn't anticipate resistance."

Ah yes, resistance. The one question Hale did have. "This other man, do you have any idea who he was?"

"I recognized him from the church. He was with Christine Lewis both times. We got this at the square."

Brand stepped toward Hale's desk and held out a small tablet with a photo of Scott Reardon and Christine Lewis entering a building. A third individual held open the door, his back to the camera. Enough of his profile was visible for Hale to recognize the features. "Sykes." He let loose a string of obscene words. He'd planned for this day to arrive, sure, but that didn't mean he had to like it.

"Nothing ever comes easy," his old man would say. And Hale had hated him every time he'd said it. This was one of those moments Everet Hale relished imparting wisdom for. And it made Hale's skin crawl to think the old fool might've been right.

"Do you know him, sir?"

Hale ripped up the image of his father in his mind and met Brand's puzzled gaze. "He actually stopped by earlier. Shame we didn't know what he was up to while he was here." Hale waved for Brand to hand over the tablet and simultaneously triggered the intercom feature of his desk phone.

"Yes?" Marissa's voice called out from the speaker.

"Can you come in for a minute? And bring the guest list from the demonstration."

The phone clicked, and Hale wordlessly expressed his amusement toward Brand as they waited in silence.

Within seconds the door to the office opened and Marissa marched in carrying a clipboard. She held it up for Hale as she walked up to him at the desk.

Hale ignored the clipboard and instead exhibited the photo on the tablet for her. "Does the man holding the door look familiar to you?"

Marissa shook her head.

"Come on now, take a closer look. You should recognize a handsome guy like that."

She hesitated, then angled her head and studied the image. Her eyes widened, and her lips tightened as familiarity dawned. She knew. It was him.

Hale let the rage bubble over, tired of feigning composure. With a ferocious cry, he pulled the tablet away from her, held it outstretched over the desk, then swung it at her face.

The tablet smashed against her temple. She spun in a circle, then her body dropped. She pressed her hands against the ground and whimpered as she failed to find the strength to right herself.

"You let a spy into my business, Marissa," Hale screamed, spit flying. He put the lid back on his anger and dropped the tablet onto the desk. He mentally counted to ten, then addressed Brand in a calm tone. "This is going to complicate things. There's no telling how much they got out of Reardon."

"There wasn't that much he could tell them, was there?"

"He knew enough." Hale pulled a handful of tissues from a box on his desk and knelt down next to Marissa. He helped her sit up and directed her to press the tissue against the bloody cut turning black and blue on the side of her head.

Satisfied in his act of hospitality, Hale stood up and took a deep breath. "Whatever happens over the next eight hours, we need to be ready to pull the rip cord." Digging his phone out of his pocket, Hale cursed as he stared at the lack of notifications.

He'd better call.

And it better be good news.

CHAPTER TWENTY-FOUR

THE EARLY RAYS of sunlight glistened in an arc behind the glass-topped roof of Hale Industries. From Christine's vantage point, the grounds were quiet save for the arrival of tenants occupying the northern wing of the campus. She checked her watch to confirm the time. Strange that the parking lot was so empty.

She didn't have much time, but just enough, so she turned away from the window and poured herself a second cup of coffee from the cardboard carafe. The CID agents kept their cups full at all times but backed up their addiction with an ever-increasing supply of fresh brew. Every time she turned around, there seemed to be a new delivery of coffee without a sign of who brought it in. There was a story in the Bible it reminded Christine of, though at the moment she couldn't recall the exact details.

She checked her watch again. Five minutes to go. They'd been in place for over an hour, yet while the CID agents busied themselves establishing all of the video and audio surveillance of the operation, there was nothing to occupy her time. So she studied the suite. More than once.

As they had with the safe house, Guin ensured the CIA booked the observation room for the operation. They spared no expense and booked an executive suite at the Dallas/Plano Marriot at Legacy Town Center, less than half a mile due west from the Hale Industries offices. The sight line was perfect, and there was even a private balcony.

Armstrong instructed his agents to refrain from using it, however, to keep from tipping off Hale.

As a result, the agents rearranged the posh furniture to make room for their telescoping cameras, audio transmitters, and computer bays. The large concave couch that once occupied the middle of the living space now blocked the entrance into the master bedroom. Tripods with mounted cameras sat staring out the balcony's sliding glass doors.

An arrangement of monitors on a nearby temporary workstation displayed the feeds from each camera. Between those and a collection of high-powered binoculars, they commanded an unadulterated view of Hale's building just beyond a handful of apartment buildings and the tree line along Parkwood Boulevard.

She'd have a front-row seat, but Christine was still annoyed at sitting on the sidelines while John, Guin, Eric, Armstrong, and a collection of CID agents executed the raid on Hale's building. It didn't make any sense for her to be with them, sure, but it pained her to not be involved if there was a chance of discovering evidence to exonerate Philip.

"You'll know when we know," John promised before he left.

Maybe.

Christine closed her eyes and admonished herself for thinking such thoughts. It was the truth. She knew it, but it shocked her to even consider Cross might be lying. Again. Without a foundation of trust between them, she struggled to imagine where their relationship would go.

A burst of static from a set of speakers interrupted her thoughts. Christine opened her eyes and watched the agents take their positions, then strained to catch a glimpse of the infiltration team on the monitors.

"Bravo, in position."

"Copy, Bravo Leader," replied a young female agent into a headset.

John and Eric's team was poised to enter through the entrance on the parking-structure side of the campus. Guin was with Armstrong and a handful of agents taking the driveway entrance.

Movement on a monitor caught Christine's eye. The camera trained on the covered driveway showed a line of men wearing identical black jackets with the words STATE POLICE in bold white letters on their back approaching the front doors of Hale Industries. Agent Armstrong led half the team to the door on the west side, a black Kevlar vest taking the place of his gray blazar. The sleeves of his crisp white shirt were rolled to his elbows, and he sported a pair of sunglasses.

Guin appeared in view of the camera on the opposite side of the entry. She wore her own body armor, but no sunglasses. A line of men in black jackets assembled behind her. Guin, Armstrong, and a few of the other men brandished handguns, while the rest carried large rifles.

"Alpha Team in position," Armstrong said with his distinct inflection recognizable over the radio.

"Copy, Alpha Leader."

A couple of the cameras moved. Christine stole a look at the CID agents repositioning the views, then trained her eyes on the monitor showing Alpha Team. The two halves of the team stood ready on either side of the entrance.

An agent manning a camera called out, "Clear."

"Alpha Leader, you're clear to engage."

"Copy. On my mark."

Christine held her breath. A sleepless night of securing the warrant, planning the operation, and assembling the teams had led to this moment. Adrenaline coursed in her veins.

Guin nodded at Armstrong.

"Breach!"

Armstrong repeated the word several times as two men rushed the glass doors and opened them as wide as they could. Armstrong rushed through the open door, his team on his heels. Guin mirrored his action on the opposite side.

"Go, go, go!"

A barely visible view of Bravo Team entering from the parking entrance appeared on another monitor. Christine couldn't make out John or Eric amid the mass of bodies storming the doorway.

"Nice and easy, fellas," Armstrong said. "It's a shooting gallery down here."

Christine recalled the plan. Armstrong, Guin, and their team would sweep the first floor while John, Eric, and the rest of Bravo Team would immediately ascend to the second and work their way across. Alpha would then take to the third, Bravo to the fourth, and so on.

"Switching to body cams."

Several of the monitors went black, then flashed on with fish-eye views of the building's interior from several vantage points. A couple monitors still displayed wide views of the building's exterior.

On one body camera, Christine spotted the back of John's head as he followed an armed escort up the stairs to the second floor. To make Armstrong happy, John accepted the offer of a handgun, but she noticed its handle protruding from behind his belt in the small of his back. She didn't know whether to admire his courage or fear for his safety.

Another camera revealed Armstrong sticking tight to the wall as he and his men checked office doors. One of the men kept his gun trained on the floors visible above.

"Clear!" shouted voices from the radio in a rhythmic pattern as the teams swept the floors.

"Moving to the third floor."

"Copy, Bravo. We're almost to the end of the first."

More confirmation of empty offices followed. Finally, Armstrong announced their intention to head to the fourth.

Christine watched as Bravo Team opened door after door revealing large rooms littered with workstations, machine parts, and robotic inventions at various stages of completion. She recognized completed versions of models the company website referred to as Bast and Heimdall, but with each successive room devoid of human life, a pit grew in her stomach.

A curse word over the radio accompanied the reveal of Ares standing stoic in the middle of a workroom as the next door was opened. It looked identical to the demonstration model but without the modified weapon.

"We found Ares," John said over the radio.

In view of the camera, he walked up to the model and examined it. "This is the nonfunctioning prototype."

"Over here," came another voice. Eric's maybe.

The camera followed John to a nearby workstation. Sure enough, Eric stood at the station holding the detached head of another Ares prototype. "It's hollow." He held it up for John to see.

"Fitted for a human head. And here's more parts of the suit. Looks like Reardon was telling the truth."

Christine's heart leapt. She'd refused to entertain the idea Scott Reardon had lied to them, despite Armstrong's insistence it was possible. Now with proof of Hale's deception, the possibility of finding the truth behind Mano Amaya's murder was real.

"Rest of third is clear, sir."

Armstrong acknowledged the report, then announced, "We've exited on four. Moving across."

"They're not here, Armstrong," John replied. "Someone tipped them off."

"Stick to the plan, Bravo Team. We check every floor, then we'll figure out what happened."

"Moving to five," Bravo Leader confirmed.

"Alpha Leader," the female agent in the suite suddenly interjected. "We've got something."

"What is it, Command?"

Christine scanned the monitors for anything suspicious.

"Activity on the southeast corner of the complex. Stand by for visual."

On a monitor, one of the cameras zoomed and focused on a loading dock tucked into the back corner of an annex to the main wing of the building. Just as the shot steadied, Christine spotted a couple of black-clad men duck underneath a large rolling door sliding to a close against the concrete edge of the dock.

"Unidentified subjects just entered the southeast annex."

"Bravo Team, you're in a better position than us to check it out."

"Copy, Alpha Leader. In pursuit."

"Alpha will divide and take on the final two floors. Officer Sullivan, take your team and head to five while we finish checking here."

"Copy, Alpha Leader," Guin replied.

The exterior views of the building offered no additional information, so Christine finally moved from the monitors and grabbed an extra pair of binoculars. She scanned the outside, hoping to spot something, but all appeared calm.

"Bravo Team, any update?"

"Entering the southeast annex now. Appears to be some form of staging area. No visual on suspects." There was a pregnant pause, then Bravo Leader said, "Wait a minute."

"What is it?"

"We've entered a large garage with a row of armored vehicles, motorcycles, and what looks like a mechanized load lifter with legs."

Chiron, the fourth autonomous robot project being built by the company. Christine wondered if any of them actually worked.

"Still no sign of—"

Bravo Leader's words were cut off by what sounded like fireworks popping near the radio.

Not fireworks. Gunfire.

Christine dropped the binoculars and turned to the monitors. The body cam of one of Bravo Team's members flashed between a wide view of the garage and a blurry close-up of pallet wood as he ducked for cover.

"We're taking fire!"

"Man down!"

"Engage! Engage!"

The shouting was barely audible over the radio as the sound crackled with the rapid pops of gunfire.

"On our way!" Armstrong's voice broke through the noise.

One of Alpha Team's body cams followed him running down the length of the fourth floor.

"They're on the move!"

Christine turned her attention to Bravo Team's camera feeds, praying to catch a glimpse of John or Eric safely shielded from the firefight. One of the team members leaned out from a corner and extended his sidearm. He fired several rounds at a fleet of black armored trucks speeding toward the bright garage exit. A rapid flash of light pulsated from the last truck, and the agent leapt into his hiding spot as bits of concrete exploded around him.

"Watch it, Benitez!"

"He's been hit!"

Christine exhaled at the sound of Eric's voice. She stole a glance at Alpha Team nearing the escalators.

"Benitez?"

John?

John's face appeared on Benitez's body cam as he looked over the man's body.

"I'm OK," Benitez responded. "It's just a scratch."

John nodded at the man, then peeked around the corner. He looked back at Benitez, then right into the camera.

Don't do it.

Without a word, John jumped to his feet and ran out of the camera's view toward the exit.

Apparently he didn't listen to telepathy either.

"Armstrong," John's voice sounded from the speaker. "Forget the garage. They're mobile."

Armstrong and his men slid to a stop. "I need eyes on the suspects."

Christine lifted her binoculars and searched out the window at the sprawling complex. The garage was on the opposite side of the building. To her eyes and ears, the exterior was as calm as when they'd arrived.

"I've got visual," announced one of the other agents in the room into his headset. "Convoy just turned west down the main drive."

Christine adjusted her binoculars and spotted the vehicles entering the campus's driveway one by one. Between the distance and the tinted windows, it was an impossible task to see inside any of them.

"Alpha Leader, suspects are mobile."

"I heard," Armstrong growled, panting. "I need every available agent to move to intercept. And somebody call in air support."

Christine tried to find him on the monitors, but there was no sign of his crisp white shirt. She turned back with the binoculars as the first of the armored trucks passed under the suspended portion of the building.

A flash of movement through the glass windows of the fourth floor caught her eye. She trained her binoculars on the inside of the building and saw a man enter the observation lounge at the base of the central structure. His white arms flexed in half arcs as he ran.

Christine followed Armstrong with her binoculars as he ran to the center of the floor and past a large bronze sculpture that looked like it featured stained glass. He slowed as he looked out to his right at the oncoming line of vehicles.

Following his gaze, Christine noticed half the convoy was already past the building headed toward the exit. She brought the binoculars back into focus on Armstrong as he changed course and ran straight for the bay of windows. He grabbed a heavy potted plant as he neared and spun with it. At the height of his spin, he released his grip on the pot and sent it flying toward the window.

The plant shattered the glass and arched away from the building as gravity took its hold. Shards rained on the third-to-last truck as it passed underneath. The potted plant struck the truck on its way down, bounced off, then shattered across the driveway's opposite lane.

Armstrong stood at the hole left in the window's place and took a deep breath. The penultimate armored truck's nose broke through the shadow of the building overhead right when he jumped.

Christine heard several profane words from the other agents as they all watched Armstrong slam onto the vehicle's roof. His body slid backward as he clawed for a handhold. His arm hooked a square emergency light protruding from the top of the truck, and he jerked to a stop, his legs dangling off the back end.

The final truck followed close behind as the entire parade, six trucks in all, blazed a trail toward Parkwood Boulevard. The first truck skidded across the asphalt as it turned left out of the exit. The next two trucks followed the leader, but then the fourth truck made a hard right. The two trucks behind it followed suit, the last truck's right rear tire skipping the curb and plowing a trough into the grass as its driver gunned the engine.

Chaos erupted in the hotel room. Half the agents ran for the door, while the other half made radio and phone calls.

"They've split up."

"Three trucks heading north."

"We need eyes on the others traveling south down Parkwood."

"What's that?"

An agent pointed out the window. Christine scanned the front of the building through the binoculars, her chest thumping, hands shaking, then spotted what he was referring to. A lone figure on a black motorcycle raced down the drive toward the exit to the campus. Just past the main building entrance, the motorcycle cut to its left down the access road to the parking structure. As the access road curved away, the motorcycle jumped the curb and tore across the grass lawn running parallel to Parkwood. The driver hunched over the handlebars as he vaulted onto the roadway and sped off.

"This is Cross," John said over the radio. "I'm in pursuit."

Christine dropped the binoculars from her eyes as John and the first three trucks disappeared from view. An agent jostled her as he scooped up a laptop and bolted for the door. She didn't mind and instead continued to stare out the window as she considered her next move. Armstrong needed help, as did John.

But first . . .

Depositing the binoculars on the table, Christine ignored the protests of the female agent at the table as she headed for the door. She was already dialing the number into her phone before she reached the elevator.

CHAPTER TWENTY-FIVE

CROSS TIGHTENED HIS grip on the throttle to the motorcycle as he navigated around morning Parkwood traffic. He swerved around a sedan, his thigh inches from its metal frame. The three armored trucks charged through an intersection several yards ahead. And yet foremost on Cross's mind was what he would tell Gary when he got home.

"You're right," he would say. "I can't do this anymore."

His quarry suddenly shifted into the turn lane and cut off the flow of traffic across Spring Creek Parkway as they turned right. Cross benefited from the reckless nature of their driving, with most cars crawling or stopped as he entered the intersection. The chaos only served to calm him. He didn't have to fight against anxiety, not like when he walked the steps to the pulpit every Sunday morning.

The road was bordered by a flat field to his left and a car dealership to his right. The blue sky cascaded down in his front field of view until it disappeared behind the familiar line of a highway slicing across the horizon.

The North Tollway. Again.

Only this time, Cross was the tail. And there were more of them. Better armed too.

Rather than ponder the wisdom of his decision to pursue without backup, Cross evaluated his options. At this point, Hale's motives were unclear. Two sets of trucks heading in opposite directions, one an obvious decoy. But for what? For Hale to escape? There was no confirmation he was in either convoy.

The only way to find him was to stop the trucks.

Easier said than done.

To Cross's annoyance, the trucks changed lanes again, this time bearing left for the on-ramp to the highway. The traffic light was green, granting them all safe passage through the intersection and onto the access road.

The motorcycle was gaining, its engine powerful but surprisingly quiet. With no time to inspect it before leaving the garage, Cross was only now noticing the machine's tactical design. Resembling more of a motocross than a sport bike, this particular motorcycle featured armored plating and two gear cases affixed to either side of the rear cowl.

A car horn blared as the trucks muscled their way onto the North Tollway. Cross used the compact nature of the motorcycle to his advantage, bypassing traffic along the shoulder. He ignored how close his right knee was to the concrete barrier as the vehicles climbed the on-ramp. The tollway was bustling with aggressive motorists trying to beat the clock into work.

The convoy merged farther to the left, but Cross maintained his position near the right shoulder. A slowdown ahead meant neither he nor they were headed anywhere soon. Cross settled on his best option: keep them in sight but don't engage until the cavalry arrived. Now was as good a time as any to make sure they were on their way.

"This is Cross. Can anyone hear me?"

He held his breath and anticipated the response of a voice in his earbud. Despite the abating noise of throttled engines, the highway was still noisy. At full speed, he wasn't able to hear anything in his ear, even if anyone had attempted to reach him. What he wouldn't give for one of Guin's molar mics.

His brain finally found the subtle hum of static in the earbud. He did a quick calculation and decided a rough estimate of two to three miles from the CID's base of operations at the Marriot. It was far, and there were plenty of obstacles between them, but still within the range capacity of the two-way radio on his belt.

"Do you read me? This is John Cross."

"Copy, this is CID Control."

Every other syllable from the voice dropped out, making it difficult to piece together the phrase. He was almost out of range.

"I've got the three trucks heading south on Dallas North Tollway, confirm."

Cross took to the shoulder of the road to bypass a nervous driver looking for an opening in the next lane. He held his breath waiting for a response in the radio, then realized a decelerating tractor trailer was about to block his view of the convoy.

He weaved across the right lane and merged closer to the center of the highway as he gunned the motorcycle's engine. Garbled radio chatter burst from the earbud, and he let go of the handlebar to cup his ear to help decipher the comeback.

"Con . . . our . . . station . . . purse . . . author . . . peas."

The signal died just as Cross passed the front end of the tractor trailer's cab. He glanced to his left to reestablish contact with the armored trucks.

The circular roof hatch of the middle truck was open. A man dressed in all black tactical gear with matching helmet and goggles overtop a black balaclava rose up from inside, carrying an M249 light machine gun. He tipped the barrel of the weapon level to the roof of the truck and pointed in Cross's direction as he braced himself against the hatch.

Ignoring the radio static, Cross slammed on the brakes and the motorcycle skidded as it slowed. The trucks disappeared behind the tractor trailer just as the man pulled the trigger and sent a spray of bullets cutting across the highway.

Horns sounded, tires screeched, and metal crunched from behind Cross. A burst of piercing compressed air bombarded him from his left as the driver of the tractor trailer fought to slow his load without losing control.

If he stayed put, he'd lose the trucks. And if he followed, they were prepared to engage, risking harm to the other motorists.

He didn't have a choice now. Cross had to pursue. He had to engage. He had to stop them at any cost. It wasn't just the training. It was his biology.

Lee Armstrong questioned his sanity as he strained to pull himself onto the roof of the armored truck. Jumping out a four-story window onto a moving vehicle wasn't something he wagered he'd ever do, preferring the investigative work of his job to the criminal pursuit. And yet his present situation was the kicker to the new man this case was forcing him to be.

Everything considered, Armstrong was growing accustomed to this new man.

The three trucks traveled down Parkwood at breakneck speed. The constant swerving hampered Armstrong's progress, and his legs still dangled precariously over the edge of the middle truck's back end.

Armstrong tightened his grip and held his breath as the trucks banked to the left and avoided a small red sedan entering the highway off a side street. Traffic was light enough to allow the high speeds but not enough to relax the erratic behavior of the lead driver.

Of course, even if Armstrong managed to pull himself onto the roof, he had no clue what he would do next. Attaching himself to the escaping convoy seemed like a good idea, but he hadn't considering anything beyond that.

Baby steps. Wasn't that what his therapist had told him to do in situations like this? Not that they ever discussed situations like *this*.

One thing at a time.

Get on the roof, he told himself. *Then figure out the next thing.*

The vehicle settled as the lead driver picked a lane and stuck to it for longer than a few seconds, the other drivers following suit. Armstrong spotted a raised metal plate attached to the roof on his right and figured it was his best option.

He tightened his core, then pulled on the light and pushed his body forward. He let go of the light with his right hand and reached out. His fingers brushed against the plate, and he closed down on a ridged lip just as the vehicle crossed a dip in the road and lurched.

Armstrong felt his legs lift, and he used the momentum to pull his body all the way onto the roof. His legs slammed onto the hard surface, and his torso twisted, forcing him to release his grip on the lamp.

The truck picked up speed and rocked back and forth, probably a retaliatory move by the driver to try to knock Armstrong off. As the force threatened to do just that, Armstrong thrust out his other hand and locked himself to the rectangular plate.

Now what?

Deciding on an objective proved to be difficult. Random thoughts kept distracting him. Who was inside these trucks? Where were they headed? What was the nature of Christine and John's relationship? Was there an opening? Guin seemed nice. What was Hale's plan now that he was out in the open? Did Armstrong's team know where he was?

The radio.

Stupid. Why hadn't he thought of it? Armstrong was sure he was within range.

"Vach, do you copy?" He pictured the round face and flat nose of the lead CID agent handling communications for the operation. Even if she vacated the hotel with everyone else to follow him, Armstrong expected her to be in position in their mobile communications van.

"Alpha Leader, this is Mobile Coms. We copy."

Atta girl.

"I'm in a bit of a pickle here. I could really use some backup."

"Agents are in pursuit, Alpha Leader."

Best news yet. Armstrong opened his mouth to talk, when he heard a loud clank. He looked ahead and watched the flat, round hatch in the middle of the roof unseal itself and lift.

Without hesitating, Armstrong pulled his gun from the holster on his vest and extended it.

The hatch opened full, and a gun barrel appeared. The man on the other end of the weapon rose from inside the truck, his black helmet followed by black goggles and a black mask covering his mouth.

Just as Armstrong pulled the trigger, the man recognized his mistake and dropped his head down through the hatch. Armstrong's bullets pinged off the lid of the hatch, and sparks showered the roof.

He was a dead man.

Armstrong wouldn't be able to hold off the armed thugs inside long enough. He couldn't stay on the roof. But there was nowhere else to go.

The truck leaned right as the driver took a curve in the road without letting up on his speed. Armstrong cursed as he held himself steady with one hand and kept his SIG Sauer P320 trained on the hatch.

A black gloved hand holding a pistol appeared over the edge of the hatch and squeezed off a barrage of rounds in his direction. Armstrong closed his eyes and waited for the bullets to pierce his skull, but without proper sight, the gunman's aim was high, and Armstrong survived the attack unscathed.

He retaliated with a shot of his own and grinned in satisfaction as the bullet grazed the hand. A yelp emanated from inside the truck as the hand disappeared.

The lead truck slowed, as did Armstrong's, preparing for a right-hand turn. Armstrong spotted the familiar blue highway sign announcing the intersection of Parkwood and Texas 121 North, also known as Sam Rayburn Tollway.

The traffic signal was against them, but that didn't stop the trucks from bullying their way onto the access road. Armstrong glanced over his shoulder and watched a stream of vehicles skid to a stop only to be struck from behind by unobservant motorists.

That wasn't the only thing he saw.

With oncoming traffic impeded, a squad of black sedans fell in place on the access road behind the rear truck, emergency lights blazing.

Armstrong let out an audible whoop. He wasn't alone.

Turning back to the hatch, he remembered his current dilemma.

CID might be in hot pursuit, but he was still on the roof, there were armed men inside, and Armstrong was running out of ammunition.

With Cross, Armstrong, and the other CID agents engaging the suspects, Guin understood the best course of action for her was to finish the search of Hale Industries. She understood it but didn't have to like it.

Cross's recommendation for her to take the role of executive director with Central Intelligence fell on deaf ears, but her role in thwarting the chemical attack in Washington and in fingering the previous executive director in the conspiracy did result in a career move out of administration and into the field.

She'd never felt more alive, and now set her sights on a ladder up the ranks she'd never before considered. Guin knew exactly where she wanted to be, and hunting down bad guys with the Glock 19 in her hand was a perfect fit.

The handful of Alpha Team agents left in her care spread out in a V formation behind her as they exited the escalator onto the sixth floor of the building.

"Look alive, boys," Guin said, the small microphone clipped to her lapel picking up her voice and transmitting it into their ears. "We don't know if everyone's left yet."

Eric's voice responded in her own earbud. "Guin, I'm headed your way with a few agents. The rest of my team ran off to pursue Armstrong."

"Copy."

Guin held the Glock out in front of her with both hands and scanned the open pathways of the sixth floor. The low barriers running along either side of the open space between the two halves were made of glass, which only added to the discomfort Guin felt all morning being exposed to potential combatants.

The men prepared to start their sweep through the offices, when everyone froze at the sound of a nearby elevator chime announcing the car's arrival to the floor.

"Eric, don't panic. We're right outside of the elevator."

"Elevator?" Eric replied. "I'm not in the elevator."

On instinct Guin and the others raised their guns and stepped away from the elevator doors. They split, three men stationing themselves on one side of the alcove, Guin and another agent pressed up near the wall on the other.

"Watch your six."

The agent behind her and one on the other side both acknowledged her order. They turned to guard down the pathway in case of an attack from behind.

The elevator doors separated and groaned as they disappeared into the wall, and a lone person walked out from inside the car.

Guin let out a breath as she dropped her gun. "It's OK. Drop your weapons."

Christine stood motionless, her eyes wide and hands up, palms open. "It's me, Guin."

"Christine, what are you doing here?" Guin nodded toward the three men opposite her, and they proceeded down the hallway to investigate the first set of offices.

"What was I going to do, sit in the hotel room by myself? I thought you could use some help finding evidence of Mano Amaya's murder."

Guin frowned. The building wasn't cleared yet, and Christine wasn't wearing a ballistic vest. But she knew there was no way of preventing the stubborn reporter from accompanying them. Not without force, which Guin wasn't about to use.

Not that she didn't consider it.

"All right," Guin said. "But you have to stay right behind me."

Suddenly, a voice said into her ear, "Officer Sullivan, we've got a situation."

Guin nodded to her CID escort, then motioned for Christine to position herself behind them. As a unit, they entered the first set of offices, Guin in the lead.

Passing through a plush reception area, they entered through a large set of double doors and found the other trio of CID agents fanned out across the width of an executive office suite, their weapons raised and pointed at the same target.

Standing in front of a massive cherry-red wooden desk, a bay of tall windows behind her, was a slender woman dressed in a gorgeous white jumpsuit. Her ruby-red lips competed for attention with an ugly bruise on the side of her face. She held a gun in her right hand, while her left was hidden behind her back.

Christine gasped and said, "Marissa?"

Guin arched an eyebrow as she raised her weapon and took slow steps toward the woman. "You know this woman?"

Marissa waved her hand to cut off Christine's reply. "It doesn't matter who I am. What matters is you have three minutes to get out of this building before it explodes."

CHAPTER TWENTY-SIX

"WE'LL NEVER MAKE IT." Guin lowered her gun and took another step toward Marissa. "Where's the bomb?"

Marissa's eyes welled with tears. She brought her left hand out from its hiding spot and held up a metal cylinder with a red switch on one end and a blinking light on the other. "How much time do you need?" she asked, choking on the cascade of tears streaking her mascara.

The situation changed. The building might be rigged to explode, but it was a manual trigger, not a timed one. Yet Marissa didn't seem like the suicidal type.

Guin holstered her sidearm and held up a hand. "OK, honey, here's the deal. I don't know what you've been told, but right now you have two options. First, you can give me the detonator and turn yourself over to our custody. I promise you will be taken care of, and if you testify against your boss, you're likely to go free, assuming you haven't killed anyone yourself. The other option is one of these guys putting a bullet through your brain before you have a chance to trigger the bomb. I don't want that option. And neither do you."

Marissa breathed heavily as she considered Guin's words. Just as she was about to speak, footfalls thundered into the room.

Guin didn't have to turn around. "Eric, stand down."

Marissa's eyes narrowed at the new collection of CID agents pointing their weapons at her. Her breathing intensified, then she opened her mouth and screamed as she raised the cylinder and extended it out.

The temperature in the room increased tenfold as the agents pressed in. "Stand down!" Guin shouted as she held up her hands. "Do not fire! Do not shoot!" Guin added an expletive at the end of her commands for added emphasis.

At the last second, Marissa turned around and slammed the cylinder and gun on the table. She released her hold on both items and fell to the floor, sobbing.

Christine brushed past Guin and ran up to Marissa. She knelt beside the woman and placed her arm around her neck. Eric led the way in securing the detonator and Marissa's handgun, while Guin took deep breaths to calm her agitated heart.

"It's OK," Christine said to Marissa. "You're going to be OK. You made the right choice."

One of the CID agents requested assistance from the bomb squad over the radio, then suggested the team evacuate the premises until the danger could be neutralized.

"What about the evidence?" Christine asked. "We can't leave here until we know what Hale's been up to."

Eric grunted as he slipped his Glock into his shoulder holster. "I'm just as eager to figure this thing out as you are, but it's too dangerous, Christine."

Christine's eyes blazed with indignation, but then they softened as she turned back to Marissa. She brushed the woman's hair aside and exposed the extent of her injury, a laceration now visible. "Hale gave this to you, didn't he?"

Marissa nodded. "He's a monster. He said he would kill my family if I didn't do what he wanted. And he'll do it too. You have to stop him."

"You have to help us," Christine replied. "What's he hiding up here? What's the Sixth-Floor Project, and where can we find it?"

Marissa shook her head. "It's not a thing—it's a plan. Anthony's plan to get away. He's going to kill the president."

Guin's mouth fell open, as did Eric's and Christine's. They stared at Marissa, then exchanged stunned glances with each other.

Guin knelt down next to Christine and looked into Marissa's eyes. "Did you just say the president? As in the president of the United States?"

The woman dropped her chin and averted her eyes, all the confirmation Guin needed for the wild claim. "Eric?"

"Already looking it up," the other CIA officer replied as he keyed a search into his phone. "Got it. The president landed at Dallas Love Field half an hour ago and is currently en route to an event with Senator Kirk Howard in Addison, Texas. The motorcade is on Dallas North Tollway right now."

Guin met Christine's wide eyes, and in unison they said the same word.

"John."

Guin jumped to her feet and addressed Eric. "Secure this location and see if she can tell us more about what Hale's plan is."

Eric nodded, then narrowed his eyes at her. "What are you going to do?"

"First, I'm going to call this in. Then I'm going to try to get to John. Somehow." She waved Christine and Marissa up. "Let's talk where it's safe—"

A voice in her ear cut off her words. "Officer Sullivan, we've got an inbound helicopter attempting to land on the roof of Hale Industries. It's a news helicopter, looks like North American Broadcasting."

Guin dug her hands into her hips as she and Eric glared at Christine.

Christine caught her breath as she shifted her eyes between them. "What?"

Cross squeezed his body as tight against the motorcycle's frame as he could and gunned the engine. Traffic ahead moved to escape the carnage of the gunman's M249, creating a clear path for the trucks to zoom down the tollway at top speed.

He needed to be faster, or risk being turned into roadkill.

The motorcycle submitted to his prayers and gained on the trucks, keeping just ahead of the bullets impacting in an arch behind it.

Cross's only option, as far as he could surmise, was to get ahead of the convoy. The gunman's view would be blocked by the hatch's lid, making it harder to sight his target.

But that meant cutting a straight line beside the trucks, and Cross assumed the gunman would figure out his maneuver in time to adjust and mow him down. That left only one additional option to make his plan work.

And he didn't like it.

Holding the bike steady with one hand as it hit top speed, Cross reached for the butt of the Glock pressed against his back.

Sure enough, the gunman paused to adjust his aim across the nose of the motorcycle as it approached. Cross pulled the Glock free, took aim, and fired.

The bullets struck sure against the hatch's lid, sending sparks into the air and the gunman down through the hole.

With a reprieve from gunfire, Cross stashed the Glock into his belt and piloted the motorcycle past the lead truck. He kept his speed as he merged into the lane in front of the convoy, now bait for their ire.

He'd bought time, but it wouldn't last. They might drift back to the right and open up a sightline. Or push their engines harder in an attempt to run him down. Whatever their options, it was their move next.

A handful of motorists ahead missed the memo about the gunfight and continued at a leisurely pace, forcing Cross to swerve at wide angles, but the gunman remained silent. Were the trucks still behind him?

The temptation to look over his shoulder was weaker than the need to concentrate on obstacles ahead. What he needed was a mirror, but one was suspiciously absent from the bike's handlebar. Instead, just to his left, was a small black box with a dark glass front.

Wait a second.

Watching the road from his peripheral vision, Cross searched the dash of the motorcycle until he spied a toggle marked CAMERA. With a switch, the glass screen powered up. Within seconds, a view of the highway from the rear of the motorcycle appeared.

He saw the lead truck still behind him two car lengths away. To his surprise, the two trucks in the rear of the convoy separated from the lead truck, one to the left the other to the right, and pulled forward until all three trucks drove side by side. The other two vehicles opened their top hatches, and identical black-clad men leaned around their respective lids, aiming machine guns at him.

Not good.

Cross coaxed the motorcycle faster, but it was hitting its limit. He needed a new plan.

One of the gunmen opened fire and pelted the concrete barrier to Cross's left, forcing him to swerve right. This opened a sight line for another burst from the middle truck, and the bullets struck a delivery van meandering along as Cross dodged out of the way.

The van's tires squealed as its driver braked and fought against the force of such a sudden stop. The armored vehicles parted to bypass the van, granting Cross a moment to consider his next move.

Just ahead of him, a fully loaded, double-decker car-carrying trailer merged left, the driver seemingly unaware of the carnage fast approaching. A plan quickly formed. The odds favored failure, but Cross's options were limited. He grabbed the Glock and did a mental count of his remaining rounds, subtracting the shots he'd taken at the gunman.

Fourteen. Should be plenty, provided he found his marks.

He pushed the motorcycle harder to catch up to the trailer. Stealing a glance into the rear camera, he gauged how quickly the trucks were gaining after their near miss with the van, the armed men no doubt readying their weapons to engage within seconds.

On second thought, the trucks could be useful to his plan.

He let off the accelerator as he neared the left rear side of the trailer. The trucks kept coming, and all three men leaned out and took aim.

A hail of miniature missiles exploded from the light machine guns and sliced through the air in his direction. Just as they opened fire, Cross cut across the lane behind the trailer, drawing their bead with him.

The bullets tore through the trailer and the rear car attached at the base level. Just as Cross hoped, the 5.56 x 45 millimeter projectiles demolished the hydraulic arms holding up the second deck. The ramp dropped, crushing the pristine white sedan underneath the weight of a midsized SUV on top.

Cross pulled along the back right side of the trailer and aimed the Glock at the chain holding the SUV in place. He squeezed the trigger and dismissed thoughts of anger and frustration as the bullet skimmed across the top, barely scratching the metal. The second shot did the trick, severing the chain in two.

The SUV's weight was too much for the nylon straps around its front wheels to handle, and together they snapped. The SUV, free from its bonds, slid off the trailer and crashed vertically into the roadway.

The armored truck failed to evade the sudden obstacle, and its nose impacted with the SUV's underbelly, lifting the unmanned vehicle into the air. The SUV landed on the front end of the truck, its underbelly facing outward and its frame blocking the windshield. The other two trucks parted from their incapacitated comrade as the middle truck's driver fought to maintain a straight path.

An air blast alerted Cross to the trailer's intention to come to a stop. He aimed his gun at the next car in line and took out the supporting chain. This time, however, the car, a blue hatchback, didn't budge.

Bullets tore through the side of the trailer's carriage just ahead of him, causing Cross to duck his head and lose sight of his target. A quick glance in the camera screen confirmed the presence of one of the armored trucks on his tail, its gunman struggling to steady the heavy M249 against the vehicle's roof.

Seconds from certain death, Cross launched a string of gunshots at the hatchback's front right tire. One of the three bullets struck the nylon strap holding the tire in place, slicing it in two.

Just then the surface of the road shifted from smooth to rough asphalt, a by-product of recent infrastructure repair. The car hauler bounced, causing the hatchback to twist in position and slide at a crooked angle off the right edge of the deck.

Cross gassed the motorcycle as the hatchback broke free and sailed off the end of the trailer, headed right for the pursuing truck. The car glanced off the truck's nose and rolled side over side up and over the roof. As it flew backward, the hatchback slammed the lid of the truck's hatch violently closed, crushing the gunman's body underneath.

The car tumbled completely over the truck, then folded in on itself as it impacted the highway in the truck's wake. The blind truck falling behind drifted into the lane and, given the driver's impaired vision, charged right toward the debris. The vehicles collided, and the SUV's exposed gas tank ruptured.

Cross gasped as he watched the SUV and hatchback explode on the screen. The fiery wreckage brought the armored truck to a complete stop, and for the first time Cross noticed the distant flashing red and blue lights of emergency responders racing after them.

The trailer slowed even more, and Cross noticed the truck behind him, its hatch now closed, doing the same. The truck merged behind the car hauler and disappeared.

Giving the motorcycle a boost, Cross moved along the right side of the trailer, peering through its collection of cars to catch a glimpse of the two remaining trucks. He backed off the accelerator as he neared the trailer's cab, wary of running afoul of the first truck's gunner a second time.

Just as he reached the cab's nose, Cross spotted the lead truck hitting its top speed as it passed the trailer and took off down the left most lane of the tollway, its companion truck following close behind.

Cross left the protection of the car hauler and pursued at an acceptable distance should they decide to pick up where they left off with the M249. For now, he was back to his original plan: maintain visual and only intervene if absolutely necessary. An even more appropriate plan now that he was down to eight rounds in the Glock and an aversion to using it against another human being.

Eight, right? Cross tried to remember how many shots he'd fired at the nylon strap holding the hatchback. It'd happened so fast, but he was certain it took only—

"Shepherd."

Cross stopped short of letting go of the handlebars as he processed the sound of his call sign broadcasting into his ear canal. He released his right hand and used his fingers to press the earbud deeper for a clearer sound. The surrounding traffic roared around him. Wind whipped at his hair and clothes.

Maybe he'd dreamed it.

"Shepherd, come in."

It was real. Thank God it was real. The voice was female. And familiar.

"Guin? It's Cross. I'm in pursuit of the suspects, Dallas North Tollway headed south. Hold on. I'll get you an exact location—"

"No need, Shepherd. We've got eyes on you."

What? How? Cross searched the camera screen for a sign of backup, but the flashing lights were failing to catch up.

"Up, John. Look up."

Of course. Cross grinned as he obeyed. Several hundred feet in the sky, flying parallel with his motorcycle, was a white helicopter with a bulbous camera affixed beneath its nose and the vibrant logo of the Dallas NABC affiliate emblazoned across its fuselage.

CHAPTER TWENTY-SEVEN

THE HIGH-CALIBER ROUNDS punctured the helicopter's body just to the right of the Texas DPS agent positioned inside the open door. He ceased fire and fell backward, his partner huddled with him, as the aircraft banked away from engaging the lead armored vehicle.

Armstrong pounded the roof of the middle truck with his closed fist and shouted a string of profanities, a useless gesture, as his words were swallowed by the high winds stinging him in the face.

The CID caught up to the trucks all right, but their hands were full when heavily armed men opened fire from the hatches of the lead and rear trucks. A silver lining for Armstrong, at the moment, was they seemed to have forgotten about him.

"Evasive maneuvers! Specter Two Oh Nine Omaha taking heavy fire!"

One of the fourteen Eurocopter AS350 AStar choppers plus half a dozen state patrol utility vehicles comprised the pursuit unit, and they'd closed the radio range gap, giving Armstrong a front-row seat to their attempts at stopping the convoy. The DPS officers were all armed but hesitant to fire, given the congestion of pedestrian traffic on Sam Rayburn Tollway.

Hale's men weren't so considerate.

Gunfire erupted behind him as the rear truck threatened the approaching patrol vehicles. Armstrong resisted the urge to look, his eyes glued to the open hatch. Since injuring the man firing at him from inside, Armstrong rode in relative peace. He wondered if the men inside expected their friends to kill him.

"Coming back around. We'll take the shot if it's clean."

Armstrong finally took his eyes off the hatch and scanned the sky for the Eurocopter. He followed the aim of the man with the intimidating rifle in the lead car and saw the helicopter making an approach from the east, straight down the truck's nose.

Perfect, Armstrong thought. The hatch's lid provided a blind spot for the chopper to engage without exposing itself to the gunman.

The truck driver must've figured the same thing, and he clipped a small sedan as he tore left across several lanes of the highway. The helicopter slowed and spun in the air, the duo of agents raising their own weapons as they came into view.

"Take the shot!" Armstrong yelled, hoping his mic picked up his voice against the chaos.

"Agent in line of sight. I repeat—I've got an agent in line of sight."

Armstrong repeated his command and added an oath for good measure.

The muzzle of one of the agents flashed in a repeated pattern as he fired on the lead truck. The truck's gunman pressed himself against the lid of the hatch as the driver veered off the left most lane into the grassy median.

Armstrong's truck followed suit, and he assumed the rear truck did as well. A concrete barrier closed the right side of the highway off from reentry just as the guardrail on the left ended. The leader gassed his vehicle and jumped the short hill off the grass and onto the asphalt, now heading the wrong way. With a clear shot, the lead gunman retaliated against the DPS helicopter, but this time his shots went wide as the pilot peeled off early.

Armstrong braced himself as his truck roared off the median and onto the highway, spitting dirt and grass in its wake. Oncoming traffic swerved, horns blaring. As the truck settled into its new route, Armstrong stole a glance over his shoulder. The rear truck retook its position in the convoy after crossing the median. The DPS unit split up, half joining the armored trucks on the wrong side, half remaining in the proper lanes.

If only they could divert the trucks off the highway. Maybe set up a roadblock farther ahead.

Armstrong opened his mouth to make contact with his team as he turned his attention forward. But no words formed, and his mind went blank at the sight of a black figure rising from inside the hatch.

He'd lost focus, his gun hand relaxed, and that meant he was dead.

The man standing through the hatch leveled the rifle in his hand, its barrel pointing straight at Armstrong's head. In a quick draw, Armstrong had no chance.

A thousand thoughts went through his head in a second, memories and regrets intermingled. Then a single thought of a question he'd long ignored.

What would come after?

Just as the man's finger twitched against the rifle's trigger, the side of his helmet exploded. A bullet exited the other side of his head and disappeared. The gunman's body went limp, and he collapsed against the roof.

Armstrong blinked. What just happened? Between the two of them, he hadn't expected the other man to end up the dead one.

He looked across the highway and spotted the deadeye aiming at the convoy from a black patrol SUV, her dark hair pulled into a tight bun and her face obscured behind the round glass of a scope attached to the top of a rifle.

Whoever she was, she deserved a promotion.

Armstrong turned to the dead man and, his mind suddenly clear, was struck by an idea. As the idea took shape, he noticed the man move.

No way. The bullet went right through his brain.

It took Armstrong a second to realize the body wasn't moving on its own as it slid back toward the hatch. It was now or never.

Armstrong used his legs to propel himself across the roof. He grabbed at the man's upper torso and snagged a handful of his ballistics vest.

Whoever pulled at the dead man's legs was stronger, and Armstrong struggled to slow his momentum toward the open hole.

His fingers finally found the small metal ring attached to a cylinder poking out from a pocket in the man's vest. Armstrong released his hold on the man's vest as he hooked the ring.

With the release of opposing force, the men inside overcompensated, and their deceased companion slipped forcibly from the roof and tumbled through the hatch. The pin snapped from the cylinder in the man's vest, and Armstrong caught himself from becoming exposed over the opening.

One Texas. Two Texas.

On the third second, a pop sounded from inside the truck, and a thin plume of white smoke snaked out from the hatch. The plume grew rapidly as the gas from the grenade filled the truck.

The driver swerved erratically on the road, and Armstrong almost lost his grip more than once. Apparently, he hadn't thought his plan through all the way. As the occupants of the vehicle succumbed to the effects of the tear gas, their odds of making contact with an oncoming car increased.

So he was dead anyway. Great.

Armstrong cursed as he considered how much easier Cross must have it in comparison.

He was alone, and they offered little help. At least that was how Christine felt watching John follow the two armored trucks down the Dallas North Tollway from the relative safety of the NABC helicopter.

Jeremy Blankenship sat next to her in the tight quarters of the rear of the aircraft, dabbing his forehead with a handkerchief, an action he'd repeated several times since the third truck exploded in a ball of fire. It wasn't helping. The front of his official NABC polo shirt was soaked.

Guin directed the chopper's pilot, an older man by the name of

Wilson Crockett, to match John's speed and stay to the left to maintain their view of both his motorcycle and the armed convoy.

Crockett, who kept insisting they call him by his air force nickname, Rocket, was smitten with the female CIA officer and more than happy to acquiesce, a permanent grin affixed to his face as he flew the machine.

"Rocket" Crockett. The man's delight was as infectious as his nickname was adorable.

Christine was thankful for a seasoned operator behind the stick, a providential blessing she hadn't expected after calling in the favor with Jeremy. The NABC reporters were along for the ride, but it was Guin and Crockett's operation from the start.

"Please repeat. I didn't catch that last part."

John certainly heard Guin's message but understandably didn't comprehend it, just as they hadn't when Marissa told them.

"Their target is the president. I repeat: the president."

The radio went silent, then John's voice came back. "The president." Another pause. "You can't be serious."

"I am serious, Cross. The president is on the highway, and Hale's men are on a course to intercept. Hale's assistant told us the whole thing. The attempt on the secretary's life was a ruse to distract from Hale's embezzlement, and now he's trying to cover his escape doing the same thing with a bigger target."

Marissa claimed to have documented evidence to back up her assertions, and Christine believed her. Hale's operation was crumbling around him, but she had to admit the plan was working. All of Texas would now be intent on stopping an assassination and less concerned with apprehending a con artist.

Christine imagined John considering the information, then presumably weighing possible scenarios. The Criminal Investigations Division was calling in every available unit, and state patrol officers were in pursuit, but there was a lot of ground to make up. And the closest available DPS aircraft chose to assist in the pursuit of the other three trucks.

Thinking like him, Christine deduced John's options were limited to himself and a lone CIA officer in a commandeered news helicopter. Not exactly the team of people you'd want intervening in an attempted presidential assassination.

"Did you notify the Secret Service?"

"Eric's on it."

"What about military intervention?"

"It's Dallas during rush hour, not exactly a war zone."

She hadn't thought of that. Christine had questioned Hale's sanity the entire trip from the top of his company's building. But now it made sense. Attack the president's entourage on a busy highway in the middle of one of the nation's most populated regions. The military wouldn't risk potential casualties with an air assault.

"I'm running out of ideas down here," John said, his tone laced with frustration.

Guin let out a puff of air that irritated her mic. "We gave you a gun, didn't we?"

Christine interpreted John's silence as displeasure at Guin's sarcastic barb. She knew his old coworker was still struggling to understand John's aversion to the very thing he demonstrated mastery over during his tenure with Central Intelligence.

He might be willing to fire a weapon at the rear end of a car hauler, but Christine knew full well he'd refuse to use lethal force against another human being. But she admitted the apparent conflict. What if it was the only way to prevent the death of President Jefferson Gray?

John would find another way. He'd have to find another way.

"What if we got them off the highway?" Christine blurted into her headset.

Guin groaned.

Oops. Christine remembered their agreement, but it was too late.

"Christine?" John asked with even more frustration apparent in his voice. "What are you doing up there?"

"Come on," Guin interjected. "You really didn't think she was here? It's her news network's helicopter."

Christine swallowed her guilt. "I'm sorry, John. But I had to come."

"We agreed you'd stay away."

"Like you agreed to not come in the first place?"

OK, that might have been too far. But it was how she felt. She didn't see a way forward in their relationship if there wasn't any trust between them. And judging by his silence, she assumed he thought the same.

"John," she said, the lump in her throat refusing to move. "We need to talk."

Crockett's tobacco-fueled voice cut in to the feed. "I hate to interrupt your lovers' quarrel, but we've got ourselves a national security situation on our hands."

"He's right," Guin said. "And so is Christine. We've got to get those trucks off the highway."

From their bird's-eye view, Christine watched John accelerate the motorcycle. The gap between him and the trucks closed.

"If I can get them off, and that's a big if, can we get air support here in time?"

"You worry about your part." Guin breathed out as she made eye contact with Crockett. The pilot, still smiling, shrugged. Guin turned to watch John as she continued, "We'll be off radio for a minute while I contact Eric. Sit tight."

"Copy."

Christine fixed her eyes on the motorcycle as she sorted through the myriad of thoughts flooding her mind. Questions, and answers, about her relationship with John begged for attention, but she knocked each one aside in favor of conceiving possible solutions to their current problem. John made it look easy, but from her vantage point, they were outgunned, and time was running out.

Her radio headset fizzed with noise, the pads encompassing her ears not enough buffer against the whine of the helicopter's engine and the beating of its rotor blades. She knew Guin was talking with Eric, but their conversation took place on a channel separate from the internal one, making it impossible to listen in.

"What's he going to do?" Blankenship half mumbled in her ear.

Oh no. In dealing with her anxiety concerning everything from Philip's possible exoneration, to stopping an attack on the president, to her conflicted emotions toward John, Christine forgot about her colleague.

She broke her concentration on the highway below and looked over at Blankenship. Guin had offered to force him to stay behind, but Christine had used his eagerness to reach a settlement concerning his curiosity toward the events in Washington.

He could come along for the ride on the condition he promise to drop the matter. She stood her ground with him, but Christine was impressed with the man's commitment to the truth. He had his quirks, but it was refreshing.

Blankenship, eager for a scoop on the biggest story of his career, agreed. Little did he know, or really any of them for that matter, what was in store.

"He'll think of something," Christine said, then reassured herself he would. "All we need to do is separate the trucks from the rest of the pedestrian traffic. Then the military can handle it."

"What, by blowing up the trucks? This is North Dallas. Even if he could get them to divert off the tollway, there's nowhere to go that doesn't have a million people. I'm sure your friend down there knows what he's doing but I just don't see how we're going to be able to stop those things."

"Let's work on one problem at a time. Just getting them out of rush-hour traffic would be a start."

Blankenship shook his head, then gazed out his window at the sprawling urban North Texas landscape. Just when she decided to leave him be, he turned back to Christine.

"OK, in about two miles he's going to hit the interchange for President George Bush Turnpike. If he can force the trucks onto the exit ramp, there might be a shot as they come out of the interchange. It's an elevated single lane with enough space to minimize collateral damage. There's only one problem."

"What is it?"

"There's no telling how packed it might be. Sometimes the interchange runs smooth, other times not so much. But honestly it's his best bet. After that it'll be bumper to bumper all the way to downtown."

Christine took Blankenship at his word. She leaned forward in her seat, as far as the safety straps would let her, and reached out to tap Guin's shoulder. Guin held up a finger, finished speaking into her headset, then toggled back into the internal channel.

"What's wrong?"

"Jeremy has an idea for John."

Guin twisted around to make eye contact with Blankenship, who smiled sheepishly and nodded. She narrowed her eyes, then turned and worked the radio.

"Cross, I've got an update."

"Go."

"Secret Service is evacuating the president, but they're just as hemmed in as we are. Air force reserve is scrambling fighters from the Four Fifty Seventh out of NAS Fort Worth JRB. They're a couple minutes out. And apparently"—Guin paused, glared at Blankenship, then said—"the other journalist has an idea."

Christine looked out the window at John and prayed. She noticed him steal a look in their direction.

"Hold on. Other journalist?"

CHAPTER TWENTY-EIGHT

TIME TO LEAVE.

The tear gas trick proving too effective, Armstrong wagered he'd fare better jumping clear of the truck as soon as the opportunity presented itself.

"A little help here!" he yelled, hoping someone was listening on the other end of his radio.

"A tu izquierda," came the reply.

Armstrong arched his head and spotted Flores at the wheel of a black SUV with a white hood approaching on the truck's left. Blue and red lights flashed in sequence on the SUV's crown.

Armstrong let out a whoop. "You came in the nick of time, my friend. I'm ready to bail from this thing."

Flores battled to stay flush with the truck as it careened out of control. Suddenly, his eyes grew big as he noticed something ahead.

Following his gaze, Armstrong cursed when he spotted the oncoming tractor trailer carrying an oversized load. He took the inevitable catastrophe as his cue and pulled himself up on one knee while maintaining a hold on the armored transport.

Armstrong willed himself into the air, but his body refused to comply. A force acting against him pulled him backward. He fell to the roof, facing the sky, and slid toward the open hatch. A black gloved hand appeared in his field of view, then disappeared as a thick arm wrapped around his throat.

Try as he might, Armstrong couldn't break the man's hold. He punched and clawed as he felt his head pass over the hole in the roof. Smoke still billowed from inside, and Armstrong felt his lungs tighten as his eyes filled with water.

Help . . .

Whatever higher power heard his appeal responded, as the truck was struck from the side. The impact caused the man's death grip to loosen for only a moment, but it was enough for Armstrong to take advantage.

Slipping his hand underneath the man's forearm, Armstrong wriggled free as he simultaneously threw a punch behind his head. He hit a soft spot and heard a grunt from behind as his attacker released him and dropped into the truck.

No time to reconsider now. Armstrong rolled onto his stomach and pushed himself up. Without hesitating, he turned, spotted Flores's car, and jumped off the roof.

Armstrong landed on the hood of the SUV and grabbed for the windshield wipers. Flores yanked the wheel, and they swerved clear of the armored truck just as it met the tractor trailer head-on.

The two vehicles seemingly merged into one as metal crushed against metal. Armstrong shielded his face from any potential debris, then stole a glance as the SUV slowed. In their wake, the tractor trailer emerged the victor, the armored truck pushed to the side to lick its wounds.

The SUV's horn blared, startling Armstrong. Flores waved him in from behind the wheel. Armstrong twisted his legs from off the hood and around into the open passenger-side window, then finally breathed as he maneuvered all the way in and settled into the seat.

For a moment they were speechless, then Flores said, "Eso fue suerte."

Armstrong allowed himself a brief chuckle. "You're telling me."

"You've only got two minutes, Cross."

He was sure Guin meant to be helpful, but Cross didn't need a reminder of urgency to motivate him. Two minutes was too long for him as he watched the armored trucks barrel their way through the morning tollway traffic. Thankfully, there was enough room for them to travel without casualty.

For now.

The plan, as outlined by Christine's NABC colleague, was to force the trucks onto the exit ramp for another highway. The ramp, if clear of innocent motorists, would offer a squad of F-16s the opportunity to stop the trucks dead in their tracks with as minimal collateral damage as possible.

The news helicopter's job was to try to clear their way. Cross's job was to coax the convoy off the road. In his mind, they were two dozen armed soldiers and a pair of Black Hawks short of accomplishing their mission.

They'd have to settle for an old air force pilot, a CIA officer, a pair of journalists, and an evangelical minister.

Concentrating on the objective at hand didn't help. How was he going to convince the truck drivers to do his bidding when all he had was an experimental military motorcycle and a gun he didn't even want to use?

Wait. The motorcycle.

As he weaved his way closer to the two trucks, Cross examined the digital screen attached between the handlebars. A menu option gave him the ability to cycle from the camera to a series of other functions related to the operation of the bike.

After dodging a slowing minivan, he turned to the screen and toggled through the options until he found a series of buttons under the heading Defensive Countermeasures.

Cross locked his eyes on the rear truck. Next step: take the lead and try out some of the motorcycle's defense modifications. He twisted the throttle and brought the bike up to speed.

"Cross, we're making our move to clear the roadway. You've got less than one hundred seconds to force the trucks into the far-right lane. And be careful. Eric just confirmed these guys are with Excalibur."

The news soured him. While the nation thought the private military company called Excalibur dissolved following multiple scandals that occurred while Cross was at the agency, they'd really only disappeared from the spotlight to resume their brutal operations from the shadows. Cross felt less secure in his chances.

But already committed to the plan, he maintained his course. He zoomed past the first truck, then the leader, before either could station a man on top to engage. He put himself in front, the convoy two lanes away from his objective.

He took his eyes off the road for a second and punched the first countermeasures button without reading it. The bike's engine suddenly went silent, and Cross expected to be turned into roadkill. To his surprise, the bike maintained its velocity. Taking another glance, he realized the first option on the screen was Stealth Mode.

Not helpful in this situation.

He registered the second button, labeled Vapor Shield, then tapped the screen. A thick white spray of smoke emanated from narrow slits in the motorcycle's frame behind him. The smoke collected into a cloud that grew in size as it trailed.

Cross saw the lead truck swerve to escape the blinding haze, but in the wrong direction.

"Not so fast," Cross said aloud as he jerked the motorcycle to the left and spread the smoke in a wider arc. The driver compensated for his move and turned across the left center lane and into the next. The smoke sputtered, then ceased as the tanks emptied.

So far so good, only he wasn't done. One more lane to go, provided the trucks kept to their current trajectory. They seemed more than happy to oblige, an answer to his prayers, as traffic on the left jammed with motorists bailing from the threat of the oncoming danger.

The hatch on the top of the lead truck opened, and the gunman, now identified as an Excalibur employee, hoisted his M249 out as he propped himself against the rocking carriage of the vehicle.

Cross figured he would deal with the man again but failed to find an adequate answer to the problem. Maybe another countermeasure.

With his eyes bouncing between traffic and the man, Cross couldn't find an opportunity to study the digital screen. He'd just have to outdrive the truck.

As he mentally scanned the road and created a route in his mind, Cross noticed the man with the M249 reposition himself so the barrel of his gun faced the front of the truck. Curious, Cross followed the direction the gun pointed, until he spotted the large green signs posted at the exit for President George Bush Turnpike.

"You've got to be kidding me."

The NABC helicopter hovered a few feet from the ground, discouraging any cars from attempting to enter the ramp.

"Guin, they see you. Get out of there before they start shooting."

There was no response. They'd be in range in seconds. The third of four buttons on Cross's screen read CALTROPS. At least he knew what that one would do.

Gunning the motorcycle's engine, Cross crossed the center left lane and pulled alongside the truck. He looked up as he passed and caught the blank stare of the helmeted driver through his closed window.

Cross winked, then maneuvered the bike in front of the left corner of the truck's nose. With the help of a schematic on the screen, he lined up the rear of the motorcycle and the tire, then released the caltrops.

The small metal spikes burst from a canister below his seat and struck the tire. As he suspected, the thick rubber refused to give and instead seemed to swallow each spike without losing velocity.

One more button, but now two objectives. Stop the gunman from firing on the helicopter while still getting the truck to change lanes.

God, help us.

Cross felt the Glock tucked into his belt pressing against his abdomen and knew it was the only option against the man with the M249. He drifted away from the front of the truck, let off the throttle, and pulled the gun from his waist.

He couldn't just shoot to distract. There was too much at stake.

Injure, not kill.

That's all.

Do it.

"Guin!" he shouted. "Get out of the road!" Sweat pouring from his brow threatened to blind him.

The NABC helicopter cleared the last motorist from the exit as the gunman squeezed the trigger. Tracer rounds shot through the air just above the helicopter's rotor.

Cross blanched as the helicopter built up speed but kept low to the ground as it met the armored truck head-on. The gunman tried to compensate, but the helicopter's speed closed the gap too quickly.

Just when it seemed the two vehicles would ram each other, the helicopter lifted. The man disappeared into the hatch as the landing skids struck the lid, forcing it to slam violently shut.

"A little help here, Cross. We need him in that lane!"

What did she think he'd been doing all this time?

Cross kept the Glock in his hand and evaluated his options. The exit was two lanes, the trucks just to the left. His gun or whatever countermeasure left on the bike was sure to be ineffective.

Unless . . .

He pushed the motorcycle to its top speed and banked to the left of a large delivery truck. Pulling alongside the driver's window, Cross pointed the Glock at the stunned man behind the wheel.

As he hoped, the man swerved away from him and cut off the lead armored transport. The transport entered the first of the two exit lanes to keep from colliding with the delivery truck.

Mission accomplished.

"John, you did it!" Christine said over the radio.

Now if they would just stay put.

Cross let the bike slow and continued his counterfeit threats toward the delivery truck's panicked operator. The trucks picked up speed as the lanes separated in anticipation of the merger.

Ten more seconds.

The leader suddenly broke free from the delivery truck's blockade and made a move to reenter the tollway. The armored truck missed the concrete barrier closing off the exit on the right and cut through the corner of the delivery truck's cab as it cleared the path for both it and its partner's escape.

Guin uttered an oath, and Cross couldn't blame her. He'd failed in his mission. The F-16s didn't have a shot.

"Cross, we've got to stop those trucks. Traffic is badly jammed a mile ahead, and it'll be impossible to mitigate the casualties."

Sirens blared behind him as the CID, state troopers, and Dallas police closed in on the chase. They'd be too late. He had to do something.

Maybe if he could get inside one.

Cross suspended any further evaluation and sped up to catch the convoy. He pressed the menu button on the touchscreen and pulled up the final countermeasures option.

MAYHEM.

Worth a shot. The readout suggested he target something behind him using the camera. Cross repeated the familiar maneuver of passing the lead truck and positioning himself just in front of its nose. The system turned green to affirm his position, then with a deep breath, he pressed the button.

A flash of pixels formed a message: ARMING MAGNETOHYDRODYNAMIC EXPLOSIVE MUNITION. A countdown from five followed.

At zero, a section of the bike's frame opened behind his seat. A cylinder with a pointed nose exploded from a tube inside the bike. Like a missile, the cylinder sliced through the air and penetrated the front end of the armored truck.

Watching the camera feed, Cross's eyes widened as several small explosions detonated inside the engine compartment. An orange glow emanated from the holes in the truck's grill, followed by bursts of hot steam.

Without warning, the front axle of the truck disintegrated, causing the front tires to twist and tear. The nose of the truck dropped into the sun-beaten asphalt and dug a trough. A combination of the impact and the truck's velocity forced the entire vehicle to flip.

He'd be a pancake in seconds.

Cross nearly broke the motorcycle's handle as he twisted the throttle. The truck's roof went vertical, then rushed toward him as gravity urged it on.

Ahead, red brake lights formed a wall across all the lanes. Concrete rose as roads and ramps crisscrossed. There was no escape.

The truck crashed down onto the highway inches from the motorcycle's rear tire. Cross lifted himself from the seat and at the last second vaulted from the motorcycle as it slammed into a parked sedan.

Carried by the momentum, Cross sailed over the trunk of the car and tumbled onto its roof. With nothing to break his fall, he rolled down the windshield, onto the hood, and off the front of the sedan. He landed on his back, the wind forced from his lungs.

Knowing better than to lay there, Cross pushed off the ground and pulled himself up onto the hood to assess the damage. He gave a quick, pained grin to the middle-aged woman staring at him from inside the car.

His grin faded as he noticed the flipped armored truck skidding toward them, propelled by the other truck having crashed into it at full speed.

Cross wrapped his arms around his head as the truck plowed into the car. The sedan lurched forward and connected with the bumper of a pickup truck.

The hood buckled underneath him, glass cracked, and locked tires groaned. Cross held his breath as he anticipated the crushing weight of both cars collapsing in on him like a vise.

But death did not come for him. The noise ceased, and the car settled into its embrace with the truck's bumper. Cross unwrapped his arms and sat up on the hood of the car. The woman inside the sedan pushed herself away from a puffy airbag and shook the stars from her eyes.

Behind them, the lead armored transport lay on its back, while the other buried its nose into its carriage. A parade of law enforcement vehicles screeched to a halt at every available angle across the tollway.

Cross laid his head down on the hood and closed his eyes as he took a deep breath and thanked God for sparing his life.

CHAPTER TWENTY-NINE

"CAN YOU HEAR me?"

The sweet voice was accompanied by the sound of fluttering wings. Perhaps he had died after all and an angel had arrived to escort him home. A warm feeling overcame him, and Cross opened his eyes to capture the moment.

Instead of an angelic being, he saw a concerned woman wearing a white cowboy hat, bending over him.

"Sir," she said in a thick Texas accent. "Are you OK?"

Cross recognized the gray shirt with blue stripes as the uniform of a state trooper. The thump of what he assumed were wings intensified, and a gust of wind threatened to tear the hat from the woman's head. She grabbed it as she looked up from him to see what was happening.

"Sorry," Cross said as realization dawned. "That's probably for me."

He sat up and ignored the shooting pain in his left shoulder as he slid across the hood and stepped to the road beside the trooper. Just behind the row of police vehicles behind them, the NABC helicopter touched down.

"You've got this," Cross said to the woman as he patted her arm and offered a charming smile. She opened her mouth to respond, but he turned and broke into a run without hearing what she had to say.

A collection of officers held the occupants of the armored trucks at bay with their weapons and shouted instructions such as "Down on the ground" and "Hands where I can see them." Cross ignored the chaos and ran a straight path through the barricade of cars to the waiting helicopter.

As he neared, the side door opened, and Christine popped her head out.

"Hey, need a lift?" she said, grinning.

Cross matched her enthusiasm as he stepped onto the landing skid and gripped a handhold securely. The interior of the helicopter only offered seating for four, with two seats in the front and two in the rear, all seats currently occupied.

This wouldn't be the first time he rode shotgun on a helicopter.

As the chopper rose from the asphalt, Christine slipped an extra pair of headphones over his ears and adjusted the microphone. She smiled again, only this time her eyes softened.

He felt the same way.

"Well, Cross?" Guin asked from the front. "You going to fill us in on what just happened?"

"You can thank Hale Industries for the high-tech bike. That last trick seemed like some kind of fragment explosive that burns through a vehicle from the inside out."

A deep laugh echoed through Cross's headphones. The pilot shot a grin over his shoulder as he lifted away above the tollway. "Stopped by the guy's own machines. That's awesome."

Cross couldn't help but smile at the jovial man.

Guin exchanged introductions for the men, then pointed with her thumb at the man seated next to Christine. "And that's the owner of the helicopter. Jerry something."

"It's Jeremy, Jeremy Blankenship," the man said as he extended his hand toward Cross. "And I don't own the helicopter. It's the property of the North American Broadcasting Channel."

Cross glanced from Blankenship's hand to both his own, then back to Blankenship. The journalist grimaced at the futility of shaking hands while Cross was bracing himself inside the helicopter, and retreated his hand.

"Technically, its true owner is a company out of California. NABC only leases the aircraft." Blankenship squinted as he studied Cross's features. "You haven't spent any time in Washington, DC, the past year, have you?"

"Jeremy," Christine interjected. "You promised to drop it."

Blankenship nodded and bowed his head as he raised his hands in defeat.

Cross would have to ask about that later. He turned to Guin and said into the microphone, "Where's Armstrong? Hale had to be in the other convoy." From the minute Guin revealed the private military's assassination plot, Cross assumed Hale was making his escape in the opposite direction, hoping the might of Dallas law enforcement would be preoccupied.

"They took out a truck of their own but are chasing down the other two headed northeast from here."

"We'll be there in six minutes," Rocket announced.

Cross and Christine exchanged quizzical looks. "Where will we be in six minutes?" Cross asked.

"McKinney National Airport. Makes sense the way they're headed. A lot of corporate air travel originates out of there. At least, that's where I'd go if I was looking to flee the country."

Cross smirked. He liked this guy.

Guin called out updates as they flew, from the president retreating to the safety of Air Force One to the bomb squad disarming the device designed to level Hale Industries. Eric, with the help of Marissa, was already collecting intelligence regarding Hale's illicit activities.

"He said he found something on Philip," Guin declared as she stole a look over her shoulder at Christine.

Cross desperately wanted to reach out and touch Christine but considered it safer to maintain his hold on the helicopter. Instead, he offered a caring smile. She nodded as she wiped under her eyes with a finger.

Their talk would have to wait until much later.

The wind beating against his body both calmed and energized Cross at the same time. He took a minute to watch them pass over square after square of suburban sprawl. The tightly packed neighborhoods thinned into blank plots ready to be developed.

They crossed another large, busy highway, and Rocket announced, "Seventy more seconds."

Guin went to work on the radio, and static suddenly filled the headset, followed by the chatter of the police band.

"They're making the turn on Industrial."

"Definitely headed for the airport."

"We're taking fire!"

"Back off. Back off—"

"Can somebody tell me the ETA on that other Airbus?"

Cross recognized Armstrong's voice as well as his signature profanities as the agent demanded anyone answer his question.

Rocket hooted, then said, "I told you. Looks like we made it in time for the fireworks."

A female voice cut in through the noise. "NABC aircraft, divert your course immediately. This is restricted airspace."

"This is Guin Sullivan with Central Intelligence. This aircraft is carrying authorized personnel involved in the apprehension of Anthony Hale."

The CID operator either didn't comprehend or chose to ignore and instead repeated her order for them to turn around.

Rocket shrugged at Guin. "What are they going to do, shoot us out of the sky?"

Blankenship's face drained of its color as he leaned forward and grabbed Rocket's chair. "They wouldn't do that. They couldn't do that. Are they actually going to try to shoot us?"

"Try, maybe, but don't worry, boy. I've flown through worse." Rocket winked at Guin, and she turned her face away from Blankenship, a gleeful grin fighting to be released.

Cross shook his head at Christine when he noticed the alarmed look on her face. Just because he could appreciate Guin and Rocket's playfulness didn't mean their green passengers understood they weren't in danger. The CID wouldn't shoot them down.

But Hale's men might.

Cross kept his eyes glued on the horizon just beyond the nose of the helicopter. The Excalibur operatives would be preoccupied with Armstrong and the CID, which meant they wouldn't be expecting resistance from a news helicopter.

"Guin," he said, "we've got to make a play for Hale's escape plan. It's got to be something already fueled and ready to take off."

"On it," she replied. With a toggle of the radio, Guin hailed the airport control tower.

Two white stripes of asphalt running north and south and flanked by steel buildings on the west appeared ahead. McKinney National Airport. Cross squinted, then spotted the intense glare of the late-morning sun off a stream of black vehicles barreling down the long roadway headed to the airfield.

"There," he called out. "Nine o'clock."

"I see them," Rocket acknowledged.

"Try to beat them to the runway."

"You got it, Boss." Rocket flipped a couple of switches, then eased the collective down. The helicopter descended from its cruising altitude.

Guin came back on the headset. "I've got a Eurocopter EC135 on the tarmac and cleared for takeoff."

"That's him. Get us down there."

Christine caught Cross's eyes and frowned. "What are you going to do?"

"I don't know," he said. "I'm making this up as I go."

Guin pulled out her Glock and unlocked the safety. "This time you're not going in alone."

The helicopter passed over the main road as the two armored trucks neared the intersection of the drive into the airport. The gunners from the two open hatches exchanged fire with pursuing law enforcement cars and another helicopter tagged TEXAS DPS.

"Hold on!"

Cross gripped tighter as Rocket banked the NABC helicopter left and buzzed the airport's brick-and-mortar tower emblazoned with a tin star below the observation deck. A few yards out, sitting in the middle of a large circle marked by cones, was a black helicopter, its blades spinning in a furious blur of white.

"Get us as close as you can."

Rocket didn't acknowledge Cross as he concentrated on making a fast landing. Cross let go of one of his handholds to remove the headset from his ears and hand it to Christine. Then, he wrapped his fingers around the butt of the gun tucked into his belt. Guin unbuckled herself and placed a hand on the door handle next to her.

They were six feet from the ground when the fencing separating the parking lot from the tarmac shred into pieces as the lead armored transport burst through. The second truck followed, as did the posse of CID agents and state troopers. The DPS helicopter cut a wide arc on the far end of the runway as it prepared to reengage the men touting the M249s.

"We've got company!" Rocket shouted.

Cross decided against jumping from the aircraft, the ground just far enough away to dissuade him. Suddenly, sparks exploded from the NABC chopper's frame as the lead gunner turned his sights on them.

Christine screamed. Or was it Blankenship?

Rocket jerked up hard on the collective control and twisted the cyclic stick. The helicopter lifted and tilted to the right as he crossed over the top of the waiting Eurocopter.

The move was sudden and forceful, and Cross's fingers slipped from the inside strap. Gravity grabbed hold of his body and pulled him from his perch on the landing skid. Time seemed to slow as he watched Christine's eyes widen. The wind from the other chopper's blades beat against the back of his shirt.

Voices shouted, but their words were swallowed by the noise of sirens blaring, weapons discharging, and engines roaring. He let go of the Glock and stuck out his hand.

Fingers wrapped around his wrist and closed tight. The momentum from his fall ceased, and he swung to a stop beneath the landing skid, his feet dangling over the Eurocopter's rotor. They cleared the landing zone, and he looked up to find Christine leaning out the interior of the helicopter and holding fast to his wrist with both hands.

Rocket leveled the chopper as they zoomed over the airfield away from the gunfire. The DPS Airbus passed by and engaged with the transport, drawing the M249s' rounds away from them.

Christine yelled over her shoulder, "Jeremy, pull me up!"

With help, Christine managed to lift Cross up and onto the skid.

"That was close," he said, panting.

Christine offered a nervous laugh in reply, her hand still gripping his wrist.

"He's getting away!" Guin's words were just loud enough for him to hear over the noise.

Two black-clad Excalibur employees covered a man in a suit as he kept his head low and ran to the Eurocopter. One of the men was struck by a stray bullet and collapsed just as they reached the door.

The second man hoisted Hale into the chopper and closed the door. He banged on the outer shell of the aircraft, then engaged the police with a handgun. The black helicopter lifted from the landing zone.

Cross slipped his headset on in time to hear the radio chatter coming from Armstrong's team.

"Target is in the air. I repeat, target is in the air."

"We're pinned down."

"I need that other Airbus in the air now. We've got to force them down!"

Guin opened her door and allowed more wind to beat against the occupants of the news helicopter. "Rocket, see if you can get me a good angle," she ordered as she readied her gun.

The armored trucks pinned down the authorities with fire from the twin M249s. As the NABC chopper swung around, Hale's aircraft shot by, narrowly avoiding a collision.

Rocket swore. "Come on you—" Another sight caused him to drop his words.

The second DPS Airbus helicopter materialized in front of the Eurocopter. It twisted in the air and exposed two armed DPS officers with their legs dangling out of the open door. They raised their weapons simultaneously and aimed.

A flurry of agitated voices mingled in a cacophony within the auditory environment of the headset. Cross picked out Armstrong's voice from the others.

"Hold your fire! We want him alive!"

Another voice, one he couldn't identify, drowned out Armstrong with repeated shouts of "Shoot!"

As Rocket completed his circle around to the left of the Eurocopter, the DPS agents opened fire. Bullets struck the nose of Hale's helicopter, then traveled up and shattered the front windshield. Smoke poured from the interior as the chopper spun out of control and descended to the ground.

"Watch out!"

"Take cover!"

The Eurocopter fell to the earth on a collision course with the two armored trucks sitting side by side on the tarmac. The Excalibur thugs ditched their M249s and jumped clear of the impact zone.

As Cross, Guin, and Christine stared in disbelief, the Eurocopter EC135 slammed into the trucks and exploded in an incredible display of fire, smoke, and debris.

CHAPTER THIRTY

CHRISTINE FAILED TO hold back tears as Philip stepped into the sunlight on the steps of the Frank Crowley Courts Building. She ran up to him and hugged his neck. He sniffed and pressed his fingers into his eyes.

"Thank you," he said as she finally released him. "Thank you for believing me."

Christine nodded, but she refrained from speaking to ensure her emotions were in check. She stepped aside as Philip noted John standing behind her.

"Thank you, Mr. Jameson."

John's lips curved upward as he shook Philip's hand. "It's Cross, actually. John Cross."

Philip arched an eyebrow.

"It's a long story." John motioned to the complex behind Philip. "I hope they treated you well."

"I wouldn't recommend it."

Christine wrapped her arm around Philip's waist. "Come on. Let's go get you something to eat."

For his first meal out of prison, Philip requested cheap tacos from a local eatery—not the choice Christine expected, though she didn't argue.

After they ate, she and John drove him to a friend's home on the outskirts of the metroplex. Along the way, they provided him additional details concerning the raid on Hale's business as well as how the businessman met his end in the fiery crash at McKinney National Airport.

Christine recounted the discovery of Hale's initial assassination plot against the secretary of defense and how the failure of the suicide bomber shifted the plan to an attempt on the president during his visit to Texas, all to try to hide his theft by disrupting the normal operation of the US government. John revealed how Hale contracted foreign cyberterrorists to leave the incriminating messages on both Philip's and Mano Amaya's phones, careful to leave Guin's name out of the story.

"What about the video?" Philip asked. "The video they said they had of me actually . . ." His voice trailed as he hesitated to describe the crime.

"After the raid, Criminal Investigations found the original security camera recordings from De Angelis," John explained. "Hale used a body double to commit the crime, then they altered the footage even more to make it look as much like you as possible. The men working with Hale were from a private security firm that's being shut down by the FBI as we speak."

Philip held his head in his hands as he processed all of the information. "This is all too surreal."

Christine assured him there was nothing more to fear, but she also demanded he promise to make plans to travel home to stay with their father immediately. Hale was dead, and his men were in custody.

It was over.

The day after Philip's release, Christine and John sat in silence in one of the many terminals of the vast Dallas/Fort Worth International Airport and waited to board the plane scheduled to depart for Washington, DC, within the hour. The plan, as she understood it, was for John to stay behind while she continued on to New York City.

She hated her feelings of distrust in the plan, the unresolved conflict that had brewed in her heart since that day in Klyde Warren Park. She needed to confess, and time ran short as she considered the reality of their paths diverging.

"John, we need to talk," she said, surprising herself.

What if he got angry? Was it even the right thing to do? More questions bombarded her frontal lobes as he closed the Bible he was reading and turned to face her.

"You're right. We do."

"I . . ." What should she say? Christine struggled to form the words, dissatisfied with every mental edit. "I think we should stop seeing each other," she finally blurted out. "I mean—" Wait. She meant it, didn't she? Christine knew she needed to have time away from him, but she wasn't completely convinced there still wasn't something possible. She cared for him, deeply. She just hadn't answered the real question yet. The question of whether she could trust him. "I have some things to figure out. I'm learning what it means to have faith. There's the United News job. And I'm starting to think I haven't spent enough time caring for my family. And, honestly, I just don't think I can—"

"Trust me."

Christine hesitated, unsure of what would come next. She slowly nodded in agreement.

"I know," John said, his eyes soft but his mouth wilted at the corners. "And you have every right to feel that way. I've come to realize that I don't really know who I am. I mean, I know certain things that are true about me, but what I'm not certain of is who God *wants* me to be. What he wants me to do. And I think if we're together, I'd be too afraid to find out what that is."

Christine looked away, as did John. Silence filled the space between them for a second time. Christine felt John's hand slide over hers and squeeze. She squeezed back. In a weird way, she felt more committed to him in their mutual decision to separate than she had even moments before.

Just as she considered delving further into their respective desires to follow divine calling into new stages of life, a uniformed man approached them and made eye contact with John.

"Mr. Cross?" the man asked as he neared.

John narrowed his eyes as he replied, "Yes?"

"I have an urgent message for you from Agent Augustus Lee Armstrong. He's requested you and Ms. Lewis meet him immediately at a specified location." The man offered a slip of paper.

John scanned the paper, then exhaled. "Armstrong's here?"

The empty hangar was open on one side, and Christine marveled at the view of DFW's Terminal E opposite them as she and John walked to the center of the bay. Armstrong's instructions were to meet him in the hangar, but as of yet there was no sign of the CID agent. Even with the massive hydraulic door open, the space was eerily quiet.

"Mr. Cross, Ms. Lewis," a man called out from behind them.

They turned to see Agent Flores on a march in their direction. Christine waved, then dropped her hand when she considered other nefarious reasons for the CID to need their assistance.

"Flores, where's Armstrong?" John asked.

"I'm afraid he won't be joining us," Flores replied, his English pronunciation strong but taxed under his thick accent.

Suddenly, Flores pulled his gun from his holster and pointed it at John. Christine gasped but held her hands steady at her sides.

"Please keep your hands where I can see them."

John glanced at Christine and gave her a quick nod to comply. She spread her fingers and widened the gap between her arms and her sides. John raised his as he stared down Flores with a furrowed brow.

Another male voice echoed from the open bay door. "Well, well, well."

Flores motioned for them to turn with his gun. Christine pivoted slowly on her heels, with John mirroring her. At the height of their turn, Christine's heart sank. She felt bile rise in her throat. Anger, despair, and confusion intermingled. She wanted to say things she knew she would regret. All because entering the hangar, dressed in a suit and tie, was Anthony Hale.

"Sykes, right? Or no? Cross, that's your name." Hale pointed a finger in Christine's direction and sneered wider. "And you're the sister. You both have proven very difficult to kill."

"We saw you on the helicopter," Christine said, still refusing to believe her eyes.

"Did you like that? Pulled the same stunt with your brother. I honestly wasn't sure it would work, but here we are." Hale stopped a few feet away and unbuttoned his suit jacket.

John kept his hands in view as he glanced from Flores, then back to Hale. "You always intended the helicopter to be shot down. That way, everyone would assume you were dead. You never intended for the president to be assassinated. It was just a distraction, fireworks to occupy the CID so you could slip away."

"But you're missing the best part," Hale said as he pulled a gun from under his jacket. "I slip away with hundreds of millions of dollars in government funding, and no one bats an eye. See, that's the fun thing about Washington. They can deposit huge sums of cash into the pockets of people they don't even know and couldn't care less if they ever get it back."

John eyed the gun in Hale's hand. "There's still the lingering question of why we're all here right now. You got what you wanted. Everyone thinks you're dead, and the US is going to write off everything they spent on your counterfeit machines."

Hale scoffed. "Did you see any of our work? Those engineers can be proud of what they did. Not everything was faked. They had to build some functioning systems in order to continue convincing the military to siphon us money."

"Proud?" Christine couldn't believe her ears. "You did nothing but make their lives miserable."

"Their lives were miserable already. At least working for me, their résumés will be thicker."

"Unbelievable. You just don't care. You took years away from hard-working people, embezzled hundreds of millions of dollars, caused a national emergency, and you really think you did anyone a favor?"

A robust laugh jumped from Hale's throat. "Sounds about right, honey." Hale shrugged, the gun pointed momentarily away. Christine wished for John to lunge for it, then remembered Flores behind them. "You can even thank me for getting you and your brother back together after all these years."

Christine's nostrils flared, and she narrowed her eyes. "Stepbrother."

"My apologies. Now, John, to answer your previous question, I knew it would be difficult to actually leave the city after yesterday's events, so I had planned on hiding out until things cooled down. Then to my delight, I hear about a journalist and her mysterious companion booked on a flight to DC this afternoon. I thought to myself, what better way to start fresh than to take the place of a man no one knew existed in the first place?"

Hale extended his arm and squinted down the barrel of the gun at John's head. "The kicker is, I get to taste a little retribution for you being a constant pain in my side."

"You won't get away with this," John said.

"I know what you're thinking, but don't worry. Christine will be accompanying me to our final destination, just so there isn't an alarm raised. After that, we'll see how I'm feeling."

Christine was furious, but she held her tongue. How arrogant was this man to think she would help him escape? Reality reminded her of their current situation. She struggled to see a way out. John was as good as dead in the hangar. Emotion clawed at her chest, demanding to be released. Her heart sank as she glanced over at John.

He was looking at Hale, his gaze piercing, and Christine detected the hint of a smirk on his lips.

"No," he said. "I mean, you're really not getting away with this."

A black SUV roared into view at the opening to the hangar. Emergency lights flashed on, and a siren sounded. Three more SUVs followed the leader in, and all four skidded to a stop directly behind

Hale. The businessman spun on his heels, his eyes wide, and bounced his aim between the vehicles.

The doors to the SUVs opened, and CID agents poured out from inside. Guin and Armstrong leapt from the lead vehicle and stomped toward Hale with their own weapons drawn and ready.

"Drop it, pretty boy," Armstrong shouted over the guttural idle of the SUVs.

Christine realized her mouth was hanging open, and she forced it closed as she turned to the sound of more footsteps marching from deeper in the hangar.

Eric led a squad of men from the back entrance, his gun pointing at Flores. As they neared, Eric curved his upper lip and said, "Fácil, amigo. Put the gun down."

Wait a minute. Christine looked from Eric back to Armstrong directing his men to apprehend Hale and then finally to a beaming John. He knew.

John smirked and arched an eyebrow as Hale was forcibly thrown to the ground and handcuffed. "Told you."

"How?" Hale spat the word to the ground from his gritted teeth.

"You can thank Flores for countermanding the order to try to take you alive. I already suspected you had someone on the inside when it seemed you were always a step ahead. The last piece of the puzzle was an unscheduled shift change in the security outside Scott Reardon's hospital room. Unfortunately, your man sent to wrap up that loose end got a rude welcome from Agent Armstrong's team."

Christine gasped as she thought about Hale making one more attempt to kill Reardon. The man was as petty as he was malevolent.

The agents raised Hale to his feet, his hands behind his back and his gray suit now smeared with dust and oil.

A hand wrapped around Christine's and squeezed it tight. She glanced at John and returned his cheerful gaze.

Turning from her, he nodded at Armstrong, then added, "I thought you might be tempted to get revenge, so we took a chance. Thanks for proving me right."

Hale's eyes darkened, and he bared his teeth. Just as a pair of agents pulled on his arms to force him to one of the cars, he spat in their direction.

"Make sure Mr. Hale is comfortable," Armstrong said with a smile.

The men dragged Hale backward as he struggled and screamed profanities. He kicked out with his foot as he passed Armstrong, but came up short. More CID agents passed Christine and John with Flores also bound, his head hanging low.

Guin holstered her sidearm, as did Eric, and they both joined Christine and John in the middle of the hangar. John let go of Christine's hand as Guin slipped her arm around Christine's shoulder and said, "You weren't really going to fly domestic when we've got a couple of open seats on a government-issued private jet, now were you?"

CHAPTER THIRTY-ONE

THEIR PARTING WORDS were brief, both promising to keep the lines of communication open. Christine left to find the gate where her plane to New York, and an offer from UNN, would be waiting. Cross left the terminal, his carry-on slung over his shoulder, to trade air travel for the afternoon train headed to central Virginia.

He spent the train ride dreaming of her, imagining a life that might still be possible. Even probable. But for now she needed to discover her new divinely appointed path. A path that didn't include a relationship, at least at this stage.

The same was true for him, Cross honestly admitted. From the minute the congregation of Rural Grove forgave him for his past deeds, he'd assumed confirmation of a pastoral career. Thinking back on it, Cross realized that his false pretenses ran deep. Running from his previous life, his vain attempt to reconcile bad decisions with good ones, all the reasons he'd formed for accepting the position were no longer valid.

And as much as he loved the members of Rural Grove Baptist Church, he understood how ignoring reality damaged the church's ministry in the community. His intentions, though good, would never be enough if God's will for his life meant stepping down.

Watching the landscape drift by, Cross turned his thoughts from Christine, and he pictured every single member of the church. No. Not the church.

Of his family.

Cross uttered an audible laugh as his heart sank, a curious but not unexpected mixture of emotions. They were his family. He couldn't help but remember the words of Jesus. "Whoever does the will of my Father in heaven is my brother and sister and mother."

If Rural Grove was his family, he owed it to them to follow God's will.

After remembering them all a second time, with his final thought lingering on Christine, Cross did something he rarely did.

Slept.

Cross diverted from his routine and sat in the front left pew as the early morning sun warmed the rich stained-glass windows of the otherwise modest sanctuary. Even with his eyes closed, he still appreciated the shifting orange and yellow hues.

He prayed some, but mostly just listened.

The door at the back of the room creaked. He opened his eyes and stood to greet Gary as he arrived for the morning service.

Cross caught his breath as he turned. Instead of the head deacon and song leader, the last person he wanted to see stood at the entrance. Cross frowned and said, "He told you."

"Gary Osborne doesn't have to tell me anything," Lori replied as she released her hold on the door and padded down the center aisle. She smiled and hugged Cross when she reached him.

Cross shook his head and, against his will, smiled back. "I don't know why I keep thinking I can hide things from you."

Lori laughed out loud. "I don't know either." She grabbed his forearm and led him to the short steps at the base of the altar. He obeyed when she motioned for him to sit on the steps next to her.

They sat in silence for a brief moment, both of them staring out at the empty, for now, pews, until Cross could no longer bear it. "Do you forgive me?"

"Forgive you?" Lori arched an eyebrow and scowled. "Now what on earth would I need to forgive you for?"

"For leaving."

Her face softened. "Oh, I knew this day was coming for a long time."

It was Cross's turn to express confusion. "You did?"

"You're a good man, John Cross. And you made a good pastor. But being a good pastor isn't the same as being the right pastor. You were the right pastor for a time, but that time is now gone."

Cross sighed. "I know. I just wish I knew where I went wrong."

"The answer is nowhere. You don't have to keep paying penance for what you've done, John. Those things were gone the minute you surrendered to God." Lori slipped her arm around his shoulder and squeezed. "You did everything you could here, and you changed this church for the better. God's got something new in store for us, just like he does for you. And even if we don't see it now, you can rest assured it's better than anything you can dream."

"I think I forgot how to dream," Cross said with a chuckle.

"Most people find it easier to do while they're asleep." Lori punctuated her joke with a wink. "No matter where the Lord takes you, just remember this is your home and we're your family."

Cross caught her gaze and held it. The twinkle in her eye assured him of everything he wanted to believe.

"So what do you think you'll do next?"

Cross shook his head. "I don't know. You don't happen to know of anybody in need of a CIA-trained marksman with an aversion to guns, do you?"

"No, not at the moment, but maybe you'll find some others just like you and form a club."

They shared a laugh, then Cross looked away as he heard the familiar sound of Gary's pickup rolling into the parking lot. Lori released her hold on him and stood.

"One last thing," she said. "Make sure to deliver a stinker of a sermon today. That'll help with the announcement."

Cross snorted as he stood up next to her. Offering her his arm, they walked together down the aisle toward the back.

And for the last time, Cross greeted the members of Rural Grove Baptist Church as they each entered for the Sunday morning service.

COMING 2021!

A SHEPHERD SUSPENSE NOVEL • #3

RIGHT CROSS

ANDREW HUFF

KREGEL
PUBLICATIONS

CHAPTER ONE

MILLIONS OF PEOPLE witnessed the arrest of John Cross, and not one of them stepped in to stop it. The video had been captured live during a campaign event in Pontefract, England, for popular but beleaguered Member of Parliament Spencer Lakeman. It played on repeat in Christine Lewis's mind over the twenty-four-hour period from John's incarceration to her arrival at Her Majesty's Prison Wakefield.

Apparent in the video, and confirmed by news outlets not long after his arrest, was John's intoxicated state as he attacked Lakeman from behind. The hammer he swung at the MP's head missed by a wide margin, uncharacteristic of the man who held all his country's highest marksman badges, and he wasn't given the chance to make up for it as Lakeman's security detail wrestled him to the ground.

The second half of the crowdsourced video evidence of John's attempted murder was more disturbing to Christine. His words echoed in her ears, a slurred monologue of dissidence and conspiracy theory mixed with prophetic buzzwords. To Christine he sounded hurt and confused, but to the rest of the world he sounded like a demented theocrat. How had he fallen so far so fast? Had his short stint as a devoted Baptist pastor been a ruse all along?

"New information today regarding the attack on a member of Parliament by an American extremist," announced every news program in the late hours following John's imprisonment. Christine's team received the same bits of information to report, though she was the only one who knew the truth. John Jones was not his real name, auditor not his real profession, and Rochester, Minnesota, not his hometown. Even in a descent into madness, John still exhibited skill in hiding his identity under layers of verifiable lies.

By divine providence, Christine was already on a scheduled leave from manning the desk of her United News Network weeknight newscast, *The Briefing*, her colleague Keaton Clark filling in as host. Her intention of a staycation focused on physical rest and spiritual rejuvenation was waylaid before it even began as the word came over the wire. Instead of dinner with Park Han, the women's Bible study leader at her church, Christine arranged transportation to JFK and caught the first available flight crossing the Atlantic. It took long enough to arrange the visit through a contact of hers with Scotland Yard that she set a record for consecutive hours awake.

She could hardly believe the video was the first time she'd seen John in the months following their separation in the Dallas/Fort Worth airport. Their decision to pursue new paths alone, she in cable news and he away from ministry, was mutual, though looking back, Christine had assumed temporary. They'd traded a few phone calls, texted almost daily, but never had a chance to reconnect in person. And weeks ago, John's texts had become sparse and bordered on bizarre. His last text, sent a month earlier, was a cryptic mixture of apology and apocalypse. Looking back, she wondered if the message had been a cry for help.

The quaint buildings of Wakefield disappeared, replaced by a stark yellow brick wall blocking the prison from view. Christine stared out the window of the taxi, though she cared little for the scenery. She had no attention to spare as she thought of John, Rural Grove Baptist Church, the attempted attack in Washington, clearing her stepbrother of murder in Texas, and how, in the midst of it all, she'd missed any signals that John was spiraling.

Recalling every past moment caused each step from the prison entrance to the visiting room to pass by in a blur. A loud buzz from beyond the door finally shook her from her trance, and for the first time she noticed both doors in the room were painted bright green.

The sandy walls and navy carpet did little to distract from the bold choice.

The eccentric design of the room's interior lost any meaning as the opposite door opened and John stepped through. If there was a guard escort, Christine didn't notice. Her eyes were transfixed on his visage.

His hair threatened to fall back into his eyes without constant attention, and the hair on his chin could officially be referred to as a beard. His skin was in dire need of care. Sorrow was etched in wrinkles under his eyes.

Or was it anger?

John sat down in the only other chair and placed his hands, bound at the wrist, on the table between them. The orange jumpsuit tightened against his chest as he took controlled breaths. He stared at her, or at least in her direction, his face devoid of any tells.

A full minute passed without a word between them. Christine assumed they were being recorded, so she'd come with prepared remarks. But now that she was in the room, she didn't know what to say.

"John, I—"

"Save it."

The coldness in his voice startled her. He wasn't angry, but worse: indifferent. She swallowed the anguish rising in her throat. "So you're not going to tell me what happened?"

"You work in news, so you already know."

"That's not what I mean."

John finally glanced away from her, the hint of a smile playing at the corner of his lips. "Oh, so now you care?"

His remark cut through her defenses, and she let out a surprised gasp as she dropped her gaze. Where was this coming from? She tried to recall a conversation or text that would help explain his animosity toward her, but none sprang to mind. As far as she was aware, their separation had been amicable.

"I don't understand," she said before regaining his eye contact. "What about everyone back home? I mean, I know you stepped down, but I thought you would stay." She kept her references to Lori Johnson and the other congregants at Rural Grove Baptist Church vague for the sake of anyone listening in.

"With those freaks?" He guffawed. "Get a grip, Christine. It was all a sham. And you know it."

All of it? What was he saying? The reality of John Cross's apostasy was dawning. She frowned as she folded her arms. "No, John, I don't know it. Why don't you enlighten me?"

Scowling, he leaned over his cuffed hands. "The man you met two years ago was a fraud. You knew that. I used the opportunity to lie low, convince the agency I wasn't a threat. This is the real me. The man who doesn't buy into any of that Jesus Christ bull—"

Christine refused to succumb to her emotions as John, filling his words with expletives, ridiculed the ideas of true life change, meaning, purpose, and love.

She interrupted before he could add another colorful adjective to the list. "So it meant nothing? The last two years. Everything you've been through, everything you've done. And us. It was all a lie?"

His eyes narrowed. "Isn't that what I do best?"

Christine flinched at the reminder of the accusations she'd flung at him. A loud buzz behind him prevented Christine from diving into the deep well of questions rising in her mind. A guard entered the room and hoisted John from the chair. Christine jumped to her feet and held out her hand. "John, I'm praying for you."

The guard paused long enough for John to roll his eyes, then they both disappeared into the hallway.

"Cappuccino for Beth!"

A short woman wearing a knit cap responded to the barista's call. Christine's eyes bounced around the large café, noting other patrons and decor, but her mind retained none of the information as she replayed her conversation with John over and over in her mind.

None of it made sense. John had been so convinced of his newfound faith in Jesus Christ that he'd left the CIA and eventually found himself as the pastor of a small community of believers in Mechanicsville, Virginia. He'd stepped down as the pastor of Rural Grove only after realizing he'd accepted the position too early in his new life, slowing down to focus on his spiritual and personal growth. How had he put it?

"I need time to get to know the new John Cross."

It seemed the time spent only let the old John Cross back into his life. And yet . . .

Christine couldn't help but ask questions. And not just why, but the entire spectrum of information-gathering questions at her disposal. None of the answers she sought were about John's attack on Lakeman but rather his denunciation of his transformed life.

There it was. The nagging question in the back of her mind. The one she wouldn't be able to shake until she tracked down the answer. The one she'd chased in the car ride from the prison to the café where she was refueling for her trip back to the States.

Was he completely gone?

John's malevolent outburst lacked two important details. He neither directed his vitriol at her personally nor made any specific denials of the Christian faith. Her mind burned under the weight of those two specifics.

Maybe the answer was no, he wasn't completely lost. This was only a valley, and perhaps the end result of this experience would be John's ascent back to where he was when they'd parted in Texas. She would certainly pray for it.

But then again . . .

Christine closed her eyes to keep her thoughts from wandering about as the left side of her brain took over. Speculating about a revival in John's heart was fruitless. It didn't mean she wouldn't pray, but despite the lingering questions, she expected the truth to ultimately be found standing right in front of her.

The John she knew was gone. The one she'd never know was back. And as of right now, nothing could change that.

"Flat white at the bar for Christine," announced a British voice. Her eyes fluttered open, and she raised her foot to take a step toward the counter. Her body suddenly froze. All the questions concerning John faded into oblivion, leaving only a single thought behind. *I know her.*

The woman in the knit cap? No, not her. Christine dismissed each person in the café through process of elimination. None were familiar. It was someone else. Someone who just walked out the door.

Ignoring the barista's second proclamation of her readied order, she headed for the exit. The coffee shop occupied the corner of a cute brick building, matching another on the opposite side of a patterned brick walkway. Pedestrians milled about freestanding vendor shops in front of her. To her right, the sun glistened off the glorious tip of Wakefield Cathedral's steeple. To her left, the walkway carried on past the pair of buildings, leading the way to a beautifully designed splash pad just off the major intersection of some of Wakefield's busiest roadways.

There. Walking away from her toward the splash pad was a woman, her every feature covered by a long black coat. Every feature but her brunet hair. It flowed over the coat, bouncing ever so gently in the light afternoon breeze.

Christine could recognize those locks anywhere. All her questions became moot. She narrowed her eyes and, with command of the entire sidewalk, called out, "Guin!"

The name arrested the woman's gait. With caution she turned until Christine's suspicion was confirmed. Twenty yards away, with her hands buried in her pockets and resignation on her face, was CIA Officer Guin Sullivan.

They stared at each other for a few seconds, the surrounding public indifferent to their sidewalk showdown, until Christine finally dug her hands into her hips and said, "He's back in, isn't he?"

Guin's sly smirk was the only answer she needed.

DON'T MISS THE FIRST JOHN CROSS ADVENTURE!

A SHEPHERD SUSPENSE NOVEL

A CROSS TO KILL

ANDREW HUFF

978-0-8254-2274-4

"An action-packed nail-biter from beginning to end, filled with enough twists and turns to put *24* and Jack Bauer to shame! I couldn't put it down."

—**LYNETTE EASON**, best-selling, award-winning author of the Blue Justice series

KREGEL
PUBLICATIONS

READY FOR MORE
CHRISTIAN SUSPENSE?

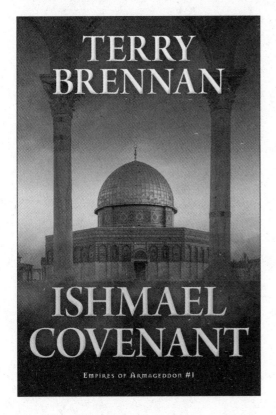
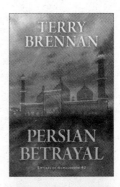